DRAGON MYSTICS

DRAGON MYSTICS
Supernatural Prison #2

Jaymin Eve

To Travis, for all the moments that loving an author is really hard work. And yet you continue to do so. Also, thank you for cooking 8 out of 10 dinners, and only complaining 4 out of 8 times

Dragon Mystics: Supernatural Prison #2

Copyright © Jaymin Eve 2015

All rights reserved

First published in 2015

Eve, Jaymin
Dragon Mystics: Supernatural Prison #2

1st edition

No part of this book may be reproduced, stored in a retrieval system or transmitted in any form or by any means, without the prior permission in writing of the publisher, nor be otherwise circulated in any form of binding or cover other than that in which it is published and without a similar condition, including this condition, being imposed on the subsequent purchaser. All characters in this publication other than those clearly in the public domain are fictitious, and any resemblance to real persons, living or dead, is purely coincidental

Chapter 1

Romania was just … freaking beautiful.

There was no other way to describe the snow-touched mountains and valleys that we traversed. Sure, in my twenty-two years I'd never been anywhere but Stratford, and now Romania, but I knew there was something special in this untouched land. It was ancient, nature at its most beautiful and brutal.

The private plane we'd used to escape had landed two hours ago, and waiting at the airport were two Porsche *Cayennes*, tires chained, gassed up and ready to go. Louis, the sorcerer, definitely had this little journey well planned. It had been easy to clear customs. Our brand new identities were barely even glanced at. And no alarms were raised when they entered the system, so Louis or the Guilds had taken care of that too.

I just wished the magic-man was here so I could ask him a few questions, like … I don't know … where the hell were we going? I also really wanted to be able to phone home and hear that no harm had befallen my parents. I worried the Four might target Jonathon and Lienda, trying to get to me, and now I had no way to check on them. Apparently, we could be traced even if we used payphones. Seriously, a payphone ... *do those things even exist anymore?*

I was slightly mollified by the fact my father was the leader of the shifter council, and also pack master – he had a lot of power and authority behind him. But still, I didn't think the dragon marked hunters cared very much about that. My one meeting with them told me they were crazy and would stop at nothing to fulfill their calling.

Breathing deeply, I forced myself to focus on the here and now. We had split into two groups. Braxton, Maximus, Mischa, and I took the front vehicle. Jacob, Tyson, and Grace, our ring-in-healer, were in the second. I'd ended up shotgun in the SUV. Braxton was driving.

There had been a bit of a scuffle between him and Maximus, striving for domination, but in the end the dragon had won. To be honest, these mountain ranges were pretty scary, especially with the snow and ice. I was glad my alpha-animals hadn't forced me to challenge anyone for control of the car. Both my wolf and dragon were content and snoozing at the moment. Despite the craziness of the last few days – what with ending up in Vanguard and being captured and almost stolen away by the crazy-ass dragon marked hunters – I was feeling pretty calm.

Still, I couldn't shake my unease.

The only information I had regarding our destination was the letter and map Louis had sent with me, which I held scrunched in my right hand. At the airport I hadn't wanted to tip off any of the staff to our destination. Paranoid I know. But the Four scared the shit out of me. Thankfully, with just a few questions – and stumbling over my shocking Romanian pronunciation – we now had a general idea of where we were going. Louis was sending us toward a range of the Carpathian Mountains at the peak of Romania, near the Ukraine border. It seemed to be about four hours from the small private airport.

I stretched out my legs; this car was surprisingly roomy. I could hear rhythmic breathing behind me, Mischa crashed out on the back seat, Maximus right beside her. My vampire best friend was staring out the window, his dark eyes assessing the craggy mountain ranges topped with pretty white snow. The broad, handsome planes of his somber face reminded me of what was weighing on my own mind. I was covered with layers of winter clothes, but I knew what lay beneath now. The dragon mark.

A visible reminder of the secret I was keeping from my sister and most of my best friends.

I hated secrets, and I was the ass concealing one. As if he'd heard my thoughts, Maximus straightened, and as I turned to meet his gaze I was knocked back by the intensity of his tawny brown eyes.

"I need to tell you something," I blurted, my nerves raising the pitch of my voice. I knew Braxton was watching me from the driver's seat. I could feel the heat of his laser blue eyes, but I didn't let it distract me too much. "Something about my dragon mark…"

I trailed off as Mischa's bright green eyes popped open. Now everyone in the friggin' car was watching me splutter and stumble over my words.

"When the energy on the mark was released, well … I shifted."

No one looked shocked yet, but they thought I was talking about my wolf.

"Into a dragon. I shifted into a dragon."

Silence descended over the car. Braxton already knew, of course, he had been in Vanguard with me. My breath caught and guilt churned my stomach. Maximus had been pretty upset the last time I kept a secret from him. I had no idea how he would react now. Mischa was the first to speak, excitement trilling through her voice, and I forced myself to pull my gaze from my vamp.

"So that could explain my dreams right? If I break the spell containing my mark ... I might shift in to a dragon also?"

Mischa hadn't grown up in our world, she'd spent most of her life with humans so she didn't understand the impossibility of what I had done. There were no dual shifters – hybrids between the races, yes, but shifters only ever had one animal to call. Even other shifters who were dragon marked could still only change to a single creature, and it was never a dragon, because dragons did not carry the mark. There was no need.

"I don't know, Misch," I said in an even tone. "I've never heard of a dual shifter before, but maybe as my twin you will find the same thing happening to you."

Her face went pensive, worrying her bottom lip, which she did when she was nervous. I could only imagine the thoughts running through her head.

Maximus still hadn't said anything, which had my heart rate increasing. I just knew shit was going to get real in a moment – or whenever he decided to explode. When I couldn't stand the tension, or my own guilt any longer, I pulled my eyes from him, turning back to stare out the window, forcing something else to capture my attention.

Wow! I leaned forward a little.

At some point during my nervous confession we'd entered a small town. I took the time to examine the colorful locals. They were scattered around the streets, chatting in groups, dining in restaurants. Warmly bundled up in extravagant and mismatched attire, they were fascinating. I'd never seen humans in books or on television dress like the ones parading through the streets.

Many eyes turned in our direction and I was thankful for the dark tint on the car. I wondered if their curiosity was simply that we were strangers crossing through their little village, or if this sort of vehicle was uncommon here. Damn, Louis should be helping us fit in, not stand out.

The signs we passed were mostly in Romanian, although some of the words looked familiar so I could probably guess at the names. At least numbers were the same, which made speed restrictions easy to maintain. I glanced down at the scrunched note again, running my eyes over the map. Judging by the distances Louis had jotted around this village, we were getting close to our destination.

"I'm not mad at you, Jessa babe."

Note forgotten, I swung around again. I was sure my blue eyes were a little desperate as they bore into the vampire. Maximus was my rock, I couldn't stand the stress of his ire. "But I need you to promise that you won't keep any more secrets from us." I knew *us* was Jacob and Tyson, his fey and wizard brothers. "How can we properly protect you when we don't have all the facts?"

Braxton interrupted then: "Jonathon was worried that when we joined together and received our calling, we might be dragon marked hunters also. He warned Jessa. Her caution is in part to do with orders from her alpha."

Braxton had been pretty quiet since the battle-of-wills with his brother over who would drive. It was nice to hear his low husky voice. I'd also like to see the dimples that graced his chiseled face, but that level of happiness seemed to be a little out of reach at the moment.

Maximus growled, low from his chest; it rumbled through the small space. "For fuck's – are you telling me your father actually entertained the concept that we might hunt you?"

I shook out my black hair, heavy and silky against my neck. "I don't think he actually believed it, but the warning was clear."

Maximus continued muttering under his breath while he shot dark glares around, but I knew they weren't aimed at any of us in particular. I glanced out to the side mirror, confirming as I had been for the past few hours that the second black Porsche was still following us. I noticed Braxton frequently checking as well.

Buildings thinned as we left the town and made our way further into the mountains. There was a steep drop off one side of the narrow path, and Braxton had to slow as the snowy, treacherous roads really began to hinder our progress. Though his hands remained relaxed on the wheel, so I didn't think he was too worried.

I, on the other hand, had never really spent much time in a vehicle. I was missing the forest of our home. I needed to run. I pushed down this need, along with all the other desires driving my body right now. Hunger was a biggie. They'd fed us on the plane, but I was hungry again. The damn cold had my metabolism shifting into high gear. Judging by my clothes, I'd already lost weight with the last few stressful weeks, and I was not okay with that. A girl needs her curves. The moment I started to resemble Giselda, BEF (bitch enemy forever), I was necking myself.

"This friend of Louis' better have food," I muttered, my eyes still locked on the towering ranges around us.

Mischa leaned forward, her face almost next to mine between the front seats. "Are we getting close? What does the letter say?"

I loosened my grip, looking down again, blinking at the crumpled paper. "What the crap? It's gone…" I immediately turned to Braxton. "It was just there a moment ago but now the writing is gone."

Braxton swore low, his eyes flicking down to my hand. The vehicle started to slow; he lowered his window, letting in drafts of arctic air before signaling something to Tyson, the driver of the other SUV. I figured they were trying to find a place to pull over. Unfortunately we were not in the best position, and we had no phones to call back. Louis had confiscated everyone's electronics so we wouldn't be tempted to use them. We were going to find some prepaid burner cells soon. Soon, of course, did not help us right now.

I flipped the paper over but the back was just as blank as the front.

"I'm killing that fucking sorcerer." The familiar lament was from Maximus. He'd also moved his massive bulk into the center of the car.

Braxton leaned forward, paying close attention to the road we were on. "We have no choice but to remain on this path. There is nowhere for me to turn around. We can meet up with the others as soon as it is wide enough. Maybe Tyson will have some insight into what happened to the letter."

Tyson was a pretty powerful wizard, but he wasn't a sorcerer yet. The quads – and Mischa and I – were twenty-two, which for a magic user was way too young to have evolved into a sorcerer. I think the youngest sorcerer in supernatural history was Louis, and he'd been thirty. Tyson was planning on giving him a run for that title. I really hoped my wizard best friend could get a read off this paper, because without it we were completely screwed.

Not only was it nearing dusk, but the snowstorm which had been holding off was starting to fall. We had exceptional night vision, and the high beams were already flooding the road, but still visibility sucked.

Mischa's green eyes darted around, examining the increasing fall of snow and shifting terrain outside the window. "Should we stop for the night?" Her voice trembled. "We don't want to drive off a mountain."

Braxton almost smiled at that one. "Have some faith … I'm a dragon, we have unparalleled reflexes and powerful vision. I'm not going to drive you off a cliff."

Dragon. His words reminded me of the moment I'd shifted to my strange, fluffy dragon. He was not kidding about the unparalleled senses part.

The colors I had seen had been so intense, as if dragons experienced much more of the light spectrum than any other creature – well, any other creature I'd turned into, which, sure, was only wolf and human, but I was probably still right. Dragons were special.

My gaze was drawn to the side mirror again. I could barely see the black shape of Tyson's car any longer. Just a shine of lights every now and then. "Ty isn't a dragon," I reminded Braxton.

Blue flashed at me, and for a moment all I could see was the cloudless spring sky that Braxton's eyes mimicked. The air in the space between us started to morph into something intense. My insides clenched in need and want and fire. I forced myself to try to remember the reasons I wasn't willing to risk our friendship, but in this moment I couldn't think of a single one strong enough.

I received a reprieve when Braxton shifted his face away. He lowered the window again to signal something else.

My breathing was a little harsher than usual as my heart and thoughts both raced. What the hell was going on?

Ever since we'd been locked up in Vanguard together, it was like our relationship had gone through an evolution. We'd been best friends for twenty years. Now, though, I had no idea where we were heading. No matter how sexified my thoughts were getting, I wasn't sure it was worth risking our friendship. What if we didn't work as a couple?

What if something tore us apart? What if one of us found our mate?

So many what if's ... it hurt my head just considering them all. But the biggest of all – what if Braxton didn't feel the same need? Maybe I was trying to force something because of my own newly discovered emotions? If I acted on it he might be the one to turn me down, and I wasn't sure I could survive that.

Shit! I was so not thinking about this any longer.

Maximus's long arm came between Braxton and me; he pointed toward a sign. "There seems to be a lookout or turnaround section just there."

It took me a moment to focus. I called on my wolf for help, and was finally able to see what he was talking about. Braxton eased our car off the main road, turning left. The wheels lost traction for a moment before we powered out of the slide and drove across the fresh powder into a large circular flat. I was relieved to see the second vehicle pull in beside ours. Of course, while I was happy to see the others, I was not looking forward to getting out in that cold. Luckily, it seemed as if they were coming to us.

How the heck was this going to work? Four large quads – I'm talking far-larger-than-was-necessary – were not going to fit in this car.

But somehow we managed it. Braxton stayed in the front and Maximus took my seat. I ended up on Jacob's lap and Mischa in Tyson's. Poor Grace, her red hair subdued under a woolen hat, had to squeeze in between us in the back.

Tyson had his usual shit-kicker grin on, and I was happy that the tension which had been very present between Grace and him seemed to have eased a little. Hopefully the witch healer was over the rejection I'd dished out on behalf of Tyson many years ago.

"You know what I'm thinking of right now?" Tyson's honeysuckle eyes were sparkling. "All of us, it's really cold–"

I interrupted him by leaning over Grace and cracking him in the side of the head. "Shut it now."

Mischa's nose crinkled a little. "Do you have to be such a pig while I'm sitting on your lap?"

The wizard laughed, dimples and white teeth flashing. "I was going to say that survival 101 was coming in handy. Sharing body heat and all that."

Sure, that was what he was going to say.

Jacob's strong arms wrapped around me, hugging me tighter. It was comforting to be in his arms, no tension like that which followed me and Braxton. There was no weird sexual pull between the rest of the quads and me.

I turned my head to see the wizard again. "Did you get anything off the letter, Ty?"

Tyson had been handling Louis' note for about five minutes, turning it over and over. I wondered if his joking around was to cover his frustration.

"Nothing. It's as if this has never been touched by magic. No spell residue, no trace marks of Louis. How the fuck does he manage to do that?"

Braxton growled. "He's a sorcerer without an equal, and I can't wait to beat his ass into the ground."

Someone was still a little pissed about the whole knock-out-kidnap-onto-a-plane plan.

Maximus caught my eye and I was reminded that I needed to tell Jacob and Tyson about my secret. But now wasn't the time. I didn't trust Grace enough to reveal something like that. Yes, I had known the witch healer for a long time – she grew up in Stratford – and I'd been okay revealing on the plane that Mischa and I were twins, and that we were dragon marked. But my dragon shifting abilities ... they were a whole other level of top-secret.

My wolf started to paw inside of me, getting a little fidgety. I was not happy being stuck in this car at the moment. I needed to run, I needed freedom.

"Can you drive for a bit, Brax?"

He didn't question me, he just shifted out of park and eased the vehicle forward. It was probably a craptastic idea to drive with a car this packed, but it was drive or I was going to lose my shit. Mischa and Braxton, as shifters, would be feeling the urge too.

The storm had eased again. We cut through the soft snow without issue, ending up back on the mountain path.

"Sorry, Jessa babe, I can't help with this." Tyson handed me back the letter, his voice rough as he cursed a few more times.

I sighed, smoothing out the paper. It was strange – it had been folded, crumpled, and handled over and over, but still ... it looked perfect. Definitely infused with magic.

We continued climbing higher, and I hoped we'd find a place to turn around. Otherwise I was shifting into a wolf and running my ass back to the other car. As I had that thought, the parchment caught my eye. *Was it starting to glow?* Very slowly it lit up, and after a minute there was no denying the brightness.

Braxton was tuned in to me. "What is it, Jess?" His eyes met mine in the rearview mirror.

I returned my attention to the letter again. "Keep driving," I said.

Jacob leaned in around me and together we stared at the glowing note. As we traveled a little further, the road dipping down and then up again to wind through the valleys and peaks, golden words began to write themselves across the paper.

You're on the right path. This is the road to the sanctuary, which at the end holds the answers. Follow the trail until you reach the barrier, and make sure that Jessa is the one to cross the border. She must vouch for the others or they will be rejected by the protections. Show them the mark. Password is in Romanian. Misticii Dragonilor: *Dragon Mystics.*

I locked eyes with Jacob. Both of us wore the same expression … what the effing fuck was this sorcerer up to? And what were dragon mystics?

"Jess, Jake…?" From Braxton's tone I knew he was at the end of his patience.

"Shit, sorry! The note has writing on it again," I said into the silence of the car.

Jacob ended up reading the letter to them – his Romanian sounded pretty sweet on the password part – I was too busy rereading the note trying to glean every facet of information from Louis' message.

Maximus drew my attention. "So we just keep following this road?"

I didn't answer right away, using my time to alternate between watching the mountain road and looking down at the note. I was expecting it, and sure enough a map started to appear along the space at the bottom.

"Yes, just keep on this path," I finally said, leaning my head out between Braxton and Maximus.

Of course, once I was this close to the dragon shifter I couldn't help myself, his scent drew me closer. Before I knew it I was pretty much snuggled into his face. What can I say? I was needing some comfort, and he was the best.

"You okay?" His low grumbly tone washed over me.

I nodded. "I just want this month to be over. I need to know if I'm going to be running and hiding for eternity, and, on a side note, this thousand year anniversary can just go screw itself. I'm over waiting to see what will happen with the dragon king…"

A shimmer caught my eye. "There!" Mischa and I yelled at the same time.

Everyone else in the car swung their heads to stare out the left side.

The opening in the side of the mountain had appeared out of nowhere. And I would bet my last piece of cake – no, wait not my cake – I'd bet the quads' last piece of cake that a human would never have seen a thing. It had that golden sheen over the entrance, the same type which protected Stratford and deterred any but supernaturals from entering.

"What did you see?" Maximus's brow was wrinkled, his brown eyes darting around.

I glanced at the rest of the car's occupants. Everyone but Mischa and I looked confused.

"It's right there," I said, turning back to the glow. I even pointed this time so there was no way they could miss it. If Braxton didn't slow soon we were going to drive right past.

I wrapped my arm across his massive chest. "Stop the car, Brax."

I had a strong suspicion I knew what was going on now. Since no one but Mischa and I could see this entrance, it had to have something to do with the dragon mark. This was what Louis' note meant about following my lead. We were going to have to guide the others in.

Although, considering Mischa had little training and was not connected to her dragon – if she had one – I was going to be the one going in.

Braxton pulled the car over to the edge of the road, onto a small graveled area with just enough room for our SUV. Actually, we were still half on the road, but it was the best we had right now.

"What's going on, Jess?" He captured my gaze, and I knew without any doubt that he was going to fight me on this.

I brought my face very close to his. I could see every facet of his stunning blue eyes, a color which had haunted my dreams of late, for more than one reason. "I need you to trust me. I'm going to have to do something you won't like."

His reply was instant. "No fucking way!" The dragon in him rose to the forefront and I could see the unmovable beast that was such a part of his personality. "You step one foot out of this car and we're going to have an issue."

My own dragon and wolf responded in kind. We did not like being dictated to, even if I knew it was because he loved me and didn't want danger slithering its slimy ass anywhere in my vicinity. I think, if he could, Braxton would have wrapped me in cotton wool and secured me in a remote location.

I caught Maximus' eye, and with a sigh he gave me an almost imperceptible nod. While my vamp's features had tightened, I knew he would back me on this. Mainly because he was not *exactly* aware of my full plan. I leaned forward, and before Braxton could reach for me I kissed him a solid smack on the cheek, flung my door open, and dived off of Jacob's lap.

Braxton's curses rang free. I didn't look back. Maximus would be using his bulk to detain his brother. I wouldn't have long, no one could hold Braxton down, but hopefully it was enough time. I didn't want to do this, running into the unknown without my pack, but Louis' note made it clear: it had to be me. And I didn't feel like sitting through the six hours of arguing it would take before the Compasses grudgingly agreed to let me go. Action was better.

Okay, and maybe my wolf was feeling a little reckless after the many hours of being cooped up.

The cold was icy enough to take my breath away, but my metabolism kicked in and heat followed the rush of blood through my body. The car had stopped about ten yards from the small opening into the mountain. The golden glow gave me a moment's pause, but I trusted that Louis wouldn't have sent me into anything too crazy.

Right?

I hit the barrier, and before I knew what was happening I was sucked through to the other side. Unfortunately, I didn't end up landing on my feet. I was strung upside down, my body constricted in a netting which was too strong to break.

My mind flashed to the letter and I decided now was the time to speak the password or forever be strung up like a piece of meat. Without thinking twice I said:

"Misticii dragonilor."

Chapter 2

The glow surrounding me made everything too bright for me to see clearly. The netting did not ease. If anything, the longer I hung there the tighter the constrictions felt. I was starting to get pissed off, and now was not the time for additional restrictions; my wolf was already cranky about the hours of travel and car time. She was ready to change, and she pretty much wanted to tear a few fresh ass-holes in anyone stupid enough to push us.

I was really hoping someone pushed us when I got free.

The frustrations riding me needed to go somewhere; it was taking all of my concentration to keep hold of my dragon. Luckily, I still retained enough mental capacity to remember that the Four were after me. I could not alert them to my location. They seemed to require close proximity, but they had told me that sometimes they felt strong dragon marked powers from anywhere in the world. And I knew mine were strong.

"Misticii dragonilor!"

I snarled the password this time, wondering if my stumbling Romanian was the reason nothing had happened earlier.

The light flared, and within my next exhalation I was freed. In the six foot drop, I managed to flip myself over and land smoothly on my feet — supernatural genetics were not just about pretty looks. My head shot up and I clashed eyes with a robed man, the dark blue of his hooded attire blending into the gray stone tunnel we were in.

He was quiet as he examined me. I made no sudden movements, except to straighten so I was no longer crouched. I was five-feet-four; he was about six inches taller than me. Which I didn't like. A few low growls rumbled my chest.

I loathed to be the first to speak – you know, alpha-domination and all that – but I had to protect my pack. "I need safe harbor for myself and my six friends." My words were hard; contrition just wasn't in my personality.

The male unfurled his arms. I was getting a weird vibe from his energy. He seemed to be fey, but also … something else … and I did not want to be around anything unknown. I tensed, preparing myself. It didn't seem he was going to attack, but I was taking no chances.

He widened his arms, as if inviting me to come closer. Not likely.

"Welcome to the sanctuary, and city of mystics." His voice was low, with a mild accent. Not Romanian though, something closer to ... Spanish, maybe? "You're halfway through your initiation. The second part requires the mark to be visible."

I didn't hesitate, I started ripping off my layers of clothes. I could only imagine how insane the Compasses were going outside. I couldn't hear anything; this side of the mountain was quiet. Soundproof. But I knew they would be losing it.

When I was down to just my bra, I spun around so he could see the black and red symbol which traced along my back and side. Twirling and twisting from my shoulders down to my hip, it was a tribal dragon. I still hadn't seen the entire image; it was difficult to capture it in one look, and really ... I hadn't had much time to examine it closely.

Only the fey's eyes moved, running down my bare body. I was getting goose bumps all over – it was warmer on this side but still freaking cold. He needed to move along this skeezebag moment.

My eyes slashed out at him. "You about done?" I swear if laser beams from eyes were possible, mine were fired up enough to shoot them. "I'd appreciate if you stopped wasting my goddamn time. I have friends outside freezing to death, so either let us in or let me go."

Mild exaggeration, sure.

He was still just staring at me. With a huff I gathered my undershirt, long-sleeved tank and winter jacket, and pulled them back on. It seemed to be the only thing to snap him out of his creepy stare-trance. I turned to walk my ass straight back out of the force field. I'd had enough of this shit. Louis was clearly deranged if he thought this was the place for us.

"Stop!" It was a command, plain and simple. I flipped him off, and was almost at the golden shimmer when he said, "I've never seen a mark like yours."

Despite my shitted off stance, my hesitation before twisting around to face him, was brief. I knew our options were limited, and I was a tad curious about his observation of my mark. One more chance for this weird cloaked dude.

Our gazes clashed. He definitely looked troubled. "You and your friends are welcome here."

I turned back to the veil just in time for it to fade away.

Shit.

Right in front of me was three hundred pounds of angry, growling, cursing dragon man. Thankfully he hadn't shifted yet, but that would only be due to his incredible control. Because he was surely pissed enough to have lost it.

Maximus, Jacob, and Tyson were beside him, and they didn't look much happier. I was guessing all four had been smashing against the barrier.

Mischa and Grace stood a little further back, probably staying out of the firing line.

"You lied to me!" Maximus snarled. "You were just supposed to check it out, not walk right the hell into the unknown."

I batted my eyelashes a few times, although my innocent face had never worked on the boys. "I did not lie, and how the heck am I supposed to get anything done when you all want to ride my ass? I can take care of myself."

Tyson was the first to wrap his arms around me. "Don't you get it, Jessa babe? Next to our mates – which we don't even have yet – you are the most important person to us. If we lose you, well … we lose everything."

Well, wasn't I the asshat of the day.

I was girl enough to admit Tyson brought a fist-sized lump to my throat and a few stray tears burning from my eyes, but I managed to keep them from falling.

Braxton growled again and held his arms out. "Mine." His voice was guttural.

All of us could see that he'd moved past the place of reasonable conversation. The predator – his dragon – was riding him hard now. Tyson did not even hesitate handing me across. Lucky I was used to these men treating me like a life-size doll.

Hard arms closed around me. The embrace was almost painful, but I was tough, I could take a bit of almost-crushed-to-death for Braxton. Then, as if he'd heard my thoughts, his grip gentled. He had his head buried in the space between my shoulder and neck, and he was breathing deeply. I knew he was calming, getting himself under control. I could feel the racing of his heart starting to slow. The scent of the shift was easing. I could always sense that hint of magic which preluded a change among shifters, almost as if a spicy heat led the way. Braxton had been damn close.

A throat cleared behind us. "You need to enter so I can resume the protective magics. We shield many here, and any delay could alert … those unwanted to our presence."

Braxton stilled, lifting his head. He locked eyes with the cloaked man. I was twisted around enough to see that for the first time unease flickered across the stranger's calm features. Good to see that Braxton's general badassery was as potent in Romania as it had been in Stratford.

As a group we stepped into the cave. My feet were still off the ground, so Braxton moved me. With barely a whistle of air, the golden sheen resumed, cutting off the black car and icy snow-laden mountain we had just left.

"Follow me." Cloak guy turned and started along what looked like a tunnel straight into the center of the mountain. It was wide enough for all of us to walk side by side as we followed.

Tyson's voice lost some of it genial charm as he called along the stone passage. "What about our car, and personal belongings?" I knew he was most worried about the fake identities and cash. They were our security if we ended up on our own in the human world.

The man did not break stride. "The car will be disposed of, and your goods are already being gathered and brought to your rooms."

Truth.

Despite the fact I scented truth, I still bristled at this man's audacity. Who the crap did he think he was making decisions for us? I wasn't the only one – more than a few growls sounded from Maximus and Braxton. Jacob and Tyson contained their annoyance better, but I knew them well enough to see the pissed-off-tension carving a path along their faces.

Unfortunately, it didn't seem that we could break the security barrier on our own, so for now we had no choice but to follow the stranger along the path. Braxton finally set me on my feet, then his right hand laced through mine. I was pretty sure he was ensuring I did not disappear on him again. Hello, hand, meet your new leash.

A flash of very blond hair had me turning to find Jacob right at my side. Staring into eyes as green as a newly formed leaf in spring, I found myself asking, "Are you getting a fey vibe off him?" Jacob generally recognized his fellow brethren, even if they were using some sort of energy to hide themselves.

His eyes creased a little. "Yes, he is fey, but there must be some hybrid to his lineage. I also sense magic, like that of a wizard. But he is not wizard."

"Definitely not wizard," Tyson confirmed.

Maximus and Braxton exchanged glances, their tense features mirrors of each other. "I don't like this," the vampire quad finally muttered. "Does Louis' note have any more information?"

I'd tucked the parchment into my back pocket when I'd first jumped out of the car. I pulled it free and flipped it open. The creases smoothed out. The writing was gone, and now just three words were scrawled across the page.

Ask for Quale.

I shook my head, a sigh escaping before I could stop it. Louis was an annoying, powerful, protective, and sexy-as-all-sin sorcerer, and if he were here right now I'd be kicking his ass. I passed the note to Braxton, who read it quickly and then sent it along the line to his brothers.

They didn't give it to Mischa and Grace. The quads and I had been a pack for so long sometimes we forgot about our newest members. My bad ... I really shouldn't forget I had a twin sister. Don't get me wrong, I already loved her – identical features and all – but she was quiet, and quiet supernaturals tended to get lost around us. Grace, I wasn't sure of – with her elfin features and low firm voice – but my wolf sensed nothing to distrust and I liked her calm nature. She tempered the rest of us a little. Healer witches were softer than most supes, more in touch with Mother Nature.

The note returned to Braxton, he slipped it into his pocket. I resisted the urge to demand its return. It was my freaking note after all, but for now I decided to only fight the necessary battles. Our group was silent but watchful as we continued along an unchanging path. The cold still prickled in the air, but it was definitely less freezing than on the other side.

I had a sudden thought. "Do you think this is where Krakov is?" I lowered my voice so as not to be overheard by any but my boys. I was sure the Romanian supernatural prison was the last place Louis would have sent us, but who knew what that infuriating mage was thinking.

Four heads swiveled in my direction, before looking between each other again. I knew, on occasion, the quads communicated without speaking. It freaked me out, reminded me of the Four and how they were clones of each other. I would be mighty pissed if that ever happened to the Compasses. Sure, they had plenty of similarities, they were quads after all, but I loved that each of them was relatively unique. I did not want that to change.

Finally Maximus answered. "I don't know, they're as reticent with information on that prison as they are with Vanguard." All the supernatural prisons were well hidden and protected. For many obvious reasons. "But I believe it's concealed somewhere in the valley of a mountain range, not halfway up like we are here."

"Yes," Braxton said, confirming this. "There's also a gateway community bordering it. This is not the prison … this is something else entirely."

Cloaky was still moving at the same even, striding rate, and as we followed his path I noticed that this seemingly never-ending tunnel was actually … well, ending. The low light was starting to brighten out in the distance, and I was astonished that it looked like natural light. Had we just walked straight through the mountain to the other side? Surely not, it was a massive range, it would have taken us days to cross. There had to be some other explanation.

Braxton suddenly halted all of us. It took him no more effort than extending his free arm. "We all stick together. It doesn't matter what is said or offered, trust no one but each other." His tone was firm, brooking no argument.

I may have accidentally elbowed him in the ribs, just because he needed to check that tone of voice when addressing the rest of us. We weren't his subjects yet. The Compasses weren't due to lead the American Supernatural Council for another three years.

Although they already had the arrogance of that position down pat.

Braxton flashed me some dimple, the first real smile I'd seen from him in a while, and I just about fell on my face. Excuse me, how was it fair to be so ridiculously gorgeous and then also powerful? All of the quads were hot … total assholes. Lucky, I adored their smug faces.

But I had to be careful, it was in their natures to dominate, and if I let them take control of me or the decisions I made, it would all be over. They loved and respected me, I knew that, but sometimes strong men think they know what is best for a woman. All in the name of protecting her of course, and I wouldn't be that girl. Not even for my Compasses.

As we traversed further into the mountain, a rumble rocked through the empty planes of my stomach. I groaned, wrapping my free hand across my abdomen. "I am so effing hungry."

I get a little cranky when I'm hungry … understatement of the year.

Braxton's smile increased, both dimples in full devastating effect, I had to shake my head a few times to clear the hotness that was assaulting every one of my senses. Damn, I needed food and sex. In that order, and not with a Compass. We had a pact, a friendship pact that was sealed in blood. It was not worth risking our dynamics for a quick roll in the hay. I was going to have to look elsewhere.

Okay, so why did the thought of having sex with a stranger kind of fill me with a blank darkness? A depression of sorts? The prospect held no appeal besides scratching the obvious itch. What the frig' was wrong with me? I loved sex.

"I love sex," I growled.

Ah, shit. I did not just say that out loud, right? That was supposed to be in my head again. All six of my group ground to a dead halt. *Oh yeah, definitely out loud.*

Mischa and Grace looked a little astounded, but huge grins had spread across the quads' faces. And then the laughter started. Tyson was actually bent over, resting both hands on his knees as his large body shook.

"Care to enlighten us to the rest of your thoughts, Jessa babe?" Jacob raised both eyebrows at me a few times, white teeth flashing as he too laughed.

Tyson straightened, mirth still rocking his body. "Yeah, what *exactly* were you thinking? Was it one of us ... please pick me." He playfully reached out and snatched me from Braxton, spinning me around in a circle.

I kicked out at him, forcing him to either drop me or cop a broken face. Thankfully he chose to place me back on the ground.

"Shut it, assholes." I started to march along the tunnel in the direction of the lit area. We were almost there. "I was not thinking about any of you."

Liar.

Yeah, so I was a liar, big deal. Better than losing my pack over a stupid hormone-induced decision. Their laughter died off as they caught up to me. Mischa pushed her way through to snuggle herself into my side. I raised my blue eyes to meet her green, one of the main differences in our looks – well, the eyes and a few other bits and pieces.

"What?" I asked, trying to keep the nasty from my voice.

She shook out her long dark hair, her woolen hat keeping it from flying away. "I know exactly how you feel." She pretty much whispered it in my ear.

Mischa was a virgin; her shifter side had been suppressed along with her dragon mark. This had allowed her a little reprieve – in the outside world – from the onslaught of hormones we were hit with around puberty when we came into our powers. Now that her shifter side was free, well, she was feeling everything intensely, and like myself had no outlet.

We were screwed … well, more like not screwed, which was the problem.

As we continued to walk, I did my best to avoid the probing eyes of my Compass quads, especially a certain piercing blue set. Thankfully, a pretty large distraction – the end of the tunnel – was closing in. Hopefully, whatever was out there would give me a reprieve from the amused looks and lessen the embarrassed heat which wanted to coat my cheeks. I managed to keep myself blush free, but damn it was hard work.

Cloaky had disappeared into the light. I really hoped we weren't heading for the metaphorical "light at the end of the tunnel." I liked living, and planned on doing it for at least another eight hundred years. As we reached the end it took no more than a moment for my eyes to adjust to the brightness. *Woah.* What the actual hell was this place?

Mischa breathed deeply. "Holy shit!" It was still odd to hear her curse. Our mother, Lienda, was fairly prim – for a wolf shifter anyway – and she didn't think ladies cursed.

Screw being that kind of lady.

We had emerged onto a dais about twenty feet in the air. Below us was what looked like an entire world, spanning as far as I could see.

Grace had lifted both of her slender hands and had them pressed against her face. "It's the hidden oasis."

I locked in on the witch. "What do you mean?"

"It was just a story my gran told me." Grace's large, very dark – almost obsidian-black eyes – were scanning the environment below. "When the dragon king was alive, he was the worst kind of dictator. If you didn't join him, you died. Some of the races banded together, witches and fey mostly, and they decided to pool their magic and create an oasis, a sanctuary for those who needed to escape but were not powerful enough to fight."

My gaze was drawn back to the scene below. This place certainly fit the "sanctuary oasis" brief. It looked to be divided into territories. Lands of ice, oceans of blue, forests of green, and deserts of red. Basically something to suit each and every one of the supernatural races, even those from the demi-fey.

But one thing was bothering me. "Why was I the only one who could enter the golden barrier?" Sure it had strung me up, but the others couldn't even get in at all. "I had to show the mark. This seems to be something to do with dragon marked."

From the side, a voice said, "You are both right and wrong. This is the created oasis, and over time it has become a dragon marked haven." Cloaked fey was standing on a small ledge which looked to lead into a crisscrossing path down into the valley. "Now is not the time for the long history of the sanctuary. Follow me, there are dangers here for those uninitiated. Do not be tempted from this path, for now you must shadow my steps."

"Are we near Krakov?" asked Braxton.

"No," was all the answer we received.

I wasn't sure about everyone else, but I was relieved to know we weren't courting the criminals of Romania. I'd heard they held the worst of our kind. Their prison was supposedly a veritable stronghold.

Cloaked dude turned and was off again. Braxton reached out then and linked our hands together. I narrowed my eyes and he leveled his stoic expression on me before he said, "I knew the moment he said 'Don't be tempted off the path,' that you'd need some help."

A few rumbling growls rocked my chest, and my eyes got even squintier. "Are you trying to say I have a short attention span? That I can't walk into this valley without suddenly being distracted by, say, a squirrel, and scampering my ass off the road?"

Jacob and Tyson both snorted. I whipped my head around to them. At the sight of my expression, they stemmed their laughter before clearing their throats and staring off into the sky.

About freaking time. I was on edge, the need to be in control, dominant, was slamming into me. Braxton had stepped up his possessiveness more than a notch since we'd escaped the relative safety of our hometown. Maybe it was that I'd never been outside Stratford before, or simply everything from the past few weeks, but now seemed to be the time to nip this bullshit in the bud.

My finger flicked around to rest of them. "Listen up and listen well, Compasses. I'm not a delicate human, or a damsel in distress. I'm a wolf, an alpha and a supernatural. If you all try to bubble-wrap me up, I'm going to rip your faces off."

Mischa and Grace seemed impressed and shocked by the attitude I was throwing at my boys, but the five of us fought all the time. It was how we related, we loved and fought hard. It was part of our pack dynamics.

Unfortunately, my five-feet-four of spitting mad shifter didn't instill even an ounce of fear in my moronic quads. They exchanged amused glances, before Maximus snatched me up and threw me over his shoulder. Braxton seemed reluctant to let my hand go, as it stretched out between us, but eventually he was forced to release it.

"It's damned cute the way you boss us around, Jessa babe," Maximus said. He sounded amused. I sighed and resigned myself to not winning any domination contests today.

I could hear Jacob and Tyson chuckling as they followed their vampire brother. Over Maximus' shoulder I saw Braxton ushering Mischa and Grace onto the path ahead of him, as he took the rear of our group.

"Are you planning on carrying me the entire way down?" I deadpanned, hugging myself into the broad, muscled back of Maximus. "I might just have a nap."

His laughter rumbled the hard body under me. "Yep ... and by the way, you're starting to feel a little light. We need to get you some food."

"Tell me about it," I grumbled.

I could hear Mischa murmuring to Grace. "Why does Jessa even have feet? The Compasses can't seem to stop themselves from carrying her around."

Gentle laughter sounded from the witch. "It's been that way since they were young. Jessa is their girl, and ... well, there is more love in their little pack than in any other I've ever seen." Her tone was hard to get a read on, but there were hints of envy. I couldn't blame her.

It was true, our pack was one big pile of love. Love, claws and cursing. We were all soulmates in a manner, destined to be friends and pack from birth. But, to be fair, some of the reason they continued to fling me over their shoulders was control. I didn't like to do what they said and this way they used their one advantage – massive bulk – to force me to follow their plans. I knew it, they knew it ... and we were okay with it. For now.

"If I could interject with some insights." Tyson's voice jarred me from my thoughts.

Someone snorted, it sounded like Grace, all light and feminine. But still irritated. Which was her usual Tyson reaction. He plowed on anyway as we walked.

"Jessa's small ... we like to bring her up to us. We're pack, we're equals. Not because of power ... but because of everything else. We actually need her in our lives ... she keeps us grounded."

"She completes your pack," Grace said, with the slightest quiver in her tone.

"Yes."

Well, crap on a cracker. Who would have thought there was so much tenderness in the quads' souls. The sharp intake of breath from Grace indicated she was in just as much awed surprise.

I bestowed a gentle smile on my wizard best friend, and he responded by reaching out and grazing my cheek with his thumb. Despite our worries, for a moment everything was right in the world.

Even though I'd been joking about the nap thing, I did find my eyes fluttering closed at the rhythmic walking. Sure, one would think the current situation wouldn't lead to a comfort level to sleep, but one thing I knew was that there was no safer place in the world than with my quads. Not a single place.

Chapter 3

It felt as if I'd closed my eyes for like eight seconds before I was jarred awake. We were no longer moving. I stifled a yawn as I looked around. We appeared to be at the start of this sanctuary and I was glad that I hadn't missed our journey through the different zones. Despite the fact it had been subzero temperatures on the outside of this cave, a desert lay right in front of us. I could feel wafts of heat rising from the red sands. There were definitely fey elemental manipulations and magic spells all over this place. The scent of ... something preternatural lingered in the air. Magic was rarely subtle; it was hard to hide.

I tapped Maximus on the shoulder. "Let me down."

For once he didn't ignore my request. I was dropped gently to the rock floor. "Did I miss anything?" I asked Mischa, who was by my side.

She shook her head, before reaching up and ripping the wool hat from her silky hair. "Nope, it was pretty quiet on the walk down the mountain, and now we are just waiting to cross the zones."

Waiting for what? I peered around the broad shoulders blocking my line of sight. Jacob might not be as big as his brothers, but he was still huge. And he was in the road. Finally, as I scooted to the side I was able to see Cloaky. He was no longer alone. The fey was in a serious looking conversation with four other males, all wearing blue cloaks. Great, it was a freaking cult or something.

I sidled closer to Braxton. He looked relaxed, but his attention was firmly locked on that group. He never glanced my way, but still knew I was there, reaching around to tuck me under his arm. "Can you hear anything?" I managed to mumble.

"They're discussing you and your mark."

I pulled back enough to see his expression. Stormy eyes, chiseled features, furrowed brows … okay, my first assessment was very wrong, not relaxed at all. He was pissed. And throwing off heat like a goddamned fire.

I started to wiggle out from under his arm. The warmth was smothering me.

"I'm wearing too many clothes," I said as I continued to maneuver myself so I could get the thick jacket off.

"Hells yes you are." Jacob the jackass was back. I'd missed him.

"Screw you," I growled.

Tyson joined his fey brother, standing shoulder to shoulder. "Well, you do love sex, remember." Tyson's eyes twinkled, which was about the only thing to save him from having his testicles permanently lodged up into his throat.

Our joking was interrupted by the convergence of cloaked figures. For the first time the hoods of their cloaks were down, so I could really see their faces. The five of them were all different, but I was surprised to see one similarity: each had a head of pure silver hair, sort of like old people gray but more shimmery. This especially stood out because their faces were young.

Could you only join this cult if you were prematurely gray?

Original dude from the tunnel still seemed to be the spokes-gray. "My name is Gerard, I am the second in charge of this *sanctuar* ... sanctuary." I noticed he lapsed into what sounded like Romanian at times, but there was no indication if this was his native language or not.

I stepped forward, my jacket draped over my arm crinkling loudly. "We need to speak with Quale."

No more screwing around. I was tired, hungry, worried about my family back in Stratford, and ... mostly hungry. Identical expressions of rapidly blinking eyes and open mouths descended over the five grays' faces. I had taken them by surprise.

"How is it that you know of Quale?" the shortest of the grays asked me. He was only an inch or so taller than Mischa and I.

The four Compasses took a singular step toward the group. I freaking hated it when they acted like a single unit. The motion had tingles racing down my spine and dread settling in my stomach.

"Take us to Quale." Braxton had also had enough, he was not even trying to hide his annoyance.

The grays didn't seem very concerned by his angry stance. Either they had no idea what Braxton was, or they were very used to dealing with dragon shifters. "Follow us," they said together.

Everyone in our group shucked off any extra layers before taking the first step onto the red dirt. Heat engulfed me and I sighed. I didn't like to be baked; there was probably some snow wolf in my lineage. Sweating, I stripped off another shirt, leaving myself in just the singlet. I hoped it didn't take us long to cross this zone, otherwise I'd be naked before anyone knew it.

Gerard started to chatter; he was our tour guide. "There are five areas here in the sanctuary. This is the desert, where the heat loving races make their residence."

So far I couldn't see any inhabitants, just long plains of red dirt with a few mountains and rocky crevices scattered around, the sand shifting as we walked. There were some pathetic plants, mostly surrounding small ponds of water. The florae were hardy, cacti-looking species.

Gerard pointed to a long, craggy cliff that was off the far edge. "Stay away from that range of cliffs. That is the territory of the Jinn. They are not very friendly."

Jinn ... *genie*. I thought they were freaking myths, or at least so well hidden that I'd never meet one. Information on their race was scarce, but we'd done one subject on them in school. Extremely powerful, they'd been rulers of the fire lands of Faerie, and there was even some truth to the wish-granting legend. Of course, you'd be an absolutely moronic moron to trust them with anything, let alone promise them something for a wish. A few desperate humans had found that out the hard way. Despite their evil doings, I was pretty sure no jinn were in the prison system. They were impossible to find, let alone incarcerate.

We were about halfway across the red plains when my thoughts on jinn were distracted by unexpected movement. One of the mounds – which I'd thought was a small mountain – was starting to rise. Holy flying crap! That was not a part of the environment, it was a red dragon. Not a shifter, but an actual dragon.

It was a little smaller, more animal looking than our dragons, but still in full possession of deadly fangs and fire.

Braxton's gaze locked onto the magnificent vision. "You have native dragon breeds here?" He sounded both impressed and hesitant.

Couldn't blame him for that. He more than anyone knew the danger of a dragon with no human instincts. Though I often thought human instincts could be the most dangerous of all.

Gerard took a moment to examine Braxton. "Yes, each of these territories has a different species of dragon calling it home. Dragons were hunted; we keep them safe. But they can be as ferocious as you suspect. Best to not approach them."

Easy for him to say, because clearly red dragon didn't know the rules and was heading in our direction. Braxton reached out and captured me under one arm and Mischa under the other. Before either of us could even blink, we were back behind him and he was stepping to the front of our group.

"Why is it approaching us?" I heard Grace whisper.

Tyson's features tightened, a reaction to the distress in her voice. Damn Louis, forcing someone as soft and gentle as Grace out into this world. She didn't need this fear. Although, as she cleared her throat and straightened in confidence, I wondered if I was underestimating her. There was fire beneath the gentle. I'd seen it before, but I still worried.

Gerard answered. "They will be curious of the dragon energy riding this group. You have two strong marked and a shifter. It's a big deal."

Wait, how did he know Mischa was marked also? Her energy and physical mark were still spelled. "How do you know there are two marked in the group?" I decided to ask.

"We are the dragon mystics," was his reply, and judging by their closed expressions, it seemed to be the only explanation we were getting.

Our attentions were diverted to the red beast, the dragon no more than ten feet from us now. I could scent the wild magic on it. Dragons were innately connected to the magic which weaved the lines of the Earth. They were unlike any other creature to roam this world, or even the fey's dying lands.

"Stay back," Braxton warned us. "If I have to shift, you're all too close."

Murmuring amongst themselves, the mystics looked like they were going to object, but they didn't actually say anything in protest. They had stepped into the role of a neutral party, giving no opinion on whether we should take on a dragon or not. Or it could be that they seemed to know that

Braxton was a dragon shifter. The race with the best chance of dealing with the natives.

The mystics moved away in a single unit, while Jacob and Tyson dragged the other girls back. Maximus and I didn't leave.

"What are you doing, Jess?" Maximus barked at me. "Get your ass out of the strike zone."

I shook my head. "No, you should leave. I could possibly help."

Braxton threw me his trademark grin, the one which gave me shivers down my spine for more than one reason. That look meant people were about to die. Then, in a blink of an eye, he had snatched me up and I knew I was about to be thrown back to one of the quads. Before I could protest, there was a horrifying roar that rocked the ground.

Braxton spun around with me still cradled in his arms. *Gah!* The red dragon was like a fucking inch away. My heart literally stopped beating. Then as I came face to face with it, the dragon's roar began to taper off and this strange purring-hum noise started deep in the heavily scaled red chest. It vibrated up through to the masses of razor sharp teeth which were far too close to my face for comfort.

Just as I was about to insist Braxton get-me-the-heck-away, heat unfurled from inside of me. Tingles started on my back and I could feel that my dragon mark was reacting to this wild creature.

Without stopping to think about it, I reached for him. Somehow I knew it was a male.

"Jess…" Braxton's voice was low. I could tell that he was trying not to set off the beast, but I heard the warning.

And yet, I still couldn't stop myself from placing both hands onto his scaled nose. A puff of smoke emerged, coating the air in the scent of sulfur. Then the dragon closed its eyes, the large black domes disappearing under scaled lids.

I don't know how long we stayed like this, but eventually the dragon pulled its snout back, gave me an odd head bob, and strode off back into the desert land it called home. As it moved further away, I started to come back to myself. I don't know where I'd gone during those moments of connection with the dragon, but it had been red deserts, ice lands, oceans of blue and green plains. Masses of dragons ruling the land and air.

I had to blink rapidly in an attempt to clear my head, regain composure.

"Did that just seriously happen?" Mischa's voice had me focusing on her tiny person. At some point everyone had moved closer.

Jacob and Tyson didn't look as calm and collected as usual. The wizard had yellow threading his eyes. He'd been pulling magic in case something went wrong. Maximus cut off my view as he stepped to Braxton's side, lowering his face to meet mine. His eyes were black, fangs partially descended. Come to think of it, he was probably getting a bit blood hungry.

"What is wrong with you, Jess? Do you have a death wish?" Maximus snarled, his tone harsher than he generally used with me. "A child listens more than you."

His anger awoke my own, clearing the last of the melodic song which the dragon had created inside of me. I struggled against Braxton, needing to stand on my own feet.

Once I was down, I stalked into the vamp's personal space. He didn't back away. I only came up to his pectoral muscles, but calling on my wolf brought forth my alpha energy. I was still dominant enough to challenge him.

"Talk to me like that again, Max, and the next conversation we have will be with fang and claws." Each word rumbled out through bared teeth.

He leaned into me, using his height as a domination tactic. "You're so frustrating. I goddamn love your stubborn, stupid ass and I can't stand by and watch you destroy yourself. I don't know what's happening to you, but it has to stop."

He was talking about more than this moment. It was still between us, me lying about the mark and taking off into Vanguard on my own. Some of my anger faded out.

"Max…" It was a warning from Braxton. The vampire snapped his head to the side and locked on his brother.

"You of all supernaturals must agree with me," Maximus growled.

Braxton's eyes caressed my features. I noticed the tension in his body, but otherwise he seemed composed. He turned those calm eyes on all of his brothers, but mostly Maximus.

"Jessa wears a dragon mark," he said. "She's special. When beings are chosen for something greater than the ordinary … well, there are always risks. We are her pack, we must support her." He softened his tone. "You fight against change, Max, you always have. But adaption is what we need now. We can still protect her, we just have to identify the new enemy."

Jacob shook back his white-blond hair. "She just patted a dragon. Where exactly do we draw the line on dangerous activities?"

I threw my hands in the air, annoyance flooding in again. "One: you don't draw any lines, I do. Two: since when are dragons the enemy? That one wasn't even dangerous."

Gerard cleared his throat. "She has a point. As long as we steer clear of their territory, we do not have trouble from the dragons. Although they don't like being challenged."

I smirked at Braxton. "Dragons don't like to be challenged … shocker," I drawled, my sarcasm alive and well.

The quads exchanged looks, commiserating mostly, but I was used to that. There was no more arguing. The fight was done. Although judging by their resigned expressions, we'd probably revisit this conversation at some point.

We resumed our travels with the cloaks across the sand. I was marching along, my feet slamming into the ground with the same ferocious beat as my heart rate. Which was racing.

I wasn't really pissed at the Compasses, I was used to their overprotective bullshit – even though they'd certainly stepped it up a notch since we'd been on the run. No, my real concern aligned with Maximus … what was happening to me?

That moment with that dragon had been weird.

I didn't know what to make of it, but there had definitely been some sort of recognition … which was freaking me out a little. Why had Gerard said my mark was different? Why was I a dual shifter? The only dual shifter that had been recorded. Why were real dragons approaching me like I was the dragon whisperer?

I didn't want this crap, I didn't ask for this crap, so why the hell was I neck deep in so much crap?

A stare was burning into me, and I knew who it was without turning my head. Braxton had defended me earlier. Generally, he was the most possessive-bossy-asshat of the quads, and yet he had defended my right to make choices. I didn't face him, but I held out my hand. My heart settled the moment his huge, overly warm palm wrapped around mine.

Touch was so therapeutic for shifters. Braxton's presence created a chemical cocktail inside of me. Similar to what I guessed a mixture of the human drugs speed and valium did. He calmed me down and hyped me at the same time.

Our group was quiet as we finished crossing the desert. The heat never abated, the sun beating down with intensity. Just as we looked to be nearing the forest zone – which I was really looking forward to exploring – the grays shifted to the left and started to walk along the border between desert and forest. After a while buildings appeared in the distance and I realized what the fifth zone was. It was a city area, right in the center of the other four regions.

As we crossed closer, I could see a dozen or so large buildings and many smaller structures scattered throughout. I'd guess it probably housed the same amount of supernaturals as Stratford, but the city part was a little more condensed.

One of the grays decided to fill the silence, "This is where everyone sleeps, eats and convenes. You will be assigned rooms, and then your personal belongings will be magically delivered."

"We need to speak with Quale," I repeated. There was a reason Louis had told us to find him.

Gerard nodded. "I will let him know, but he appears only when he wants to."

Well that sounded promising.

We hadn't seen any other supernaturals except the weird fey grays, but once we entered this main center zone, filled with the many varied stone buildings, there were a lot of them mingling around. Old and young alike. I felt joy flitter through my body as I locked in on some of the tiny faces. I hoped this was where all those children who had been imprisoned were now enjoying life.

I was barreled to the side as a group of six young supernaturals rushed through our group. The sound of their laughter trailed after them.

This was what children should be doing, not chained up and locked away. Thinking of what the Four had done had my temper spilling over, rage as strong as I'd ever known searing through me. They had to be punished, it was not right. I couldn't even think of the years of suffering endured by so many.

Several of the faces which turned toward us were more weathered than I'd expect from supernaturals. And all of them appeared to be distrustful and suspicion.

Cataloguing the inhabitants I noted supernaturals from all five races, including demi-fey, and many more were adults than children. Trolls and gargoyles lined the buildings high up, some made of stone, others wood. They often sought out the high and safe harbors. The gargoyles flew in the light of the moon, spending most of the sunlight hours as stone. I wasn't sure how it worked in a world which had fake skies, but probably still the same way.

Conversations seemed to cut off as our group strolled along one of the laneways.

"I'm guessing they don't get many visitors," I side-whispered to Mischa.

She ran her hands up and down her jeans, a nervous gesture, fitting for all the wary glares smashing into us. I had so many questions to ask, but the grays didn't seem to be interested at the moment. They were conversing amongst themselves. They spoke about the weather outside, the dinner last night, and a few other random things. But something told me there was more to the conversation than what I was picking up.

More supernaturals appeared as we traversed further into their territory. It was like a small town here, cobbled paths through shops, houses, and large buildings. Everything was in neutral colors, nothing bright that stood out. Quite bland, eerie even, especially with what felt like seven thousand eyes on us.

"We will spread the word of your arrival, the curiosity will die down soon," said the gray closest to me. I nodded my head, but didn't drop my gaze. I was focused on not locking eyes with anyone. In my current state-of-unease my wolf would see it as a challenge, raise her silky black head and shit would go down. And right now I just wanted to clean off the shit already coating me; too much drama could wear down even the most resilient of us.

A few shops caught my eye as we weaved through the streets. They seemed to be pretty self-sufficient in this little mountain range. I was guessing if they never wanted to leave, they never had to. There were grocers, hair dressers, restaurants, clothing stores, spell weavers, apothecaries – shit, even a movie theatre. They were actually better outfitted than Stratford.

The Compasses – who moved in a single line of muscle – were definitely on high alert. A regular supe wouldn't see anything besides the calm and controlled exterior they presented, males without a care in the world, but I knew them as well as I knew myself. There was tension riding every rigid plane of their bodies. Not to mention their smiles didn't reach their eyes and not a single dimple was in sight.

We veered sharply into what seemed to be a deserted alley. But before I could express any concern, another turn had us arriving at the front of an enormous apartment building. A skyscraper.

I tilted my head back to try to take in its full height. I'd seen skyscrapers on television of course, but had never been in one. There were none in Stratford.

My wolf whined a little inside. Even my dragon started to move around. As shifters, all of that stone and brick and timber piled on top of each other made me quite nervous. It wasn't natural.

The grays paused just before the revolving door. Gerard waved toward the glass monstrosity. "My brethren advise that we have three dwellings available. You can split and be in two double-bedrooms, or stay together in a four bedroom. How would you prefer to stay?"

"Four bedroom!" all the Compasses shot out.

Mischa, Grace, and I exchanged commiserating grins and sighs. Over-protective and domineering men were fine ninety percent of the time. But there was always that ten percent you wanted to fight them on.

Right now I was in the ninety. I wanted everyone together and safe. The only problem with this was finding a moment away from Grace so I could tell Jacob and Tyson about my dual shifting ability. I was done having any more secrets within my pack.

We were led into the building. As I stepped into the rotating doorway, I somehow managed to get my arm caught, almost killing myself. Thankfully, Jacob was quick enough to yank me free before the next go-around snapped my bone. I seriously needed less metal and more forest around me, I wasn't cut out for this shit. When the silver elevator doors opened I clenched my hands tighter in the jacket I was holding. Once inside, the small panel numbers lit up as we rose in the tiny death box. I was astonished that a place like this existed within a mountain – a place so rustic seeming to have such modern, human amenities. It was weird, and after all that had happened, weird put my senses on high alert.

The Compasses pretty much filled the elevator with the rest of us crammed in around them. Including the grays. I glanced between them. "I'll bet we're over the weight limit with you four in here."

The quads just grinned.

I felt a small hand snake its way into mine. I looked down. It was Mischa. She appeared to be as freaked as I was, but one would assume she'd been in a lift before.

"Sometimes I'm claustrophobic," she said, as if she'd heard my thought. "Elevators are one of the things which trigger it. I avoid them at all costs."

It had probably been her suppressed wolf trying to force its need forward. She'd never known about her heritage while living in the human world. I'm sure it made for some confusing little quirks.

"Almost there. Floor twenty-two," Gerard said.

There were only twenty-four floors. We were right near the top, which I did not like for many reasons, but escape and safety were number one.

"What you stressing for, Jessa babe?" Maximus murmured as he sidled closer. "You're safer than most of us."

Oh, that's right, I could fly.

But it wasn't as simple as that. I leaned in closer to the grays. "Does this sanctuary hide and contain the power of the dragon marked?" I asked. All eyes were suddenly on me. "If we use our powers, can the Four find us?"

Those scary-ass quads, the only other foursome in the supernatural world besides my boys, were constantly on my mind.

Gerard smiled. "You are safe to free your energies. The protections here are unparalleled. You're more secure here than anywhere else. You will have time to learn, train, and expand on any and all skills of the marked."

A surge of relief flooded my body, some of the tension that had been riding me eased a little. Though Braxton's expression did not shift, and I knew he was reserving judgment.

Often when things seem too good to be true...

Finally the ride from hell ended and we exited the metal box into a long hallway, which then branched out to four doorways. Gerard led us through to the furthest door. It had a large number on it: 2244.

Seemed we had found our home for the time being.

"Your bags should be inside by now, and you're welcome to shower and relax. We eat in one hour. We will meet you downstairs then, for the rest of the tour."

Gerard bowed his head and then the grays left us at our door.

Grace flicked her red hair over her shoulder as she turned to watch them leave. "How do we get into our room?"

Her quick dark eyes had picked up on the fact that there was no lock or possible way to access this room.

The cloaks did not turn back, and seemingly before we could blink twice they were on the elevator and gone. I huffed, exasperated. I really needed a shower and I really needed food. This friggin' door had better open soon. I kicked at the wooden structure, missing it by a few inches. I'd been standing a little far back, and I didn't really want to break their door down. I'm sure the mystics would be pissed if I started damaging their stuff.

A snort of laughter had my head flipping around. It was Braxton, actually laughing at me, which would be a real dick move, except his laughter was the most beautiful sound I'd heard in days.

"What?" I couldn't stop a return smile from crossing my face. "You questioning my door breaking abilities?"

In one rapid movement, he leaned forward and kissed me on the forehead. My heart pretty much stopped beating. I stared up at him, my eyes wide and unfocused. That had come from nowhere, and it had hit me. Right. In. The. Feels.

Tyson distracted me then. "There is magic riding this entrance." He gently shoved me aside and started running both hands over the wood without actually touching it. He remained calm, clearly not sensing anything too worrying. Finally after a few more circuits, he slammed both hands down, right in the center of the white barrier.

The door disappeared. Like one minute it was there, and then ... gone.

Maximus snorted. "Looks as if they have the rooms magically protected so only those residing may enter."

So if my foot had connected to the door, it would have most probably gone all the way though and I'd have landed on my ass.

Tyson took the first step inside, acting as the guinea pig in case there were any other securities. I couldn't see much beyond his broad frame, but when he didn't get smashed by another force, I knew it was okay to follow him across.

We were about to see our new home.

Chapter 4

The space inside was huge, the size of any single level house in Stratford. The open living room and kitchen was spanned off by a hall and three doors. As we spread out to explore I noticed – just as the mystic has said – that through some sort of magical happening, all of our bags were on the white carpeted floor of the lounge. Piled together next to the dark red, leather couches. And on the glass coffee table were our passports and cash.

Stepping past this, my gaze was drawn to the large glass windows that spanned one entire side of the space, allowing for an uninterrupted view of the land. Our apartment faced the side of the sanctuary which was made up of forest and desert, and from this lofty height I could really appreciate the full scope of the zones. They were massive. The sun was shining in the sky, but I knew it was fake because there was clearly the rock of a mountain above us. Luckily magic could imitate most of the life-giving nature of sunshine. Otherwise the city would be filled by some pretty depressed, lacking-in-vitamin-D inhabitants. Yep, even supernaturals need the hit of the sun.

Tyson's voice startled me and I spun around from the view. "Who wants to sleep where? There are four rooms, two beds in each."

Mischa's eyes met mine. "I'll bunk with Jessa," she said.

I gave her a smile. Sometimes it felt as if my twin was trying really hard to build our relationship. I wanted that too, but it was going to take more than forced proximity. Only time could create the bonds we should have had. I didn't mind sharing with her, though I'd have preferred one of the quads.

"Sounds good," I said. The joy that shone from her expression was reward enough.

Grace was perched in the doorway of the spacious, white-tiled kitchen. "I'm happy to be by myself. I'm used to it, and magic users don't have the same pack tendencies. It will be easiest for me."

Jacob shoved some of his white-blond hair back, ruffling its smooth strands. "Alright, well, I'll share with Tyson's lazy ass, and that leaves Max and Brax, the dynamic duo. They take up the most space anyways with their brooding and general pretty-boyness."

Tyson snorted. "Yeah, we'd better give them the biggest bathroom, their *beauty* crap takes up a lot of space."

The wizard barely had time for a second snort of laughter before he flew through the air and smashed into the glass windows to the left of where I'd just been standing. He clattered to the floor in a messy tangle of limbs. I was surprised to see that that the glass and paneling seemed to have suffered no damage. They must have been reinforced to withstand the weight and strength of supernaturals crashing into them. A great idea with our hotheaded natures.

Braxton was standing in the spot from where his brother had just taken his little flight across the room. He looked calm, deceptively so, arms hanging loosely as he locked eyes with Tyson. The magic user was already on his feet, streams of gold threading the brown of his eyes. This was about eight seconds from World War Ten – the other nine counted only the major battles between the quads over the years – it was time to end this now. I stepped to the center of the room, between the boys, and held up both of my arms.

"Stop! If you two fight, I'm going to tear you both a new ass–"

"Jess!" Horrified, Mischa cut me off. Her over-the-top fear of crudeness of any description was enough to lighten the tension.

"I'm going to shower and change," said Grace gently, as if the boys weren't squared off to fight. "We should all hurry. We only have forty minutes to meet back with those fey."

She maneuvered through the room, avoiding Tyson, before grabbing her bag and entering the closest bedroom. Within moments I heard the sound of running water.

This was my chance to end the secrets between us.

I waved my arms. "Bring it in."

Our group tightened until Mischa and I were the center of a hulking mass of males. Five sets of eyes locked in on me. Tyson's were back to honeysuckle brown, already over his shitted-at-Braxton moment.

"I need to tell you something." I focused on Jacob and Tyson. I didn't mince my words, quickly detailing the dragon marked abilities, my dual shifting and what had happened in Vanguard. "I didn't say anything when we first escaped because of Grace. It's not the sort of information which should be general knowledge."

The silence was heavy, filled with anger and slivers of hurt and mistrust. I didn't drop my eyes. I forced myself to see and feel every facet of pain visible in Jacob's leaf-green eyes and Tyson's honeysuckle.

The quad wizard was uncharacteristically somber. "Do you have any more hidden information? Because I'm about done with all the secrecy."

Braxton and Maximus stepped closer into me. I'm not sure they even realized they had done it, their instincts always to protect me, even against their brothers.

I shook out my hair. "No more secrets, I promise. I agree with Max, we can't fight effectively if we don't have all the information, so full disclosure."

It might have been what I said, or the fact that *truth* rang clearly in my tone, but the tension slowly filtered out of the boys.

Jacob folded me in his arms. "I adore you, but sometimes you're a real asshole."

I chuckled. He was right, sometimes I was.

With everything fixed between us all again, I gathered my bag – a large black duffle which had been stored in my closest for emergencies but never used – and followed Mischa into the second door past Grace's. I had no idea what the hell sort of clothes Louis would have packed for me. It didn't much matter anyway, I didn't care as long as it wasn't ruffled or lacey. Once we stepped into the surprisingly large room, decked out with two double beds and a full length mirrored-door closest, I threw my stuff down and crashed onto the soft bed.

Mischa stood over me, hands on her hips. "You doing okay? I can't even imagine how you're still going after the last few days."

I scooted forward, placing my elbows down on the bed so I could prop myself up. "I've never understood why people say things like that. It isn't as if I had a choice. Trust me, I would much rather be lying bikini clad on a beach getting my tan on."

Mischa laughed. "You've never even been to the beach."

Rub it in why don't you.

I shrugged. "We have to keep moving forward, there's no other option."

My bluntness didn't seem to offend her. Instead she smiled. "You are so literal, I was really just sympathizing with everything you've been through."

Oh, right. Humans were weird with that "say one thing and mean another" crap. Mischa had zero actual human in her, but some of their tendencies rubbed off on her while she'd been hidden in their world.

"You want to shower first?" she asked.

I dropped myself back onto the comfy bed. "Nah, you go ahead."

She turned away to riffle through her bag. "So do you think this place is just a sanctuary for dragon marked?"

I'd been running the possibilities through my mind since we'd entered the mountain. I had many theories. "I do get the feeling there is more to it than a simple sanctuary." It was pretty ironic that a world which had been allegedly created to shelter supes from the wrath of the dragon king, was now used to protect his "marked" supernaturals. Someone, at some point in time, had manufactured a genius switcheroo.

Mischa continued to chatter about the different zones, leaving the bathroom door open. I mumbled and nodded, but truth be told I think I might have fallen asleep for a bit.

"Gah!" I yelled as hands shook me, bolting upright. "What? What happened?" My head swiveled left and right, but there seemed to be nothing in the room except my clean, soapy-scented sister. Her hair was damp and she had on new jeans and a long-sleeved tank.

"Your turn." Her grin was a little wicked, as if she'd enjoyed shocking the shit out of me. *Nasty.* Probably payback for falling asleep on her.

I rolled off the bed, the little nap I'd had rejuvenating me. My main exhaustion was due to an egregious, horrific, shameful lack of food. I was used to eating regular meals and that had not been happening much lately. My last full meal had been … shit, at least twelve hours ago.

My bag looked to have all the essentials. I just grabbed what I needed and stepped into the blue tiled bathroom. I didn't close the door either, naked wasn't a big deal.

"Holy freaking hell!"

I spun around, my shirt clutched in my hands. Mischa had actually cursed so I was expecting, like, flying vultures to have descended in our room. But no, her eyes were locked on me, and suddenly I remembered the mark on my back.

She took a step closer, one hand raised as if she couldn't stop herself from reaching out. "Is that … the dragon mark?"

I twisted so she could appreciate the full picture, it was so difficult to see in its entirety, the black and red continually moving and shifting. Almost like the shimmering scales on a dragon in flight.

"Will mine look like that?" She touched a single fingertip to one edge, I guess to see if it felt different than skin. It looked like a three dimensional image. I'd expected it to feel raised too, but it wasn't.

"I have no idea," I said, "Gerard did say that my mark was larger than any other he'd seen, but I don't know about you. If the Four weren't hunting our asses, I'd say we should get Louis to remove your spell."

It was the only way to find out.

Mischa must have realized that I was still standing there, half naked and waiting to shower. "Sorry, I'm wasting your time," she said, backing across the room.

I finished undressing, forcing myself not to dwell on the massive mark. The shower was awesome – large powerful jets, plenty of hot water. I washed away the last twenty-four hours and almost felt like myself as I dressed in ripped black jeans and a simple white tank. After brushing out my long hair and securing it in a ponytail, I pulled on black biker boots to finish the outfit. I was ready to go.

The bedroom was empty. I noticed Mischa had unpacked, putting our clothes into the large wardrobe. Our crap took up about an eighth of the space provided.

I could hear voices as I ventured into the living area. I was the last out; they had been waiting on me.

A knock on the door had us all spinning around. I was closest, so I started along the hall, but before I could press my hand to the panel and activate the unlocking mechanism, I was muscled out by four large pains-in-my-ass. The quads formed a line of defense before Tyson triggered the magical opening. I wedged my way through to find a male standing on the other side.

He was average height – short for a supe – and had a head full of silvery hair, another one of the mystic cloaks, only he was sans cloak, wearing a simple pair of cotton slacks and a loose-fitted white shirt.

"I am Quale." He did not smile or encourage any sort of warm feelings, but there was something around the dark blue eyes, a few shades off purple, which told me that this guy was pretty closely linked to Louis.

The Compasses backed up a foot or two, and with a wave of Maximus' hand, he was allowed to enter. It was pretty hard in the supernatural world to prove anyone was who they said they were. Firstly, we didn't carry identification, and any we had was generally fake. Mostly we judged on power level and whether we could kick the stranger's ass. If we were weaker, we proceeded with caution. If they were weaker, we didn't really give a shit who they were.

This male was strong, but there would be very few beings who could take on our pack. We were pretty secure in our awesomeness.

The door slid shut behind him, fortifying our apartment again. I backtracked to the living room, sinking into a sofa, next to Mischa and Grace. The quads spread around the room but didn't sit. They wouldn't give up their dominance. My animals were starting to demand I stand too, but before I moved, Quale sat across from us. My wolf settled again.

The male tented his hand in front of him. "I'm glad you made it here safely, Louis contacted me a few hours ago. I have been waiting for your arrival."

I leaned my upper body forward, trying very hard to get a read on him, but he was like the other cloaks. Some sort of weird hybrid fey.

More than ready for food, I didn't waste any time. "How do you know Louis? And can we contact our parents?"

His expression remained passive as he focused on me. "There are no traditional contact methods out of the sanctuary, but Louis wanted me to assure you that all of your parents are fine." No traditional contact, but clearly there was some way. "The Four are still around Stratford, but they have caused no further trouble."

That was a huge relief and worry at the same time. Those other quad bastards just did not give up.

Quale's piercing eyes roamed over all of us, as if he was memorizing our features. "As for Louis, well, I'm his older brother."

I froze, my mind taking a few moments to register what he had just said. "I don't …

understand. Louis did not seem to know much about the dragon marked. If you're his brother…"

"I am a much older, half-brother. I was born with a head of silver hair, as all mystics are. My mother recognized the signs and knew I was just like our grandfather. I was sent to this sanctuary long before Louis was born. We have never met, only communicated."

Maximus hulked his massive body closer to Quale. "What exactly is a *mystic*?" The others hadn't been forthcoming with information. Hopefully Quale would be more inclined.

"It is … complicated." For the first time the fey seemed unsure of his words. "Since you are here, it is best that you understand … our fey forefathers were chosen, they formed a council to the dragon king – they were destroyed with the king, but in the next generation some of their offspring were born with the mystic's traits. We bore silver hair and also have a mark, but it's not the same as yours." He nodded at Mischa and me.

"You were hunted also?" Braxton asked.

Quale lifted a hand and rubbed at the corner of his right eye, looking uncomfortable. "Yes, we were. And still are."

"Why?" I asked.

He worried at his lips, just for a split second, before the stoic expression descended again. "We are to form the new council for the dragon king. It's our duty to protect his marked ones and to make sure he rises again."

Well, fuck-a-ding-dong.

Louis said I would find information I needed here. Did he really think we should be in a place clearly designed to support the rise of the king? I didn't want that effing tyrant to rise, even if I did wear his mark.

I was struck by a sudden notion. I rose to my feet. "Gerard said we weren't near Krakov, but … are we actually in Mount Drago?" My eyes locked in on Quale as my wolf's shackles rose. Rumbles shook my chest.

Quale fidgeted under my stare. "No, but Drago is close by. Louis sent you here to protect you. Legend says that if the king rises all marked who are not in this sanctuary or Mount Drago will die."

I recalled the legend, but still wasn't sure I believed it. Either way it gave me bad juju to know that the king's body was nearby. Even if he was currently missing his head.

Grace let out a gurgling cry. "If the king rises, he will destroy the supernaturals. He almost succeeded a thousand years ago, and now, well, this sanctuary suggests that this time he'll have an army of marked at his disposal."

Quale pulled himself to his feet. "I was born into my role. I have never met the king nor worked for him. I don't know if I agree with him rising. For now there is no chance it will happen. So let's not worry ourselves."

"Did Louis clue you in on how long we're supposed to stay here?" Jacob asked. "We have responsibilities, we are to be the next council leaders. We cannot disappear indefinitely. What's the long term plan?"

He was right, they were giving up an awful lot for me and I should encourage them to go home. My mouth opened but I couldn't make the words exit.

Quale waved toward the door. "You are more than welcome to leave. None of you are in danger except for the twins. They need to stay for the next month, in case the king rises. I'm sure none of you want to see them self-destruct."

Well, didn't that just sound like an assface way to die.

Braxton joined in now. He'd been quietly observing until this point. "Jessa and Mischa go where we go, and right now our duties in Stratford don't mean shit." He leveled a glare at his fey brother. "Our focus is here."

Jacob brushed Braxton's glare aside. "You know I never meant we would leave without the girls. No responsibility trumps Jessa. But we still need to know the short to long term plan."

"I admire and respect your loyalty," Quale said as he started to move toward the doorway again. "It won't be all bad here. You will learn about the marked and the abilities that your females will develop." He gestured for us to proceed before him along the hall. "And you will all be safe. In here, you will only find others who have searched for security."

Judging by the dirty looks we received as we entered, that wasn't completely true. There were definitely some here who'd do anything to keep their sanctuary untainted by strangers.

The trip down in the elevator was as shittastic as going up. Two mystics were waiting for us outside, neither of them Gerard.

"How many of you are there?" I asked Quale.

He noticed the way I was eying the grays through the front glass. "There are twelve mystics. We spend our time in the different zones. There are about two thousand supernaturals in here."

Wow, that was a lot, especially if most of them were dragon marked.

"We've recently added quite a few hundred to our ranks."

My brain clicked on about the same time that Braxton spoke. "You mean those who were freed from the various prisons?"

The dragon shifter never missed a beat.

Quale leveled his stare on the black haired quad. While he didn't look surprised, something told me he had not expected us to know of this. "Yes, the twins free them and then send them back here to us."

Out the doors now, the two cloaks joined with Quale to lead us back through the town. At the mention of twins I ground to a halt.

My eyes narrowed on the three mystics. "The two women who have been breaking into the supernatural prisons and freeing the marked are twins?"

My voice might have risen a little louder than I'd intended.

Quale nodded. "Yes, we have quite a few twins here, but they are the oldest I know of." He paused for a breath. "And you two are the youngest."

I didn't like the sound of that. Anything that paralleled in life … well, there was always a reason. And that reason had better not be that the two oldest and two youngest dragon marked twins were the four needed to open the tomb of the king. If that was the case, they were going to be shit out of luck. I wasn't freeing that crazy bastard … not in this lifetime.

The quads exchanged glances, doing that thing where I knew they were reading each other's thoughts. I wondered if they were having the same panicked heart palpitations I was. Tyson reached out his long arm and snagged it around my shoulders, pulling me into his side. As the familiar wizard energy surrounded me, I calmed.

"Don't stress that pretty face, you'll get wrinkles," Tyson jibed at me, his tone light.

I managed to free an arm and flip him off.

Maximus grinned. "He's right, no need to stress. We'll stop you and Misch from sticking your fingers where they don't belong."

I was too far away to retaliate, but thankfully Mischa got in a decent whack on his arm. Sure it was a girly, open palm slap, but still it was good to see some violence in her soul. Character building.

I wondered what was happening between Mischa and Maximus. Having spent most of my life with guys, I wasn't one for girl gossip. I just accepted that supes had their own business and mostly I cared very little what it was. But my twin and the vamp had been all touchy, hot and heavy – well PG hot anyway – and now they seemed to be a little distanced again.

I reminded myself to ask Mischa tonight when we were back in our rooms.

There were less of the hardened supernaturals in the street now. Since food was a pretty huge part of our culture, most of them would be at lunch. We crossed through a paved section that had lots of diminutive stalls, like an open air farmers market. Scents were emerging, foods of many different flavors tantalizing my senses, and then as we left the market I almost squealed as I saw the next street.

Jacob leaned in close to where I was still under Tyson's arm. "You're drooling."

I didn't blink or remove my eyes from the scene in front of us, but I did lift my hand and wipe at my chin. Jacob was right, there had been a little drool.

But for reals … it was a street of food.

I mean the entire length, which was probably about a mile, was filled, both sides, with eateries. Each one seemed to represent different international foods. From my position I could see Chinese, Thai, Indian, and Turkish, and I was sure many more cultures filled the shop fronts.

We started to move again, and if it wasn't for Tyson's arm I'd probably have been running. Scents were hitting me hard from all directions, and actually … not all of them were pleasant. As we moved further through I understood the stench. Scattered amid the regular eateries were quite a few specialty cafes. The first I saw was a raw seafood center filled with the water loving demi-fey. Down the alley, beside the café, was a stream occupied by chattering mer-supes.

Nearby, another eatery advertised – in big letters and with disgusting graphics – that they catered to carnivores of the raw meat variety. Ogres, gargoyles and trolls looked to be the large – and I do mean large – majority of their clientele.

The grays halted just past the meatery. The taller of the two said, "You'll need no money here. Simply choose your taste for each meal and order. In return we expect you to help. There is a roster rotation and you will be advised of your shifts."

We nodded and they left us there. Quale stayed with us.

This was different than the way Stratford worked. Sure, everyone pitched in to run our town, but we also had jobs that we applied for after school. Some of them were limited, and you might miss out, but mostly we chose the career we were to have.

I hadn't had to work yet because I was still in college. And the quads, well, they didn't have to worry for a long time about menial labor, since they were to be the next leaders.

The boys took the news of their impending dish-pig duties like real men, not a single whine, moan, or bitch to be heard.

Quale patted Jacob on the arm, before snatching his hand back at the look on the fey's face.

"Don't worry on it too much," he said, covering his nerves with words. "I will make sure you don't receive any of the particularly distasteful tasks. With so many supernaturals here, it takes quite a while to rotate around duties."

Great. Awesome. All fantastic news.

But let's bring the focus back, Mr. Gray Fey – *food me now*.

"Guys, Jessa has the look again." Tyson pretended to struggle and hold me back. At least I think he was pretending, since my feet had started to move on their own.

Braxton laughed. "Time to feed our girl."

Quale was more talkative now, giving us the reviews on each place we passed by. There was something from every culture and country … but my heart was set on Italian. It was one of my favorites and it felt like years since I'd seen pizza and pasta. I didn't even need a guide; the scent of garlic and oregano led the way. I could have found the sidewalk eatery with my eyes closed.

I barely took the time to notice the red awnings and jumble of white-clothed tables in and outside the roomy space. I escaped Tyson's clutches to run inside, ignoring the glances from the dozen or so supernaturals who were already eating – lucky bastards.

A shifter was behind the counter. I didn't have time to scent his animal, I was too busy starving to death.

My words came out in a rush. "I'm going to need one of everything." There was probably a menu somewhere, but who the hell had time for things like that.

The male grinned, and I was distracted for a split second. He was cute, but way too soft for my taste. I liked my men large and hard. This shifter screamed gentle. He was probably a rabbit or something prey-like.

"Well, yes, ma'am, I'm more than happy to oblige your request." Flirting, and a southern accent … interesting that the first supernatural I talked to here was American.

A shadow fell over us. "If another *ma'am* comes out of your mouth, you're going to be bouncing on one leg, rabbit." Braxton looked unamused. And I'd totally guessed the animal correctly. "We're going to need enough food for eight hungry supes."

The lanky rabbit, with his caramel skin and black hair, seemed to actually pale under the stare of the dragon. Braxton had that effect on most males.

The server scurried off to pass the order on to those out the back. Braxton laced his fingers through mine, and without actually dragging me, made it very clear that we needed to go back outside.

I didn't fight him. We had to present a strong united front against all those watching us. But what the actual heck was going on with Braxton? Sure, he was always protective and dominant, but that right then had been mate-like, the way he had declared me his territory. Okay, he hadn't said those words exactly, but the gesture was clear. He was staking his claim on me.

Which was not awesome. I was seriously going to get zero action with his brand of ownership across my back.

My dragon and I were going to be having some words soon. That was for sure.

Chapter 5

Our food took an exorbitantly long time to arrive. I started tapping my foot after five minutes, and by the ten minute mark Mischa was practically sitting on me to keep me in my seat.

"Come on, let me go in there, this is freaking ridiculous."

Mischa was grinning. "Jess, it's been like twelve minutes, that's not a long time to wait."

I was a growling, spitting, hissing mess. Okay, probably not that bad, but I was getting mighty pissed. It wasn't the same for all the supernatural groups, but shifters were part animal, and if you let an animal get hungry … well, we were likely to rip your face off, or some other body part you were probably quite fond of.

I was exactly three minutes from the point of no return.

Thankfully, at that moment rabbit boy strolled out the front door holding two large plates, and moved toward the section of the patio we had commandeered. He carried pizza.

"Seriously," I snarled at him, "what sort of Italian place doesn't even have bread on the table."

He didn't blink twice. Clearly I wasn't the first to snap at him. Instead he produced a basket of bread with a dish of garlic-infused oil balancing precariously on top – *Where the hell had that been?* – and placed it right in front of me.

Mischa held both hands in front of her as if appealing to someone with common sense. "Sorry about Jessa. She's not herself when she's hungry."

My gaze snapped across to her. "Did you just quote a fucking Snickers advertisement at me?"

We had human television, I knew what she was doing. I opened my mouth to rage at her further, when Jacob leaned over and dunked a slice of bread and shoved it in my mouth.

"Run while you can," Tyson side-whispered to rabbit boy, and sure enough, true to his breed he scampered away. I glared at the grinning mage, but truth be told I was already feeling better.

Damn, this bread was fragrant … and soft … and delicious. Maybe I wouldn't have to kill myself a rabbit after all.

Food continued to arrive after that: masses of pizza, pasta, breads, salad. I ignored the green stuff, except to dig out the cheese, but managed to sample everything else. The Compasses and Quale did me proud by demolishing every scrap of food not tied down. Mischa and Grace made pitiful attempts to keep up.

It was remarkable Italian fare, rich and authentic. Someone knew what they were doing in that kitchen. I couldn't wait to dine at the other restaurants. Maybe being stuck here for the next month wouldn't be too bad.

As I was stuffing my mouth, I noticed two little girls sitting at a table across from us – a different restaurant, but right in my line of sight. They looked so familiar.

I leaned in Braxton's direction. "Are those young supes from Nash's group in Vanguard?"

They were dead ringers for the two who had torn my heart out, hugging each other. Braxton followed my gaze and stared for about three seconds before nodding.

"Yes, they were in the room."

He'd probably scented them from over here. Dragons were scary like that.

I examined the girls again. They were sitting with other children, and a few adult shifters. It was no wonder I didn't immediately recognize them. In Vanguard they had been thin, dirty, and expressionless. Here they were well dressed, clean, and clearly filling their mouths with food. They looked almost content. Well, except for the shadows deep in their eyes. No matter how relaxed they appeared, their body language still screamed of fear and wariness ... yeah, not a huge surprise. Those poor children had been caged their entire lives.

I just hoped they found a semblance of peace in this sanctuary. The Four needed to die. Braxton distracted me by reaching across and grasping my hand. He didn't say anything, but the look on his face said enough. He got me.

Rabbit boy appeared again, dropping off dessert before scampering away. I was almost too full to enjoy it, but I'd push through. Braxton released my hand, allowing me to reach for the chocolatey goodness.

Just as I was about to bite into my pastry, a nervous tension filtered through the street. Followed by an excited cheer that echoed around the market square, I dropped my uneaten sweet back to the plate. Then, as we stared around, supernaturals started running along the streets. Chairs were flung free and left overturned in their place, as if no one had the time to stop even for a moment.

I locked in on Quale. "What's happening?" This secure – and suspicious – little community didn't strike me as the type of place where supernaturals went nuts and started running in the streets. They were a little too dark in nature, dark and damaged. So what the hell was happening?

Quale rose and the rest of us followed. "The last time it was the twins," he said, and then he was moving. "They must have returned with the next lot of marked ... I have to find the mystics."

We were totally not missing this. I snatched up my pastry and let my feet hit the pavement.

Braxton grinned at me. "Couldn't leave your dessert."

My mouth was too full for speaking, so I just gave him a return smile, one which explained exactly how delicious this chocolate-filled, flaky, buttery ... oh, God...

His grin broadened. "Damn, I should have grabbed mine."

I hesitated just before I was about to shove the last of the morsel into my mouth. Instead I extended it toward him.

His blue eyes heated until they were a melted pool of liquid. *Holy eff me. How the hell did he do that and what's happening to my insides?* I was, like, burning up or something.

"Thank you, Jess, but I would never take the food intended for your enjoyment." He was growly ... his tone layered with a heat that completely matched those eyes.

I had to wrench my gaze away. He'd just pulled some more mate shit on me. Male shifters don't take food intended for their mates, not when they knew she still wanted it. Some sort of macho provide-for-all-their-female's-needs thing.

It was odd, Braxton had definitely stolen off my plate through the years, but if I thought back, really thought about it, well ... he had never taken food until I was done with it. And he always let me have any of his food ... pretty much. How had I missed that he'd been acting mate-like for freaking years?

Jacob's laughter broke through my thoughts and I was relieved to have something else to focus on. "Did Jessa just offer up her dessert? You okay, babe?" The fey reached out and gripped my chin, turning my face toward him. "Did you hit your head or something?"

I whacked his hand away, shaking my head at his stupid antics.

Our pace slowed as we neared the gathered supes. They had congregated at the edge of the town. Clearly not every marked supernatural had dashed over, but there were about two or three hundred hovering around.

Before us was the red sands of the desert, bordered on the right by the endless greenery of the forest, and on the left the blues and greens of the ocean area. The salty air was distinct and actually quite pleasant. I'd never change out my favorite forest scents, but damn, the ocean had it olfactory appeal.

Even though we stood at the back of the group, we still managed to gather a crap-ton of stares. Somehow they all knew we were there.

"What's with all the gawking?" I asked a nearby female vampire, blunt as always.

She had long, midnight-black curls and eyes the color of rich, newly-turned soil. She was stunning, and not much taller than I was. Her fangs were hidden, I knew, because she snarled at me.

"We do not trust strangers, and not all of you are marked. The mystics told us that you were the protectors of the marked twins, but you're quads. Quads are hunters."

I understood their fear, they didn't know and love the Compasses the way I did. And the Four were scary effers. But how had they even known my boys were quads? Clearly the mystics had big friggin' mouths.

Maximus took a little step closer. "If you pose no threat to our pack, we mean you no harm. But spread the word that if any of you come at us with hostile intentions, we will respond in kind."

Seeing the vampires face to face, I was reminded that Maximus needed to feed, and soon.

Braxton closed in on his brother, broad shoulders side by side. "What Max is so eloquently saying ... we *will* kill anyone who touches our girls. End of story."

The pale skin around the female vamp's eyes tightened. But there was also something more in her expression, respect and acceptance. "Message received loud and clear. You will find no trouble from me or my nest mates."

Speaking of, I could see quite a few hefty males moving in our direction. Definitely vamps, and they had that look in their eyes. It was a look I was more than familiar with.

"I'm Cardia. Feel free to find me if you need the rundown on the workings of the sanctuary."

There was less sneer and more smile on her face as she turned. It was then I noticed the small mark on the back of her neck, visible above her strapless top. It was a miniature version of my dragon mark, about a hundred times smaller.

Shit. Did they all have marks that tiny? No wonder Gerard had freaked when he saw mine.

Cardia didn't look back as she used vamp speed to intercept her worried nest mates. The four of them leaned in closer and I knew she was spreading our message. It would be in the ear of every supernatural by nightfall. Some would see it as a challenge and come at us accordingly, others would respect the sentiment and deal with it by leaving us the hell alone. I couldn't wait to see which was which. I had plenty of aggression and sexual frustration to work off. Beating the shit out a few morons might just be the ticket I needed.

"What are you looking so animated about?" Mischa asked, examining my face.

Jacob and Tyson both chuckled. "That's her happy-violence face," the wizard said. "If that face is ever directed toward you, I suggest you run."

"Shut it, you not-so-funny-fu—" An excited shriek ran through the crowd and cut me off. Supernaturals screamed and called out names.

Braxton, who was about a head taller than most here – everyone except his brothers – only had to crane his neck slightly to see. "They seem to be finding friends and family in these new arrivals."

I wondered which prison they had been rescued from. It could be anywhere in the world.

The recently arrived supes – from those I could see – remained separate from the current residents of the sanctuary. Staying together in a group, their movements were jittery and nervous as they closed in protectively around the young in their midst. It looked like there were only three children and no babies. They were a little cleaner than the group I'd seen in Vanguard's secret marked room, but not by a lot, their clothes old and tattered, eyes heavy and weary. If the king thought he was coming back to an army, he was in for a shock. These supes were damaged. The Four were so far up on my shit list … I didn't even know I could feel hate this strongly.

A witch standing near us broke down into tears. The scent of her emotions floated through the crowd. She drew more of my attention when she started to murmur, "Lacey … Lacey…" over and over. Her tears increased as a witch with short, ragged black hair broke away from the new arrivals and without hesitation ran straight into her arms.

They embraced as if they had not seen each other in years, which was probably true, and I was pretty sure they were sisters, or cousins. They had the same Asian features and thick, coarse hair, though the first female was decidedly better kept.

How many dragon marked were still out there, hidden, tortured? I turned back to my pack. "I know twins are often marked, but does the mark generally run in family lines?"

Quale appeared out of thin air or something – like *bam*, popped in right next to me. I didn't jump though, I have reflexes like a ninja. Okay, maybe not, but I took a moment to be thankful I managed not to squeal like a bitch.

The mystic's voice was low. "Dragon marked are mostly in the same family line, so not always siblings, but sometimes aunts, uncles, grandparents, cousins. Most marked supernaturals will have other marked family somewhere along the line of the last thousand years."

I wondered if Mischa and I had any relatives in this group. No one had ever mentioned other marked in the Lebron line, but I should ask Dad about it one day.

My heart clenched then. I missed my father ... even my mother, although she hadn't been in my life for long, so it wasn't that strange to not have her around. But Jonathon, well, we were a team, and I was missing the heck out of him. I knew he would be worried about Mischa and me too. I hoped Louis was keeping him updated.

Louis. That damn sorcerer.

He was moving us around like chess pieces and it pissed me right off that half the board was hidden. It meant I had no idea when I was about to become a pawn.

I was no one's pawn.

It was time to start demanding answers. "Is Louis coming here?"

Quale looked uncomfortable, shifting on the spot from one foot to the other. "I'm actually unable to contact him right now. We spoke yesterday, but since your arrival, no response."

That better mean he was currently twenty thousand feet in the air flying himself and my parents to Romania. I knew he could step through one of his portal things, but I wasn't sure he had enough power to move three supernaturals this sort of distance. He'd most probably be on a plane.

"I'm sure he is on his way here," Quale said, following my train of thought. "It will be very strange to meet him after all these years of simply being *pen pals* of a sort."

My mind flashed to the tall, powerful presence of the violet-eyed sorcerer. He was nothing like the semi-timid Quale. I wondered why the mystics had inferred that Quale was a badass who listened to no one. Heck no! He was more like a nerdy airhead who wandered off and got lost a lot. Either that or he was hiding his true self from us, and doing a damn good job at it.

My eye caught on Maximus. I sidled closer to the vampire. "You need to feed." His fangs were partially extended. Normally, I couldn't see them unless he wanted me to.

He brushed aside my concern. "It's fine. I'll find out soon enough what the vamps do for blood here."

I swung around, my gaze hard on Quale. "Where is your feeding zone?"

The fey shifted toward the massive vampire. "We don't have blood donors here, you will need to find a willing partner, or we have bottled available in the Redcell Restaurant."

Maximus' lips curled in a sneer. He hated the taste of *old* blood.

"I volunteer."

My eyes flicked to the left. It was Cardia again, and I could see by the way she was eye-effing the heck out of Maximus that she was hoping to get plenty out of this offer. Two vampires feeding from each other probably seemed like an endless cycle of stupid, but as long as one of them, at some point, also fed from other supes, they could sustain each other.

Mischa bristled at the female vamp. I could see her wolf rising. If she had been covered in her fur, it would have stood on end. "You can feed from me," she blurted to Maximus.

Cardia turned slowly and scanned Mischa from the tip of her black hair down to her toes. With a dismissive shrug, the vampiress didn't seem impressed or worried about the competition.

Maximus' brown eyes were dancing. He appeared to be enjoying this little showdown. *Asshat*. I elbowed him, working extra hard to get him right in the sensitive zone under his ribs.

He narrowed his eyes on me before baring his teeth in a snarl. I flipped up my middle finger, just to let him know my feelings on this.

With a snort and shake of his head he turned to my twin. "Thank, Misch, but it might be a little intimate for you. Just wait here for me, I won't be long."

Okay, clearly he knew about her issue. The virgin shifter.

Maximus gave Cardia a single nod and then the two of them wandered off through the crowd. Mischa looked like she'd been punched in the gut, her eyes following until Maximus' broad back disappeared. I slung my arm across her shoulders. I really felt for her. I knew she had feelings for Maximus, she'd made that perfectly clear. But I was worried that she didn't really understand the way supernaturals worked.

We tended to change partners a lot, unless we found our true mate. Sure, we might date the same supe for a year or even ten, neither of which are considered long term when you live to almost a thousand. But unless it was a true mate, there were no guarantees. Mischa had grown up with humans and had too many of their ideals floating around her head.

Although from what I could see, even humans struggled to make the whole mate-marriage thing work for longer than a year or two. Probably they were trying to force pairings that weren't true matches as well. In the supernatural world that sort of mateship never ended well.

There was a surge in the crowd then, and with a hard jolt my arm was wrenched from Mischa and I was shoved aside.

What the hell? No one had been close enough to move me like that.

I took a step back toward my friends, but before I could take a second step a mass of supernaturals crowded between me and them. I was forced further back, losing sight of my pack.

Great.

I decided to just hang out on the edge of the forest until the new arrivals cleared off. Surrounded by greenery, the earthy scents enveloped me as soon as I stepped into the shade of the trees, and I realized how much I missed home. The cool, damp green reminded me of Stratford. The minute details of the scents differed, but it was close enough for now. My wolf rose, pushing me further into the shadows, she was keen to change and run. Giving her an ear scratch I pushed her back again; it wasn't time now to run off into the unknown. I was reckless, not stupid. *Well, most of the time.*

My sensitive ears picked up the rustling long before the shine of eyes appeared in the dark undergrowth. A rabbit sprang free, not a shifter, just the natural kind. Probably destined to be someone's dinner. The creature showed no fear, bounding across the free space and back into the undergrowth that littered the forest floor.

Another noise filtered through to me.

Shit!

I'd been so busy following the little animal and trying to stop my wolf from giving chase that I'd missed the subtle tendrils of magic beginning to weave around me, surrounding me in an invisible energy cage.

It didn't even matter that I was no more than ten feet from the crowd of supernaturals still greeting their new arrivals. There was no safety with magic.

A hazy figure glided in from the general direction of the desert zone.

Hazy ... what the hell?

I forced myself not to panic, even though I had no idea what the freak was coming. I thought I knew every type of demi-fey, but I could sense that this was more ... something which was nailing all kinds of scary. I couldn't think of a single demi-fey that possessed this sort of magic – that which coated my skin in power and raised the fine hairs on the back of my neck. This was energy unlike any other I'd felt.

Not the earthiness of the fey, or the natural magic user, this was cold and ancient, wrapped in a metallic taste that coated my tongue. Still elemental, but from the hard rocks, the minerals, the blood of sacrifice. *Freaking blood magic.*

As the figure moved closer, some of the fuzziness lifted from its facade. My heart stopped dead, like literally froze in my chest. And then my blood trickled in icy tendrils until I became no more than a frozen block staring at my death.

No wonder I didn't recognize the demi-fey.

It was a jinn.

But nothing of the ordinary jinn, I was pretty sure this was one of the gods of their kind. Pure fucking legend. And it was staring at me from across the forest. I'd seen an image of one once, in my history class. Vendir Vamissa, the teacher, had raved on and on about how this species had either escaped to another dimension or were somehow wiped out from their own warring.

Jinn had not been seen for a thousand years. Hence why I had been so shocked to hear Quale say they were in the desert – and a jinn elemental … I did not have a clue how long since they'd last been seen. The lore said one could tell an elemental by the intricate black markings which began in the center of its forehead and spanned outwards to stop at the top of the cheekbones. This one had very pronounced markings.

It stood in shades of red, its skin like a burnt sunset, its features elongated and jutting, with black glittery eyes. The jinn were from the land of fey, or so the legends said, but sort of from their underworld part. Not evil, per se, but definitely had a streak of "don't mess with me or I'll stomp your ass."

I could only wait and see which side of the line this one was on. If it was here to eliminate me, I had no doubts it could. The Four might not have found a weapon to kill dragon marked yet, but I just knew there were plenty of other creatures who could bring about my demise.

No worries.

Despite my instinct being to attack first, I didn't challenge the jinn elemental. I had the very faintest of hope that it was just curious of me and not looking for blood.

Those hopes were soon dashed.

"You shouldn't have come here," it said, its words like whispers on the wind, weight to each and every syllable. "You are north, and north is the most important direction for the king."

Well, shit, it was getting harder to pretend I wasn't one of the four points to open the damn tomb. And apparently north at that. No movement from the jinn, but my survival instincts quickly rose to epic levels. Something big was about to happen.

And I was probably not going to like whatever it was.

I finally found my voice. "Are you going to kill me?" There that wasn't so rude, I even managed not to call it an asshole.

Black eyes glittered as they scanned my face. The force of its whispered words slapped me in the face. "I did plan on it, but ... there is something about you. I'm curious to see this play out now."

From the tiny fraction of information I had on jinn, I knew they possessed foresight, scanning the ever-changing future to see a multitude of possible outcomes, which could change depending on the choices made by those involved. But according to the texts, they didn't usually interfere in free will – fate – whatever you want to call it.

This jinn had seen something which forced it from the desert. It had wanted to eliminate me ... but now it was stepping back again. What it did here would change the future it had seen. I wondered what path had opened up now.

Its scare-the-shit-out-of-me talk wasn't done yet. "I won't kill you, but I will also not make it easier for the king. It is time for you to demonstrate your ability to live. I will let the fates have you."

What the freak did that mean? Something bad for sure, something very, very, very bad.

Screwed. I'm so screwed.

The winds swirled around us, those unblinking black eyes still locked on me. It was next to impossible for me to read a creature so doused in magic, with the most alien of features. Hell, trolls and ogres were easier to glean information from.

The pressure was building, but I held my ground, feet as solidly planted as I could get them.

"Jessa!" The bellow was the only thing since stepping into this clearing that really threw me. Sure I was scared, but I was not thrown ... until Braxton's voice broke through the magic.

For the first time the elemental jinn tore its gaze from me, and after about two seconds of scanning, focused on a spot to my right. I did not turn to look *– enemy in front of me, friend at my back.*

The jinn moved, gliding back, its words just audible. "I do not know how you have broken the ancient energy, but fate has intervened. There are three paths for you both now ... one is ... survival. Good luck." It disappeared into the other side of the swirling energy mists.

Arms surrounded me then, Braxton's heat and scent engulfing me.

"Hold on to me." He had to yell to be heard over the jinn's increasing enchantment. "This is going to hurt."

That was the last thing I heard before there was an inward ricocheting of energy and the circle of power surrounding us suddenly imploded. I couldn't be more grateful that Braxton was with me.

I wasn't even going to question how that was, not yet anyway; it was time to prepare for … for…

The strike of the energy was direct, and no matter how hard I fought it, I was forced to surrender consciousness.

Everything went black.

Chapter 6

I'd been knocked out once before, in sparring. It was tough to hit a shifter hard enough to render them unconscious, but when I was about seventeen a lion shifter got me a good one, out cold for fifteen minutes. So I knew the sensation of waking from a blow like that, the haziness and disorientation of my synapses trying to fire in some semblance of order again.

Waking from the jinn's spell was nothing like that. A slow haze of consciousness started to filter in, measured increments of awareness. I knew my body was moving on instinct without any actual recognition of the motions. Eyes open, chest rising and falling, lungs filling, hands scratching at the rough dirt beneath my body. I couldn't say how long it took for memory to creep in, for images to filter into my brain past the lingering magic. Whatever spell that elemental had hit me with, well, it had knocked me out in more ways than one.

My eyes were tracking small wisps of what looked like dandelion. The air was neither hot nor cold, and there was plenty of light, but I wasn't outside. It was like a wood-lined cave, which was … odd. Maybe a round cabin?

Bit by bit, piece by piece, the parts that made up Jessa started to fit back into their places. My wolf rose, along with my dragon. When I was unconscious, they seemed to be out as well. As the fluffy aura of my dragon snarled and flicked metaphorical wings, I suddenly remembered that Braxton had broken through the energy cage. What the hell had happened in that clearing? Where had the jinn sent us?

A slice of agony split through my head, as if the clarity of events had reminded my poor abused body that it had just been hurt. *Badly*. I couldn't move my head, but that didn't stop my hands from searching for my dragon shifter.

What if something happened to him? What if that jinn had taken or hurt Braxton?

The wolf and dragon inside both started to howl, a long mournful cry of pain and loss. We couldn't survive without Braxton. There was no Jessa without him.

I was distracted by a low growl behind my head. I was still struggling to move myself, having to force my limbs through magic that coated my skin and held me immobile.

The contents of my stomach started to roll as the agony of my head intensified. I was about five seconds from hurling. Eff this. I knew what I needed to do.

I reached for my wolf, fighting the remnants of the jinn's spell on my skin. The shift to animal often cured many ailments, and she was quite impervious to magic, so it was my best option. I was going to destroy my clothes, but I'd deal with that later.

The change was seamless. Four paws hit the hard, rocky ground, and without much hesitation I began to scan and scent the place. It really did look like a round wooden room. There were two doors. From the one in front I could scent something damp and decaying, like the forest; the other held the hot and smoky aromas of the desert.

There was no roof, the ceiling was a natural skylight, a glass barrier in which beams of light caromed in an array of arcs and lines. They must have been the dandelions I'd followed with my eyes.

Circling the room twice, there was no sign of what had growled before. It had to have come from outside. The monochromatic nature of my wolf vision didn't give the variation that my Jessa eyes would have, but I was guessing there wasn't much in the way of color in this room anyway.

The growl sounded again, louder this time, and then everything clicked into place. I knew that sound, I'd heard it many times before. It was Braxton. Dragon Braxton.

Door number one. The forest. Which was good, since I wasn't taking the desert door. It reminded me of the scent of the jinn, and it seemed avoiding their kind was in my best interest.

Shifting back into human form, I rose from my crouch, the light reflecting off my nakedness. I gathered up my rags of clothing and managed to clothe most of myself. Luckily I'd been wearing a reasonably loose shirt. My ragged pants covered my ass, but not much else.

Striding forward, I shoved back strands of black hair which had fallen across my face. At least I seemed to be back in control of my senses and body, and the pain was gone. The jinn's spell was dissipating and I couldn't be more grateful.

I was going to rewrite those fucking history books. There was no way they properly prepared me for the piss-myself-fear the mere presence of a jinn had induced.

I reached for the handle on the forest door, expecting it to be locked, but it clicked open without any effort and I was hit with a blast of damp warmth and the scent of home.

The moment I opened the door, the forest started to intrude through the doorway, vines snaking inside. Okay, that wasn't normal plant behavior, unless this vegetation was filled to the brim with magic, which, recalling the cunning in the jinn's eyes, was a very real possibility. The general vibe from the elemental hadn't indicated that it was sending me off for a nice, relaxing holiday.

I took a hesitant step, slowing my breathing until there was virtually no sound from me except the rush of pulse and beat of heart. Even I couldn't hide those from beings with advanced senses. But still, I needed to be cautious until I knew for certain there was nothing out there but Braxton.

My creeping was slow, silently placing one bare foot in front of another, the ground prickly – soft undergrowth, but there were sticks, stones and other unknowns. I thought briefly of shifting to wolf again. I knew I was faster in my other form, but I wanted to focus, and while my wolf could be the queen of focus at times, if a rabbit bounded past I was screwed. I was scanning as fast as my eyes could process images, my nose elevated as if that would help with the detection of enemy.

Outside the door of the cabin the landscape was overgrown, tangled, ancient. Forest, but unlike any

I'd seen before. I catalogued the scene: trees, vines, bushy undergrowth and large, probably poisonous, pink flowers, the kind that drooped over and had some sort of sticky dew rolling out of their center. They lured their prey in with beauty and then killed them.

Where the hell am I? This place was one giant plate of freak-me-the-hell-out.

The growling started again, louder than before, coming from the left, sort of through the vines and on the other side of the round cabin. There was no clear path for me to take, blocked in a cage of greenery so tightly interwoven that I had no idea how to get through. Shifting my hands into claws, I started to rake across vines in the direction of the growl.

It took me a while, but I managed to force a path, the vegetation scratching my exposed arms, but I barely noticed. A flash of black and blue caught my eyes and my heart rate both sped and calmed at the sight. I knew those scales. Braxton was close. But, judging by the vinery around that scaled leg, he was pretty tangled in the vegetation.

I let my claws fade away and whispered in his direction, keeping my tone low and soothing. "Shift back, Brax, you're too large to fit through this dense undergrowth."

The growling cut off, and I knew he was working to calm himself. I could sense a minute variation in the air. Usually it was very distinct when a shifter pulled energy to change, but the air here felt so dense with power it dulled everything else. Still, I knew when he was shifting back. And sure enough, within seconds the scales had disappeared. Then I heard the most beautiful sound in the world. Braxton.

"Jessa babe ... are you okay?"

He was trying to be calm, but the undercurrents of stress strained his voice. The forest rustled as he plowed through to where I stood. Unlike me, he seemed to be cutting a path no problem. His face appeared in a small gap and he wasted no time tearing a larger entrance. It felt as if we'd been apart years rather than mere moments. As more of him was visible, I saw he was wearing just a pair of low slung jeans. He must have removed his pants before shifting earlier. They'd never have survived the change to dragon.

My mouth went a little dry as I drank in the sight of him. Damn, those pants ... they were really low, I could see each defined muscle of his two-hundred pack and that delicious "V" which men were blessed with as a tool to tempt women. The pathway to the goods, a pathway I'd like to lick my way along...

Wait, what? Down, hormones, down.

Braxton finally destroyed the last of the vines, and before I could blink he slammed into me with the force of three hundred pounds of muscled dragon man. His arms wrapped around me and lifted me off the ground. There wasn't much room here so we ended up planted against a large, gnarled trunk, his hands roaming over me. Not in a feel-me-up way, more of a check for injuries and make sure all limbs were accounted for. Of course, someone forgot to tell my hormones that those large, bronzed hands caressing my bare limbs were just checking for injuries.

My hips arched up as his hands crossed over my thighs, the heat of his palms intense through the ragged tears. I almost moaned but swallowed the sound down. What the fuck was Braxton doing to me? I was about to self-combust.

I wasn't sure when it happened, but the line I'd drawn in the sand with all the Compasses ... well, it was blurring between Braxton and I. Very, very blurry. I was starting to think our friendship pact was going to be tested very soon. Like in the next five seconds.

Braxton had been so focused on examining me for injuries, making sure I was safe, that he'd missed my rapid breathing, dilated pupils, accelerated heartbeat, and that distinctive scent of arousal.

I knew the exact moment he realized. He stilled, his pupils stopped darting across my face, and something dark and dangerous rose in his eyes. Low growls started in his chest, enough to rock us both, a predator in his gaze, built on instinct evolved over the last million years. Both animal and supernatural instinct.

His full lips parted. I could almost taste the scent of him on my tongue, and not only was it his usual combination of spice and heat, but also arousal. *Holy shit.* Braxton wanted me, in a way I'd never felt from him before.

My eyelids fluttered down, lashes tickling my cheeks. A relief to block him out, but the pulsation of energy between us was too tantalizing. I couldn't keep my eyes shut.

Unable to pull away, I was almost a hundred and fifty percent certain I was about to burst into flames. My skin was surely an eruption of scarlet, the hot pumping of my blood a roar in my ears. *Kiss me,* I silently begged.

I'd never wanted anything more in my life. More than want, *needed.* If he didn't move his ass, I was going to take what was mine.

Braxton leaned into me, and just as those delicious, morsels-of-sin lips were about to close the final millimeters between us, he stopped. Mere inches from me.

"There is something moving out there," he said, husky tones brushing over me. "It's close enough that I don't think we should be staying still right now."

I could hear his resigned disappointment as he shifted into protective mode. Probably the only thing which could have stopped him.

I sucked in a few deep breaths, trying to fill my oxygen-starved lungs. He let me slowly slide down his body, his attention still firmly on me as though he was very reluctant to end this moment. As I descended, my bare feet landing on the rough ground, I could feel that Braxton was hard … everywhere. That moment had affected him as much as me. His arousal had not left his melting blue eyes, it had just been shelved while we tried to stay alive.

"Where are we?" I said softly, facing the tawny skin lining his rock hard pecs, still trapped between him and the tree.

He didn't answer immediately, which was a worry. He was shifting his gaze around the area behind me. What the hell was he seeing?

Finally he focused on me again, still pressing against me pretty intimately. I expected him to move back, place some space between us, but he didn't.

He dropped his chin so that our faces were closer together. "I have no idea where we are, this is not a place I've been, and the scents are ... unusual."

Not reassuring.

I pouted in false annoyance. "You could have just lied and said we were still in the sanctuary. You suck as a friend."

His expression softened, a ghost of the dimple even appeared. "Sorry, Jess. While your happiness is my number one priority, I'll never lie to you."

I thought he was kidding around, but the serious tilt to his head indicated that wasn't the case.

"Do you think we should start moving? Shouldn't we wait here to be rescued?" I shifted my head, the rough bark catching in my hair as I attempted to see the room I'd woken in. Maybe it was time to take the other desert scented door. But, of course, a thorough scanning of the area indicated that the forest had eaten the round room.

I wondered if that door had led back to the desert part of the sanctuary. I'd be okay with taking it now, even if we had to deal with the jinn, but it seemed that avenue was gone. Typical magic. I'd chosen the forest, chosen Braxton, and that had negated the other doorway.

Braxton looked around us again. "No. We definitely shouldn't stay put, the noises are closing in. Let's move to somewhere higher so I can get a lay of the land. Plus, I need room to shift."

He was right. If we could get out of the dense jungle, both of us could turn into dragons and fly our asses right out of the Congo, or whichever mess of wilderness held us. I didn't even care about releasing my marked power. Now was not the time to give a shit about the Four. Let them come at us. I was tired, hungry, and pissed off … it was lucky that wolf shifters only had a fertile window once every three months – and I was still a month out – otherwise we could have added PMS to that list of personality traits. It was only four times a year – useful in preventing unexpected pregnancy – and there was no mistaking when the time was upon us.

Braxton seemed reluctant to let me go, which I was kind of liking … a lot. As his heat finally escaped from me I almost swooned like some human in a romance novel. I hadn't even noticed how much of my weight he'd been supporting, and despite the fact it was not cold at all in this place, I already missed the warmth of his body.

Braxton forced me to focus: "We should move. I don't see a sun to track, so it's hard to determine how much light we have left." He turned, and I was drawn to the sight of his muscles rippling across his broad back. I leaned forward, my tongue already extended. I was so licking him.

Wait, what? *No, Jossa!*

I lifted my hand and unobtrusively slapped my cheek. I had to pull myself together. This was not the time. Not. The. Time.

Braxton started to walk. I managed to suck my traitorous tongue back into my mouth and follow him, focusing on the simple task of stepping right into each of his footprints. He was clearing the path beautifully.

"Have you ever seen plants like this?" he asked, a trace of unease in his voice.

Braxton's words had me looking closer at the greenery around us. I knew this place felt strange, like old magic, but until I really looked I hadn't noticed how odd the plants were. First, the colors were off. Not only were the leaves a bright, fake green, the trunks and branches were too. Plus the trees were massive, trunks as wide as a building and towering into the air. This forest was ancient. I also noticed that on top of the poison pink flowers, there were other strange blooms, yellow, looking like mini suns with petals like beams of light, and … they were warm. I could feel heat emitting from them.

This sort of weirdness continued as we pushed further through. Braxton stayed in front of me, making sure to clear the path the best he could. The terrain was rugged and I knew without him I'd still be back in the original clearing. I had no idea what the dragon man was using as a guide, but he seemed to be following a line only he could see.

We didn't talk a lot, attempting to stay below the radar as much as possible. I was mainly trying to figure out where the hell we were. I studied our surroundings, searching for just one defining characteristic. I'd never been out of Stratford before, but I'd paid attention to at least seventy percent of school, and I knew of lots of places in the world. Especially if they were connected to supernaturals.

There was nothing recognizable here. I tilted my head back as far as my neck would reach, scanning hard for a sliver of sky or cloud. I could only see green. Which made no sense, the canopy was thick, but not so thick that I shouldn't be able to spot blue patches.

It took Braxton a few moments to realize I'd stopped following him. In a flash he was back at my side. "What did you see?"

He followed my line of sight into the canopy.

I rubbed a hand over my eyes; they felt tired and gritty. "Why can I not see sky?" I worked hard to keep my voice low. "It's not dark, there are gaps in the trees, but all I see is green."

I looked up again, just in case I'd missed something.

Braxton cleared his throat, a sound I was familiar with. My chin dropped so fast I swear I jarred my neck. "What? ... Brax, what do you know?"

While his expression didn't reflect any unease, I could tell he was worried. "I'm pretty sure you are seeing sky."

I shook my head, trying to understand what the underlying meaning to those words were. I slowly raised my face again. "Are you telling me the sky is green? That's why I keep thinking it's the canopy?"

I didn't want to comprehend the repercussions of this. Sure, I'd seen a bit of a green sky when massive storms had rolled through Stratford. But there was no storm here, it was light and warm. So that meant, if Braxton confirmed my thoughts, that this was just a plain old green sky. The color of leaves.

"Yes."

Oh shit-ass-face.

"I need a drink," I sighed, "preferably of the Faerie wine variety, and ... a burrito. Yep, definitely. Plus a cookie for dessert. No ... two cookies."

I continued to mutter away to myself before noticing the look Braxton was bestowing on me. I trailed off. I tended to put that same faintly amused, faintly exasperated expression on all the quads' faces, but Braxton's held a little more. Memories of our "tree" moment before.

With a shake of his head, he turned again and resumed our journey. I grudgingly trudged along behind him, still suffering from the rough ground, but I'd heal those little nicks quick enough.

Why the hell is this forest not getting less dense?

I was half tempted to shift back into a wolf, but I didn't want to lose the scraps of clothes I still had. Most of my body was covered. And the way I was practically dry humping Braxton's leg, I was way too sexually deprived to be naked right now.

Although ... *no. Jessa, no.*

Our journey continued for hours, and even though the silence was as comfortable as always, I could tell both of us were reaching the end of our patience.

"Where the hell are we, Brax?" I tried to dial back the anger, but I was still a little snarly. "Are you just randomly walking or is there some sort of path?"

He stopped moving, the first break we'd had in ages. "I'm following a scent, something a little different from the forest we're in. It's the only thing standing out to use for direction."

I hadn't scented anything, but Braxton was pretty good with those things.

His features were hard; his jaw would probably break a brick wall if he threw it in that direction. I knew the next words out of his mouth would not be good news.

"I'm pretty sure I know where we are," he sighed, running a hand through his black hair so it stood up a little. It kind of freaked me out to see even the slightest falter in confidence from my usually unflappable best friend. "If I'm right, we're … in big fucking trouble. Jacob told me a little, but he only knows secondhand … and from memory transference."

Surely Braxton was kidding me here. I looked around the unusual forest again, and then up to the green sky. Comprehension hit me like a fist to the face, and for the first time the dread was real and heavy.

"We're in the undying lands of Faerie!"

I didn't ask it as a question, but Braxton nodded anyway.

Awesome, we were in the lands which had something so rotten in it there had been a mass exodus of a multitude of magical races.

No worries there. We should be just fine.

Chapter 7

Braxton and I were doing our best to ignore the fact that we were probably not on Earth. The jinn hadn't been kidding when he said I had to prove I was supposed to live. He'd dropkicked my ass right into a pretty big challenge.

The fey were secretive old bastards about their lands, so I had next to no useful information to ensure the maintenance of our health and safety here. We could only keep moving and deal with whatever came our way. So far we'd managed to stay out of harm's way. We just had to remain alive long enough for one of the other Compasses to realize we were missing. And hope they could trace us to Faerie land.

We could be here forever.

After hiking for about fifteen hours straight, we had to stop and try to get some sleep. We ended up slumping against a rather large tree trunk, covered in a soft moss.

"I was hoping we'd find somewhere with more space," Braxton said. I raised my eyebrows wordlessly at him and he grinned. "I'd be able to protect you better if I was in my dragon form; no one gets the drop on him."

He looked relaxed with his massive limbs spread out in front of him, but I knew the look in his eyes; he was alert and on guard. I was equally tense. Who knew what creatures still walked this world. But … I was also pretty tired, so I decided to be alert and comfortable at the same time. I let my head drift to the side and rest against his shoulder.

Which was not exactly the comfortable surface I was looking for.

Was it too much to ask that I have at least one best friend who was less muscle and more squishy. The quads were all hard planes, which made sleeping on them difficult. My eyes traversed the length of said hard planes and muscles … actually, scratch that last thought. Squishy wasn't going to work for me after all, I'd just take the shitty sleep.

I picked at the sticks and rocks littering the ground beside me. "Why do you think the jinn sent us here? Despite these unknown Faerie creatures around us, we haven't been attacked."

Braxton laughed. "You mean yet, we haven't been attacked *yet.*"

My head lifted as he raised his arm and draped it over my shoulders. Now I was more comfortable, able to snuggle into his side.

"I get the feeling the elemental wanted you out of the way," he said.

I sat up straighter as a thought hit me. "How were you able to penetrate the veil of magic the jinn created in the forest clearing?" I hadn't even stopped to think how lucky I was that he had managed to reach me in time, otherwise I'd be here alone. I shuddered, and Braxton tightened his arm, pulling me back into his heat.

"When we were separated I kept an eye on you, following you into the forest. I'm not sure why, I just knew something was about to happen. The way you'd been driven from our group … it wasn't natural."

Thinking back, he was probably right about the unnatural part.

"By the time I reached you, the jinn was already there. I could see you, but couldn't make it across the barrier. Eventually, I partially shifted and lunged through. My dragon can go where no supernatural has gone before."

It was true, dragons were resistant to most magic, with protections the rest of us could only dream of. Yeah … I still couldn't really think of myself as a dragon. I'd shifted once, and who even knew if I could do it again. My dragon raised her head then, snarling little wisps of smoke, which trailed around her. She was definitely flipping me off ... it was so bizarre how I could internally see the movements of my shifter animals. Truth be told, it was something I really treasured.

Tilting my head so Braxton could see my face, I smiled. "Despite the fact we seem to be stuck in the ass end of Faerie land, I'm really glad you're here."

He was staring down at me, the weird undying light of the sky highlighting every dark facet of his beauty. "You have no idea how relieved I am to be here," he said. "If you'd disappeared on me, well, right now there'd be a fire dragon ripping apart the sanctuary."

Snorts of laughter shook me. "I'm sure you wouldn't have destroyed the mystics, marked, and their little world."

I expected him to laugh with me, but there was not a trace of mirth in his expression. "You have no idea what I would do to keep you safe, Jessa. No idea."

I was sure the awed shock registered on my face, just for a moment, before I managed to control my features. That was without a doubt the hottest thing I'd ever heard. The surge of attraction which blasted through me every time Braxton was close was getting worse, clawing through my body, leaving jagged rips in my heart and soul.

I blurted, "I'm tearing up the friend contract."

Fuck. Me.

I really should learn to think before I speak.

A flash of surprise crossed Braxton's face this time, soon to be replaced with the heat of a thousand suns. "Be very sure about what you want, Jessa." His husky voice was a low growl which turned my insides to liquid. "You've been a long time without sex, so right now it's like being hungry and going to a buffet."

He was calling himself a buffet ... oh my.

Squeezing my thighs together to hold back my urges, I suddenly felt like the neediest supernatural in the world. As in, I *needed* to be butt naked and claiming myself a dragon shifter.

"... there is no going back," he said.

I realized that in my roar of desire I'd missed some of what Braxton had said.

I didn't want to ask him to repeat it, so I had to guess. No going back ... did he mean that once the sexual relationship ran its course we wouldn't be friends any longer? Surely not – there was no way that would happen.

A half grin lit his features. "Get that look off your face, sweetheart. There is not a single scenario that would result in us not being best friends."

Relief.

Except … there was a scenario. What if one of us found a mate while we were together and the other wouldn't let go?

Thinking it through, I was sure that even if I found a true mate, I'd still choose Braxton. I didn't care what a true mate bond felt like, I was stronger than that. Plus my relationship with Braxton and the other Compasses was pretty close to mated relationships anyway. We ate, slept, and played together. We made joint decisions and consulted each other for the important things. We were a pack and a family. The only thing that I didn't share with them was sex, but in every other way I was hogging those four morsels of deliciousness to myself. We all knew other members of our community thought I was banging all of them, but I'd never given a single fuck what others thought.

It just didn't feel like it was enough anymore, not with Braxton. I wanted more.

The dragon shifter seemed to be following along with my thought processes. Probably the emotions were showing themselves clearly on my face. "Sleep on it, Jess," he said. "I know what I want, now it's time for you to decide."

He knew what he wanted? Shit, while I had been slowly coming to the conclusion that he was attracted to me, the serious nature of his tone ... spoke of much more than a quick dalliance.

"You want me?" I braved the words and asked the big question.

I waited breathlessly for his reply.

A slow grin, followed by dimples, assaulted me. "Fuck ... more than anything." His words crashed into my heart, giving it what felt like wings. Then he leaned forward and the air between us shifted to full throttle again. I could practically see the sparks.

His full lips descended, pressing softly to the corner of my mouth. Gentle was not in his nature, but somehow it was the most tender touch I'd ever experienced. That tantalizing taste of Braxton was enough to have me clawing my hands into the ground to stop myself from yanking him into me.

As he pulled back, I swallowed down my scream of protest. I wanted more. *More, more, more.*

"Your dragon is rising, Jessa." Braxton's voice went even lower, but I barely registered it in my need. "Calm yourself, babe."

The fire started in my center; my gut burned. Rising in plumes were the flames of my desire, my need. My dragon wanted Braxton and I had no idea why. My eyes locked on his with an animalistic intensity. His irises were no longer my favorite blue color. They had threads of yellow, threads of his dragon, as if our beasts were trying to get to each other.

"What's happening?" My voice was harsher than usual. "I'm not sure I can control her."

Braxton growled, loud in the cloying silence of the forest. "I know the feeling."

I jumped to my feet. "We have to go." I had to start moving again, I had to escape the emotions. Braxton must have understood my desire. Gracefully, he unfolded his lengthy limbs and rose to his giant height.

"Stay close," he said.

My heart skipped a beat. He didn't have to worry, I didn't have the strength to pull my dragon from his scent and heat ... even if I wanted to. Which I didn't.

We trekked for a long time, the daylight never waning, and since there was no way to tell time, we could only guess at how long we'd been in Faerie. We didn't touch each other; it felt unnatural and I knew it couldn't last much longer. I needed to decide what I wanted, because something told me we were already past the point of no return, that our relationship would never be the same no matter what I chose.

A branch smacked me in the face, distracting me from my endless thoughts. *Shit, I am so sick of this forest*. I was about five minutes from throwing a tantrum that would make any two year old proud, when finally something changed.

Braxton sensed it first, but I wasn't far behind. The random noises were different. We were now being followed, in a stalking-our-ass kind of way.

Braxton reached out and captured my hand. "Move," he said, his voice a snap of emotion.

It was the first touch since the whole almost-tearing-his-clothes-from-his-body incident, and it felt right to be in contact again. It wasn't natural for us to hold back.

We were flying along now. Braxton was a speed demon when he hauled ass. His bulk cut through the greenery, making the journey far more comfortable for me. On the other hand, he was covered in many nasty-looking cuts and bruises. I was thankful he was a fast healer; within an hour most of the damage would be gone.

But that only worked if you stopped getting damaged.

Trees crashed to our right, far closer than before. And as I caught sight of what chased us, it gave me a moment's pause. *Sweet baby ogres.* Faerie was now actively trying to kill us. The creatures were as large as a grizzly bear, but with the dexterity of a monkey as they swung through the closely-knit tree line. The worst was the humanoid face peeking out from the masses of thick black fur coating its head.

Braxton and I were at a disadvantage in this terrain, unable to shift to our large animals, and we couldn't use the trees the way this massive bear-monkey was.

"What do you want to do?" I spoke around my clenched jaw.

Braxton's grip tightened on my hand. "We're almost free of this forest. They're coming in from all sides, but I think we'll make it out before they reach us."

All sides … that was freaking great.

I was not stopping, that was for sure. Thank the gods it would be pretty rare for a supernatural to do the whole "trip over a fallen log" cliché of just about every horror and action movie. Even though we were moving at super-speeds, for our senses it was slow enough that we wouldn't miss anything in our trail. Plus, Braxton was nailing the whole bulldozing-all-obstacles in our path thing.

I still couldn't see a break in the tree line to indicate we were almost out of this greenery. I was just wondering if Braxton was mistaken, when we suddenly burst free from the jungle.

Weird. Major weirdness.

Normally a forest started to thin before reaching the end, but this had just cut off. The outer tree line was just as dense as the rest of the jungle had been. In front of us I could see a long expanse of thick-grained sand, a dark watermelon color. The briny quality Braxton had been scenting was very strong now, and I could hear the crashing of water in the distance. We were still moving, the warmth of the shifting sand soothing on my ravaged feet. I wished I had time to truly admire the beauty. This world thrummed with magic, the colors unparalleled with anything I'd seen on Earth, serene and beautiful, but it had a sense of being *off,* and it was hard to pinpoint exactly what the problem was.

The bear-monkey-people things burst from the forest. I didn't so much see as hear their massive bulk hit the ground. They didn't sound as if they were as agile on the sand, there were many thumps and noises of collisions echoing toward us. Braxton was practically flying along the beach, his strength lifting me to keep pace.

"I'm going to shift," he said. I could hear him clearly, despite our rapid trajectory. No wind, the land was eerily calm.

And that was why Braxton was running and not fighting, he was trying to gain enough space between us and our pursuers to shift. Normally my dragon quad never ran from a fight, it wasn't in his nature, but his priority was protecting me. He flung me forward before grinding to a halt, covering my flank. I just barely stayed on my feet, and spun away from the water line, turning to find Braxton had shed his jeans and was about to shift into his dragon.

I forced myself not to stare at the double perfection of Braxton ass. His perfect, sun kissed, tightly muscled … *shit*.

The horror coming at us from the trees helped to cool the raging torrent of my hormones. Twenty of the beasts – did they call for a freaking family reunion or something? – were galloping across the sand. I couldn't see any wings on their mishmash of features, so we might have flight as an advantage. I felt the pull as Braxton gathered his energy – strong, almost visible in waves around him.

He never even had to bend forward or drop to all fours. His shift was so fast that one moment he stood six and half feet of muscled male and the next he was fifteen feet tall of powerful dragon. His black and blue scales glistened under the sunless green sky.

The creatures must have had at least half a brain. As Braxton tilted back his snout filled with razor sharp teeth and roared to the sky, they skidded to a halt. About fifty yards separated us from them, just enough distance that they were safe from Braxton's flames which would strip the flesh from their bodies in seconds.

I edged myself closer to the dragon's tail; somehow I knew he wanted me as close as possible. A thump sounded behind us. I spun around and my heart dropped, pretty much ending up at my feet.

Crap, shit, ass.

"Brax!" I shouted, already sprinting, and in about five agile steps I was moving along the thickly scaled tail and up onto his broad back.

The dragon snorted but didn't eat me, so he wasn't taken by surprise. Maybe he'd also seen the creatures which were dragging themselves from the water. Not only were we facing mutant bear-monkeys, but behind us came the serpents – shaped like water dragons, but on a dinosaur scale, and there were literally hundreds of them.

I settled into the groove just behind the dragon's wing joints. Those powerful appendages thrust outwards and within a few swift beats we were airborne. It wasn't the first time I had flown with Braxton, but generally he lined his hide with a saddle so the scales wouldn't rip my skin to pieces. The armor plating of his skin was smooth, but the impenetrable strength and immoveable nature of them made them hell on my skin.

As we ascended, the view from below became startling clear. The fey might have left Faerie land, along with many of the demi-fey, but those which had stayed behind were giant and scary, bad ass mothers.

"What's the plan, Brax?"

He couldn't answer me, but I was hoping he'd be able to mime or play friggin' charades or something, because I had no idea what we should be doing.

Where should we go? How did one escape from this land? No one ever spoke of it. I wasn't sure if Jacob even knew. Sometimes he went off and had clandestine garden parties with other fey, but wasn't allowed to share too many of their "ancient secrets" and we didn't push him. I could only hope he had spoken to his brothers a little more, giving Braxton some insight.

So far we were clear; nothing followed us into the air. However a battle was about to take place on the sand. The water dragons had not been emerging just for us, and a pissing contest was about to erupt. They didn't want the bear-monkeys on their sand. Which was great for us and as long as nothing was in the air.

A blur whooshed past us. Okay, note to self: don't speak or think here. Faerie land had an asshole sense of humor. My head snapped to the side as I tried to see what was coming at us. Braxton was doing the same; his large eyes and advanced sight would be picking up far more than I could. Another blur flew by, this time much closer. I shot to my feet, both hands resting on the scaled back so I could keep my balance. If I had to fight I needed to be up and ready.

Braxton roared again. I jumped a mile and almost slipped off his back, catching my balance at the last moment and orientating myself again.

Wafts of simmering air surrounded me, as smoke emerged from Braxton's mouth and nostrils. This was followed by his flames, a long, uninterrupted plume of red and blue fire. The heat that came after was extreme ... I swear my skin started to bubble a little. On occasion he forgot that fire was fluid, and that it could spew back on me.

Shadowy shapes flew in from all sides, and I finally got a decent look at what we were facing. A giant eagle – long feathered wings, sharp talons, and a beak which looked lethal. Riding on its back were demi-fey, not exactly like any we had on Earth, but I still recognized the *otherness* of them. In fact, judging by their long hair, claws and screeching, they were my first glimpse of the famous battle-hungry harpies, female warriors who were well known for their bloodthirsty nature.

As Braxton caught sight of a harpy about to launch herself off the eagle and at his head, he let out another blast of fire. She ducked the flames, somehow managing to stay on her bird. While that distraction came at us front-on, two flanked me on either side. I rose to my full height; Braxton was sort of hovering, so it wasn't hard to keep my footing. A harpy flung herself at me. I braced myself, calling on my wolf for extra speed and dexterity.

Just before the creature's claws were to pummel into me, I shot both hands out and attached to the harpy's forearms, spinning in a half circle and releasing her off into the air. The second hit me from behind and together we tumbled down. Thank the gods Braxton was a massive monster and had a broad back; otherwise that hit would have sent us both free falling. We scrambled to our feet, and I finally got a good look at the demi-fey.

They were definitely female, their bird-like features holding a semblance of a humanoid shape, hunched over a little in the shoulders and with defined breasts and hips. Her skin was gray and leathery looking – I guessed tough and hard to penetrate. Small, squinty eyes watched me as we circled each other. Braxton was still keeping the others at bay with claws, teeth and flames. My opponent opened her beak-like mouth and squawked at me.

"I don't speak bird … or bitch," I snarled at her. Not a total lie, I really didn't speak bird, but I was damned fluent in bitch. Some would say expert levels.

The harpies didn't appear to have any weapons, but seeing how lethal their hands looked, they mightn't need any. I loosed some of my shifter energy and transformed my hands into claws.

It was on, bird-biatch. We were going to rumble.

Her movements were strong and confident as she took a large step across the scaled hide and came in swinging. I knew her style of fighting – direct, no illusions, so I was ready for that first move. I had my hands up protecting my face. I deflected her jab, mindful of how sharp her clawed hands looked.

Wide eyes and a snarl were my indication she had not expected me to match her in speed or strength. She clearly hadn't fought a shifter before. I came back at her straight away, my jab combo slipping past her defense and clipping her chin. She shrieked as her head jerked back – this wasn't a sparring match, I was not tempering my strength at all. I followed my punches with a roundhouse kick, which was harder than it looked considering I was on the back of a flying dragon. I knew Braxton would have landed to help me, but there were even more enemies on the ground.

My kick hit her in the gut, and it was enough momentum to fling her over the side. I threw myself down and crawled to see over Braxton's edge, watching as she fell, her face contorted in fear, but there were no more shrieks. She took it like a warrior.

Right at the last minute, before she was about to become harpy pancake, her eagle caught her. I pushed myself up. Braxton was flying again, his movements reasonably smooth, although without my wolf reflexes I'd definitely have fallen by now.

There was another thump. I spun around. Two harpies. They rushed me as one, clearly not underestimating me any further. I shifted my hands back to claws; it took very little effort to hold them in this change. I expected the two to stop right before they hit me, but they barreled straight into me, pushing me back. Their talons cut across my biceps, my right arm copped the worst damage.

The scales were too slippery to gain traction, so I did the only thing left to me – dropped to my knees and clawed upwards to grasp two handfuls of leathery gut. My claws slid through easier than I'd expected, and my biceps burned as I strained to lift both harpies above my head, splatters of their watery orange blood raining down on me as I hurled them backwards over the edge.

I didn't bother to check if they hit the ground or not. There was no time. A sharp pain hit me in the back almost knocking me off the edge. Talons had pierced between my shoulder blades, the harpy pushing in hard, trying to get to my heart. Through the back door.

Not today, warrior-witch.

Ignoring the pain, I threw myself back into her, slashing with my claws over both shoulders. I must have hooked something. She let out a low wail, although she never lost her hold on my flesh. The surface of Braxton was slippery with blood and sweat now and since my pain was pretty intense, I knew a fair amount of the body fluids were going to be from me. My wounds were deep.

I slashed again. My claws caught, ripping out a mass of whatever I'd connected to. Her hold loosened enough for me to roll free. I hooked both legs under her and flipped her over the top of me. She landed on her back, too slow to get her hands up, and I didn't hesitate to dive across her and start laying into her face, slashing at her until I had her teetering on the edge of consciousness. Then I snapped her neck and threw her off the side.

Yeah, I was pissed now, and it was about to get fucking bloody if anyone came at me. Well, more bloody. I could still feel the hot pulse of fluid down my back. The deep wounds would bleed for a while, but I'd heal up soon enough. Braxton started to dive, and I'd been on him enough to know what was coming next. Evasive flying. I lowered my aching body down to his back and kind of hugged myself as close as I could. Where I was positioned I didn't have much to hold onto. The spikes on his tail would have been good, but I wasn't close enough to them.

He dived faster, swift as the wind, his wings flattened to his side. When he was at an angle where I was seconds from sliding off, his right wing shifted around and I felt a heavy weight descend across my legs. He had me pinned to his back. I could hear blasts of fire, screeches and snapping of jaws, but I couldn't see much of what was going on.

Eventually he freed my legs. He needed to fly.

Braxton flapped his powerful wings and we were ascending again, following a path along the coastline. On one side I saw a massive body of water, and on the other the never-ending forest. Staring out across the falsely green expanse, I was starting to realize how lucky I was that Braxton was with me. He'd used his dragon nose to scent for the ocean, and I had no doubt that without him I'd have been lost wandering randomly in that forest for weeks.

Was there was more to this world than forest and water?

Spinning about the best I could, there didn't appear to be any harpies around. Had they retreated or had my dragon taken out the last few? As I had that thought, something huge crashed into the underside of Braxton. He twisted to avoid another attack, and my precarious hold on his scaled back was lost. Both arms flailing, I grabbed for anything but there was nothing.

With a gasp I found myself tumbling backwards, spinning downward toward the ground.

Chapter 8

I was a long way up, so I had a long time to contemplate my death as I fell. I saw Braxton react, his dragon twisting, prepared to dive after me. I had no idea if he could reach me fast enough, but I spread my body eagle-style to slow the descent. I had to give him a chance.

He moved swiftly, his bulk cutting the distance between us like a bullet, rapid and lethal. A sliver of hope lit up my heart, then something smashed into Braxton again and knocked him off course – another large creature, bigger than the eagles the harpies had used. Probably the thing which had knocked me off his back.

The ground was closing in, I could see the ocean and tree line. I was about to become intimately acquainted with one of them very soon. I shut my eyes, the descent making me dizzy. Inside, my dragon raised her head and growled.

I knew immediately she wanted me to shift into her and save all our asses. My wolf joined in with the growling, her hackles raising along her silky back fur.

Well ... right now the Four were not my biggest worry, and who even knew if they could feel energy in Faerie.

I reached for the dragon energy the same way I would my wolf's. I couldn't remember what I'd done the one other time I'd dragon shifted. There had been so much panic and pain in the prison, but surely it was simple.

Nope.

The energy was there – I could feel it, but it didn't encase me as my wolf did. The dragon growled again, bashing against the cage which held her. At this stage, even if I managed to shift into her, we wouldn't have the space to prevent the inevitable smash into the ground. My only other hope was the dragon's strength. She could possibly survive this plunge, which was going to kill me in my humanoid form.

I reached for her again, and at the same time she gnashed her teeth and lunged for me. We collided against the barrier. What the hell? Was this the protection from Louis? I thought he said he was just hiding the energy, not locking it away.

No ... I was pretty sure it was something else.

I still had my eyes closed. I didn't know how far until my life ended, but it had to be soon. I screamed as something wrapped around me. I was jerked to a grinding halt. Well, actually, I was still descending, just slower this time. I opened my eyes to find a pair of talons wrapped tightly around my middle. I was going to be very sore and sorry tomorrow. But Braxton had saved my life, so I couldn't really complain.

Flickers of blue light caught my attention, and I noticed that parts of his tail were covered in flames. But he'd managed to keep the rest of himself fire free. Which I was thankful for.

As I had that thought, we were attacked again.

Holy eff me sideways. Is this shit ever going to end?

Something pierced through my right thigh. I screamed again, long and loud as whatever had speared me attempted to wrench me from Braxton's grip. I doubted the spearer was stronger than the dragon, but the two forces were going to tear me apart.

More cries ripped from my throat. My dragon was still smashing inside, but we couldn't touch each other.

I slipped through Braxton's claws; the pain in my leg did not ease. I couldn't see what had attacked me, but as I started to spin in a circle, whatever held my thigh released me, flinging me into a straight downward plunge to the ground. This time there was absolutely no chance to be saved.

I closed my eyes again and prepared myself for the impact. In my mind all I could see was Braxton, the beautiful dragon shifter trying his absolute best to save me. As long as he survived, I would be okay with dying. And maybe there was a chance ... I hadn't been as high this time ... maybe I'd survive. I was strong, I was dragon marked

Wait.

The dragon marked were supposedly unkillable. Such an insane concept. I'd always been well aware of my mortality, so to start thinking of yourself as immortal, well, it would take some getting used to. But surely the Four had tried dropping us from a massive height in their quest to find the right weapon. Guess I was about to find out how immortal I was.

I hit the ground.

The sensation of bones crushing, organs pierced, blood splashing around ... it's not something I could really describe. Or the pain. There were definitely no words for the pain. I would have done anything to escape the agony ripping through every part of my body.

I sensed thumps landing around me, but I was too far gone to wonder or care what the hell they were.

Even the flash of blue light which washed over my closed eyelids barely registered.

My dragon roared then, and this time I didn't have to reach, she smashed her barriers and the power of her energy flooded through my weakened body. Had I been holding her back?

Either way, the pain receded. It seemed even my nerve endings were afraid of my dragon. I shifted, and this time the sensations were not so strange – the weird rainbow spectrum, the sense of smell which allowed me to actually taste the different scents on the air. Strength coursed through me, knitting bones together, sealing organs and flooding my massive veins with blood. Blue and silver flashed in the sunless light, and I could finally see the wash of iridescent ocean colors which threaded my scales and fur.

It took a few tries to get the feel for my other body. I'd landed on the pink shifting sand and dug my talons in, but I was still a little unsteady on my large, clawed feet.

Something caught my attention. A black dragon was barreling toward me. The expression on his huge head was ferocious. I'd never seen Braxton look so feral; he was beyond a nightmare, especially with the blue flames. I should have been deathly afraid, but I was pretty sure fear wasn't an emotion dragons felt. And, like the very first time, the flames called to my dragon. I strode across to him, the heavy tail thumping behind me.

Would the flames burn me? Before I could even contemplate the complexities of what might happen – and trust me, the dragon brain seemed to be capable of calculating pretty much every variable of a situation – Braxton shot his head forward and wrapped his long neck around mine, intertwining us in a sort of dragon hug. A strange humming sensation started low in my chest, the vibrations weak to begin with but gathering strength, and pretty soon I was thrumming loudly. Braxton's dragon returned the motion, moving his body even closer. The flames did no more than warm the fur and scales covering my hide, despite the fact I expected to scent burning hair.

I sensed the creatures surrounding us before I saw them, a mixture of bear-monkeys, water dragons, harpies, eagle flyers, and another massive looking octopus animal. I eyed the newest freak-show: the octopus. It had a large spear-like tentacle scattered throughout its other appendages, and I guessed this was the culprit for the sharp pain I'd felt through my thigh.

Fucker.

I pulled back from Braxton, rolling floods of anger ripping through my dragon self. These Faerie creatures had tried to kill us. Now we were going to return the sentiment.

Our dragons fell in back-to-back. The fey-land inhabitants hesitated. I guess after seeing what Braxton's dragon was capable of, they were afraid to face two of us. Which they should be.

Sure, I was pretty useless, lacking the years of training that dragons required to master control of their beast. But I was still dragon and dragons had no equal.

I was delighted that my beast and I seemed to be thinking in sync, even more than the last time I'd shifted. In the prison my dragon had wrested control from me; this time it was still me, even more than when I was in my wolf form.

Lifting my head, I freed the growling howl which had been building in my body. Flames followed, and I was both impressed and astonished, since I hadn't called for fire. Maybe that buildup I'd felt had been fire?

The creatures still weren't attacking. Their caution was clear, although I could see in the distance they continued to fight each other. I was sick of waiting for something to happen. I was going to make it happen. I lunged forward, and even with my lack of knowledge – and some would say coordination – I was a weapon. My dragon claws sliced through bear-monkeys like a hand through air, and my teeth had no problem snapping the water dragons in half. Although, I soon learned to avoid this, they tasted like moldy ass.

Braxton and I were just finding our groove, carving a path of destruction, when a shout drew our attention.

"You two about done?"

I recognized that voice. Lifting my snout familiar scents floated on the air particles toward me.

Jacob and Louis. *Family. Pack.* They were here.

Their shouts had drawn the attention of the other fey creatures, but Louis just lazily waved his hand, murmured some sort of spell, and faerie-freaks blasted off in all directions.

Damn that sorcerer, his power would have come in handy before now.

"It will be easier if you shift back into your human forms," Louis said. They were pretty much at our feet now. "I'll clothe you."

Jacob looked hesitant, but also fascinated as his eyes flicked between me and his brother. My dragon didn't fight me at all, she simply slid away and I was Jessa again. I slumped forward onto the sand. Jacob had me in his arms so fast I barely even hit the ground. There was no pain. My previous injuries seemed to be healed, although I felt sore and feverish. Strong arms tightened around my shoulders in a hug, leaf-green eyes bore down into me.

Jacob's voice was a strangled whisper. "I can't believe I'm looking at you again. Are you okay, Jessa babe? We've been going out of our minds." I could hear the anguish in his soft words. "We didn't know if the Four had found you…"

He trailed off.

My poor family. I knew when I'd gone missing they would have contemplated the possibility that the Four had me and had locked me under the sea.

"How did you know we were in Faerie?" My voice was hoarse, the words scratching over my throat.

Louis crowded up behind me, and despite the growls from Braxton's dragon, and Jacob, he didn't hesitate to touch my shoulder. In an instant clothing covered me, jeans and a white shirt. Underwear also, perfectly fitted by the feel. Magic could kiss my ass … it was way too awesome and I wanted some.

"Tyson couldn't sense you or Brax," Jacob said. "We were dealing with the mystics, trying to get answers, when Louis and your parents arrived."

My head shot up. "Dad and Lienda are in the sanctuary?" I turned around to find Louis. "Thank you."

He gave me a nod. "No problem. I needed to get them away, the Four are not above using leverage."

I sucked in deeply. "What about Jo and Jack ... and Nash?" I didn't want the Compasses to suffer either, or their new little dragon marked charge.

The wizard's violet eyes darkened. "I tried to bring them also, but they refused. They should be okay, I have a few friends keeping an eye on them."

I struggled in Jacob's embrace, my feet were still off the ground. "Put me down," I ordered, and he actually complied. My bare feet hit the warm sand. Braxton's dragon crowded in a little closer to me. Warmth washed over my neck, shifting strands of black hair.

I crossed my arms over my chest, my gaze drawn to the sheer number of creatures that surrounded us, seemingly unable to penetrate the bubble of magic Louis had erected.

"Can you take us home?" I asked the sorcerer, who was clearly the reason we'd been found.

He nodded. "Yes, though getting into Faerie is easy. Coming home ... not quite as simple. But I'll manage."

I'm sure he would. No doubt the wine he'd given me long ago at dinner had been procured directly by the sorcerer himself. He seemed to know how to wander in and out of this land.

"You don't seem surprised that I'm a dual shifter?" I had concealed this from the sorcerer last time we spoke of my marked abilities. Thankfully he didn't seem that upset by my previous evasiveness.

He smiled in his enigmatic manner. "Let's just say this does not come as a huge surprise to me, I sensed more from your energy. You are called for something higher."

Great. I loved being *called* for something.

Louis turned to Braxton then: "You can shift back now, I will keep us safe," he said. The dragon snorted again, growls ripping from his open jaws. "I know it chafes at your instincts to let others do the protecting, but for once you're just going to have to deal with it."

Braxton threw back his massive head, jaws wide as he roared to the sky. As his snout lowered, I narrowed my eyes, before reaching up and tapping him once on the nose.

"Bad dragon," I said, striving for some humor. Hopefully the lighter tone would help him regain some control.

He snarled at me, and I sighed before waving his anger aside with a swish of my hand. I wasn't afraid of Braxton. And clearly neither was the sorcerer. Louis turned his back on us and started a complicated set of movements, opening a doorway home.

I felt a surge of energy, and in a rapid change Braxton was back on two legs. Louis did not stop his hands moving, although he dropped one finger onto the dragon shifter's shoulder, clothing him.

I drank in the sight of my best friend, his startling blue eye, hair as black as night. He had been my last thought before I plunged into the earth and I didn't want to wait one more minute to tell him how much he meant to me. Without Braxton and all the Compasses I would be nothing. I threw myself into his arms and without hesitation he pulled me close. His strength surrounded me, and for the first time in hours I breathed easy. I gently nuzzled my face against the soft shirt he now wore.

"I couldn't save you." I heard the low anguish of his words, each ripped from his throat. "I had to watch as you plunged into the ground ... I heard your bones break." The anguish turned back into fury and suddenly his grip on me was even tighter. "I'm going to kill every last creature on this world, one by one, piece by piece."

Jacob's face popped up over the side of his taller brother. "This is the reason the fey abandoned Faerie. No longer is it safe for us here, and all the fighting is too much."

I managed to wiggle my face free so I could see my fey best friend … and I needed to breathe – breathing was really important.

"Have you been here before?" I asked.

"Yes," was all the reply I received.

Jacob was always quite cagey about this place and the tales of his people. We had few secrets in our pack; Jacob's reticence was not of his own choice, they made all the fey swear oaths. He told us what he could, but it was very little.

"The doorway will be open in about a minute," Louis said, sporting that half-grin cocky expression I associated with him. "I doubt you're going to have time to go on a murderous spree, lizard, even on your best day."

Braxton lifted his head from where he had it buried in my neck. I couldn't see his expression, but I felt the sudden tension which filtered into his already hard body.

"Don't push me today, Sparkie."

Silence descended; Louis didn't reply. I was surprised by his lack of smartass retort. Sparkie was a derogatory name for magic users, for two reasons. Firstly, their spells often lit up in sparks, which alerted enemies to their location. It was as if they couldn't be stealthy no matter how powerful they were, and shifters especially loved that weakness – mainly because magic was an unfair advantage, and our strength was in stealth. And secondly, according to our history tomes, most supernaturals descended from non-humans ... probably fey. But magic users were different, they'd definitely evolved from humans, just one chromosome removed or something. They call humans their "spark of life," and since we all considered humans to be ... well, sort of beneath us, that riled the magic users.

Braxton released me, allowing me to step free and fill my oxygen-starved lungs. "Where exactly is this land in reference to Earth?" I really should have paid more attention in geography and history, but I'd had better things to do. Like sleep. Although, since it was about Faerie, the information probably hadn't been in any school lessons.

Louis tilted his head back toward me. Over his left shoulder I noticed that the portal was opening. "This is the next dimension across. These two worlds sit parallel to each other, on either side of the great divide."

I furrowed my brows. "The great divide?"

Braxton answered. "The divide is the "rumored" plane which exists between Earth and Faerie, a land of fire, mists and souls. The dead who have not been reborn or crossed to the gods reside there."

I was trying to work the logistics in my head. Seemed as if these three "dimensions" sort of existed within the same space, but on different planes. Weird, but acceptable.

I wondered what a supernatural had to do to end up in the great divide.

"It's supposedly where the dragon king's soul rests, in the divide," Louis said, before indicating I should step through the portal. "This is how he can return, his existence is stuck in limbo and hasn't moved on to the gods."

I was troubled by these words as I moved toward the doorway home. Louis reached out and halted me just as I was about to cross over. "Sorry it took me so long to get to you." His sincerity bled into me. I almost lost myself in those hypnotic eyes, and the power which rode along with his words.

I shook my head a few times, clearing the vagueness which had descended. "It's not a problem." I pulled my arm free. "You're not my keeper. Besides, we were doing okay on our own."

That smirk crossed his face again, and I noticed the quick circumnavigation his eyes did of the scene around us — the mangled fey bodies, the creatures snarling and trying to break past the magic barrier – and I thought, for a moment, there was a sign of strain, just very mild around his eyes. I was probably imagining it.

Louis leaned in to whisper his last power-laden words. "Yes, you did very well on your own.

Thankfully … *they* didn't wake or it might have been a different tale."

I wasn't even going to ask what *they* were. Right now I didn't care.

Just as I dropped my leg into the shimmery portal, I heard Braxton ask. "How much time has passed, Jake?"

I swung my head around, leaving that leg hanging in the unknown. What did he mean? We'd only been here for like a day or so.

"Almost three weeks."

Uh, what?

"Time moves differently in Faerie land?" I was proud there wasn't even the slightest waver in my voice.

The Compasses both rested their gaze on me. Jacob was the one to answer. "Yes, time is much slower here, which is why the fey can live many more millennia on this world. We are practically immortal here, and yet there are so many dangers that our lives ended up being much longer on Earth."

I rubbed my right hand across my face, trying to arrange my thoughts into a semblance of order. "So the rise of the dragon king…"

"Seven days," Louis answered, with no extra frills.

Holy hell. Schooling my features, I finished stepping through the portal. The trip back was more intense than usual for a step-through. I felt extreme pressure and a mild turbulence, but eventually I made it to the exit. I arrived back on the edge of the sanctuary-forest-zone from where I'd disappeared.

I waited for the others to finish their journey back, and even though I was exhausted I didn't let my guard down. I walked in a circle, keeping an eye on all angles, making sure nothing or no one got the drop on me. I wasn't sure what the hell was going on with the jinn, but if they came for me again I needed to have a plan. But how was I supposed to find any helpful information on a race, that until this moment, I'd thought was no more than a supernatural fable?

A shimmer appeared in the air right before Jacob exited the doorway. I reached out and captured his hand, holding it tightly in my own. I was so glad to see him again. Braxton was next, and Louis the last through. He'd have held the shield until the rest of us were safe.

Braxton straightened to his full height, which was like somewhere in the clouds, his head shifting around as he took in the surroundings. He got right to business. "First thing, we need some rest, and then we have to deal with the potential future threat of the jinn."

He'd had the same thoughts as me.

"A jinn sent you to Faerie?" Louis showed no surprise or fear in regards to the appearance of these ancient fey. Of course, he didn't seem to fear anyone, so that wasn't the best indicator.

Braxton growled low in his chest. "Yes, it was a jinn. I just managed to grab on before she disappeared."

Louis' expression didn't change. I wasn't sure he was grasping the true seriousness of the situation. "It was an elemental jinn." My voice had a ring of challenge.

Louis pushed back strands of his light hair. Something flashed across those eyes, but still his relaxed expression remained. If it was still there in a minute, I was punching it right off his face.

"An elemental you say … well, there was no way lizard here just attached himself. That jinn allowed him to go with you."

I wasn't denying that. I remembered the words the scary-ass thing had spoken. "It seemed to think I was dangerous and was sending me to Faerie to die." I looked between my friends. "The Four said that dragon marked can't die, so… what was that all about?"

Louis answered: "Just because nothing on Earth can kill you, doesn't mean nothing in Faerie can."

And suddenly the jinn's actions moved up to another level of deadly.

On that ominous note from Louis, we started to trudge toward the main part of the community. I was actually looking forward to the death ride up in the elevator, just so I could fall into bed. Even food wasn't number one on my mind, although I wouldn't say no to a piece of cake if it landed in front of me. My stomach rumbled then, as if it had been slumbering and my thoughts had awoken the beast.

My eye started to roam over Jacob and Louis, as if I could discern their secrets with a glance. "Did you bring me any cake?"

I growled and Jacob actually paused. "She's got that look on her face again." His tone was as wary as it should be in these circumstances.

Louis' laughter rang out, breaking whatever tension had been layering our group since we ran into each other in Faerie. Braxton even joined in, his deep tones sending those tingles down my spine. These two supernaturals were so powerful that to watch them together, well, it was beyond captivating. Jacob could hold his own with almost any other supe in the world, but he was not of the level of Braxton and Louis.

With another chuckle, Louis waved his hand, and in the blink of an eye he was holding a medium sized white plate. Resting on it was heaven. Chocolate ... and caramel ... with flakes of dark chocolate coating the side.

He held it out to me and I actually drooled a little. "I'm sure they won't miss this in the dessert shop," the sorcerer said, and he rapidly moved up my list of favorite people in the world. He might be in the top ten now.

Wait a minute ... there was a dessert shop?

I pounced on the cake. The first bite crumbled in my mouth and I had to close my eyes. It was so good that it took every part of my control to not shove the entire thing in in one go. Rich creaminess danced across my tongue, the bitterness of dark chocolate tempered by the velvety ganache and caramel filling.

Holy shit.

My eyes flew open to find three males staring at me. Each expression was a little different, and I was reading a hell of a lot in those gazes.

"You will be showing me which shop this comes from," I warned Louis. He had created a monster. I was hooked.

Jacob was the first to straighten. He looped an arm over my shoulder and pulled me into his side. "Come on, Jessa babe, it's time for you to get some rest ... and a shower wouldn't go astray."

I elbowed him, although he definitely had a point. I smelled like old ass that had been left to sit in the sun for a week. We made quick work of the distance to our room. I finished the cake and Louis kindly disappeared the plate for me. He grinned when I asked him he wanted a tip. If this sorcerer thing didn't work out, he had a very successful career in hospitality waiting for him.

The ride up in the elevator was as horrible as always, but clenched hands were the only sign of my discomfort. I hoped anyway. I couldn't wait to see the rest of my pack, and Mischa too. I'd actually missed my sister, she was working her way into my life.

Exactly how it should have been over the years.

Louis opened the door to our rooms. I didn't bother to ask how he got himself onto the security. He was Louis, that was all I needed to know.

The main living area was empty, the floor soft on my poor abused feet. I turned to Jacob. "Where is everyone?"

"When Louis arrived, we were spending our time searching for you. He pretty quickly inferred that we were all dumbasses, and that you were most certainly in Faerie. I was the logical one to accompany him, since the land would recognize me as its own."

"*Inferred,*" the sorcerer murmured. "I'll have to work on making myself clearer."

I ignored the idiocy in the room. "Are you telling me that the *land* could have started attacking us too?"

Jacob gave two hard nods. "Yes."

Great! Sign me up for the all-inclusive week at Faerie land. Holiday from hell.

I moved across the room and opened the door to the bedroom I shared with Mischa. It was empty. I poked my head back around the corner. "Where's Mischa?"

Jacob's expression shuttered before recovering in almost the same moment. I narrowed my eyes on him. "Speak, Jake, or I'll have Braxton beat it out of you." I liked to fight my own battles, but with the Compasses, Braxton was the true threat.

The fey ran a hand through his white hair. "Something happened while you were gone. We all kind of lost our shit and … things went down between Mischa and Max." His full lips thinned. "Tension has been pretty high, and, well, she hasn't been around much."

I couldn't imagine my slightly timid sister wandering around this place on her own. What were they not telling me? I furrowed my brow and opened my mouth to blast the shit out of him, but Louis interrupted me before I could let loose.

"She's fallen in with the twins."

My heart stuttered in my chest. I almost wheezed as I tried to suck in my next breath.

"What?" I stepped back toward the males in the living room, blinking a few times in rapid succession, trying to clear my thoughts. "You mean the twins who were breaking all of those marked out of the prisons? The twins who are trying to bring about the rise of the dragon king? The ancient twins who are probably manipulating Mischa without her even realizing it?"

Holy fucking fuck. This was why I needed to stay here at all times, supes went stupid without me. I rubbed my temples, exhaustion pressing down on me. A weight only sleep could ease.

I sighed. "Right now I'm useless. I need some rest. But we have to deal with this Mischa thing, she's not used to our ways. If the twins were looking for a way to infiltrate our pack, she's the weak link."

Braxton and I locked eyes, and I could read the same worry in his that I'm sure were reflected in mine.

I got a sudden whiff of my own disgustingness, the scent tingling my senses and not in a good way. Definitely time for a shower.

"I'm going to clean up," I said, "and then before I hit the bed we need a game plan."

I turned back to enter my room, but paused as I heard a noise. I'd thought everyone was out, but someone was moving in the room Braxton and Maximus shared. I caught a familiar vamp scent.

I dashed down the hall. I couldn't wait to see my vampire. I'd missed him so much, and I knew he'd have been completely pissed and worried when both of us disappeared. It would be cruel to not let him know straight away that we were back.

"Jess!" I heard Jacob yell for me, but I was already at the door.

I flung it open and stepped into the dimly lit room. Only one bed was occupied, a sea of blankets piled up high. I had just a moment to wonder why the hell Maximus was in bed in the middle of the day before more scents hit me hard. I gasped as two heads popped up from the covers.

My eyes had adjusted to the lack of light, so I recognized the tousled dirty blond hair of my best friend, and the tiny beauty queen vampire who'd taken Maximus away right before I'd disappeared. Cardia. They were intertwined, lingering traces of sex in the air. Sex and blood.

Chapter 9

I just stood there in the bedroom doorway, my hands hanging limply at my sides as I tried to process my emotions.

Maximus sprang out of the bed, as lithe and agile as only a supernatural could be. "Jess!" His exclamation was loud as he dived toward me, naked in all his glory, but not aroused, so clearly I'd caught them between rounds. I had just enough time to register the darkening anger on Cardia's face before I was hit with a wall of muscle.

"I've been so damned worried about you, Jess." His voice cracked a little as he pulled back, both hands gripping my biceps. "Where the hell were you?" His emotional tone shifted into a growl, fangs slightly descended and his eyes shaded to black.

I'd never seen him vamp out in such a short time, especially when he wasn't hungry. But that wasn't my most prevalent thought. I was having a breakdown similar to the one I had the time I thought Mischa was a dragon shifter. I knew the only way Maximus would be in bed with this chick while his brother and I were missing was if she was his true mate. Not to mention he generally never slept with the same female more than a few times. He liked to cut them off before they got attached. It had been three weeks with this Cardia.

The first few months after finding your mate were intense. Supernaturals had trouble leaving the house and going out into public. Plus, I had not missed the vamped-out nature of the interloper. Her clawed hands and descended fangs screamed of a territorial reaction.

I was pissed. Anger coursed through me with the force of a speeding train, flooding my gut and ricocheting out. It wasn't that I felt the way for Maximus that I did for Braxton, but still, this was the beginning of the end of our perfect pack life. I would have to pull back from the very close proximity I had with the Compasses. Cardia would not tolerate that.

I let my expression dissolve into blankness, taming my inner turmoil. "It doesn't really seem as if you were too worried about me."

It was either cut him down or lose my shit and cry like a baby.

Yes, I was being a bitch, mate bonding couldn't be fought against. What my parents had done was insane in the scheme of supernatural relationships, separating themselves to protect Mischa and I from the marked hunters; it was unnatural. As I had this thought I realized I wanted to see my parents. Where were they? I assumed they had been given their own apartment close by.

Maybe somewhere for me to escape to.

I was avoiding thinking about Maximus, even though he was standing before me, seemingly trying to figure out what to say in response to my anger.

Tears pricked at my eyelids. I refused to let them fall. I deliberately removed both of his large hands and took a step back, working hard to calm myself. I hit a hard wall of warmth, and for a second I sank into the comfort that was Braxton. My shock and pain had been so great I hadn't even realized he'd been standing behind us.

I tore myself from the dragon shifter. "I have to go. I need some air."

"Jess..." Maximus' voice was hoarse now. He held out a hand toward me. "Please, don't go, we need to talk."

I shook my head. I needed to grieve and come to terms with everything I'd lost. And I needed to do it alone.

"Don't follow me."

I issued the last warning before I ran out of the room, and using every facet of my shifter speed dashed across the apartment and out the front door.

I was in the elevator when three Compasses burst out the door – Maximus ripping his pants on, the doors sliding closed between us.

"Jess, it's not safe for you to be on your own," I heard the vampire say desperately, right before the metal sealed them away from me.

Silence descended. I sank against the cold steel wall, my heartbeat erratic. Damn, I was hurting, a pain that was soul deep. I knew I would eventually be happy for Maximus. I wanted my boys to have love and a mate. I wanted to be the aunt to their kids, but I'd thought that was a long way in the future. Not today. Not when there was so much shit happening in our world. I wanted to climb into bed between my dragon shifter and vampire, have my fey and wizard there also, just like we'd done so many times over the years.

But it would never again be like that.

Instead of crying, I channeled the crap-ton of emotions churning inside into anger, my weapon right now, and exited the building on a wave of self-righteous rage. I stormed along the streets, aimlessly wandering and yet still finding myself in that main street of food.

What can I say, food and I have a bond which I'll probably never replicate with any male.

I stopped near a colorful falafel store, though I wasn't really reading the menu in the window. I was actually paying attention to the small group which had been trailing me for some time—not the Compasses—and I was starting to get the feeling they had more than fun on their minds.

Since I was in a shit of a mood, I decided to get off the main path and have a little stress-relieving entertainment. If I couldn't have sex, maybe some fighting would help.

I strode between two Chinese food stores. No dead end, so I wasn't boxing myself in. Rocks scuffed on the path behind me. I smiled. Three supernaturals. I scented two shifters and a vampire. They'd decided now was the time to approach.

Turning, I lowered into a fighting stance.

Front and center was a tiny brunette – her hair braided down her back in a single line – female, a shifter but not wolf. Something close … fox maybe. Flanking either side of her was another, much larger male shifter, also fox – and third was a vampire. They continued straight at me. I waited, poised on the balls of my feet, hands relaxed but ready at my sides. I also had an ear out for any approach from behind, in case they were going for the whole distraction ploy.

"You shouldn't be here," the fox girl said, showcasing her pointy little teeth. She'd been spending too much time in her animal form. It was starting to bleed into the human. "You have brought unease to our sanctuary. The Four roam the mountains around us, and you pack around with another set of quads. You must leave."

The Four were here, in Romania! Shit! Another awesome piece of news to add to my shit-cake of a day. Would December hurry up and fuck off already, it was turning out to be my least favorite month. Supernaturals don't celebrate Christmas, that was a human tradition, but even if we did there wasn't anything jolly going on right now.

The male fox distracted me from my thoughts. "You must leave!"

I raised my right eyebrow. "And if I don't?" It wasn't a blatant challenge, but it was close. I hadn't really scented aggression from them. I was pretty sure they'd just followed me as a warning, but I was in the right sort of mood to push them.

The three took a step closer, barely five feet between us. "Then we will make you." Finally the vampire got to speak, and compared to Maximus this guy's balls hadn't even dropped. It was as if he was trying really hard to deepen his voice to that scary octave which the quads were kings at. He missed it by about a mile.

I pushed aside thoughts of my vamp, now wasn't the time to drown in heartache. I was ready to work off some of the anger which was riding me like a mermaid in a seaweed storm. I slowed my breathing, taking a few moments to size up my opponents. The chick was the leader, and the one I was most wary of. When you're smaller than most supes, you had to rely less on strength and more on developing skills. Something told me she had some mad skills.

The three of them exchanged a glance; an unspoken something passed between them. They somehow mutually agreed on an order, and the vampire came at me first, gliding over. A vamp's speed is their greatest asset. But shifters were fast also.

He flew straight at me, fangs bared, hands aloft. Definitely untrained. I took two steps and after a combo one-two hook, smacked him straight in the nose. Cartilage fractured under my fist, but I didn't stop there, turning with a spinning heel kick and cracking him in the jaw. As he hit the ground, I was over the top of him and had his left arm twisted behind. The distinct crack of bone breaking echoed through the silent alley.

He let out a whimpering scream. *What a bitch.*

I dropped my knee into his temple and just like that he was out cold.

Bouncing back to my feet I eyed the other two waiting their turn. "That was fun," I said, not even remotely out of breath. "Next…" I smiled, and the fox male almost took a step back. I must be wearing a hell of an expression right now.

I assumed he would come at me next and I wasn't wrong. He strolled closer. The fox was all long lean lines, but I could see lithe muscles in his lengthy limbs. His eyes were dark, almost a gray and his hair orange, like a carrot, which I'd guess was also the color of his animal's fur. Generally, that's how it worked.

He was less bouncy and eager than the vamp, and hopefully equally skill-less. But something told me it wasn't going to be quite as easy. Standing motionless, all of a sudden he leapt for me, trying for the take-me-by-surprise plot. *Sigh. Amateur.*

I sidestepped the first swing and he tried to counter with a backwards kick to my gut. I saw it coming from a mile away. Using the narrow walls I gained height by running up the stone, launching myself off the side and landing a massive Superman punch on his jaw. He smashed back into the wall behind, and I followed, landing in a crouch over his body.

The fox tried to wiggle back to his feet, but he must have been seeing stars because his movements were jerky and he ended up falling down again. I sensed footsteps and knew the female was going to come at me while I was occupied with the male. With this in mind I swung my left elbow into his face, I heard bone crack, and since I'm not a healer I could only guess that I'd broken his jaw. He didn't move again.

I pushed both hands onto his chest, and using his ribs for leverage flipped myself backwards into another crouch. The shock on fox bitch's face flashed in the dim light. Yes, I had some mad skills too, let's just hope they were enough.

I could tell that she hadn't expected me to move so quickly; however her recovery was admirable. Her footsteps were swift, short brown hair bouncing on her shoulders.

I tried to slow my rapid pulse so I could focus on what was coming at me. Her movements were smoother than the males. She'd had training. I brought both of my hands up to guard my face. This was going to get interesting.

Two steps in and she swung a left-right-left-cross combo at my face. I ducked the first and blocked the second, before countering with my own combo. Which she managed to block. She had fast hands, really fast. I decided to change strategies. Just because she was good with her hands didn't mean she could grapple. I needed to get her to the ground.

When she came at me again, I waited until the last second and let her punch graze me before dropping to the floor and smashing her in the stomach. She wheezed as the air left her lungs, then I wrapped myself around her legs and took her down. Her head smashed into the stone floor, and I swear I heard that dull echoing hit of skull on cement all the way into my bones. I hated that wet, bouncing sound. It turned my stomach.

She got her elbows under herself, trying to arch up and flip me off her. It wasn't happening today. I smashed both knees into her chest and she hit the deck again. Her eyes rolled back in her head. I waited for her to react, but she looked to be out. Guess I needed to downgrade her skills from mad to mediocre. I pulled myself wearily to my feet. Now that my adrenalin and anger had been worked off, I was feeling every inch of the exhaustion which was about to level me.

"You about done, Jess?"

I spun and shrank into a crouch. How the hell had Louis crept up on me?

The sorcerer was leaning casually against the wall at the entrance of the alley. He had that smile on his face which he wore when he thought I was amusing. I didn't ask him why he hadn't helped me. He knew I wouldn't have appreciated his interference. I strolled across to his side, and as he straightened his expression sobered.

"So besides that…" he said, waving toward the carnage I'd left behind, "are you doing okay?"

I swallowed, all the events of the past few days crashing in on me. "The Four are here, outside of the mountains."

He nodded. "Yes, they have been seen on multiple occasions, but they are not welcome in the sanctuary. You'll be safe here until we figure out a plan."

My voice cracked on my next words: "I don't know what to feel about Max." My pain could no longer be pushed aside, and it seemed Louis was the one I'd bare my soul to. Despite everything I trusted the sorcerer. Well, trusted with some reservations.

He examined me, as if trying to burrow into the deepest of my emotions. "You don't lose anything by this, Jess, you gain another sister into your pack. Maximus will not abandon you ... I can't imagine a supernatural who could willingly walk away from you."

Well, that was uncomfortably intimate.

Since exhaustion and heartache had negated my already faulty brain-to-mouth filter, it was time to get this shit out in the open. "What do you want from me, Louis? Why are you helping me so much?"

His expression closed down, more unreadable than it had been before. I was sure he wouldn't answer. Then he said, "I had a mate ... a long time ago. She was killed by another witch. One who wanted her power." His voice broke. I strained to hear every soft word. "I went crazy for a long time. I was unstable, no one could touch the bubble of pain and anger I had wrapped around myself. Eventually, I was able to control myself again, but no amount of time could heal the pain. Up until the day I touched a tiny twin with a dragon mark."

My heart dropped, I really didn't want to hurt Louis, but I wasn't sure I could give him what he needed.

"It was as if your power wrapped around me and soothed some of the ragged edges of my soul."

He reached out and grasped my hand, pulling me closer into his side. "I thought maybe you would be a mate-of-sorts for me, that the tie I felt toward you had to mean something. I watched you grow up, kept an eye on you, protected you when I could and waited for the chance to be in your life."

Okay, a tad creepy, but on some level I understood.

"Louis–" I started, but he cut me off with a chuckle.

"Stop panicking. It didn't take me long to realize that the emotions you created in me were not romantic, but ... family. You feel like my kin and I consider you to be mine ... in a purely platonic way."

It was strange, but I felt something similar when Louis was around. I'd always thought it was to do with his power being the one to spell my mark, but maybe there was something more there.

"Do you think we share a common ancestor?" I squeezed his hand tighter, wanting to erase that agony which flashed across his eyes. Talking about his mate had cost him something, brought him back to a dark time in his life.

The gentlest of grins graced his lips. "All supernaturals share common ancestors, but possibly you and I are a little closer."

I pulled my hands free, and when his sadness didn't disappear I opened my arms and wrapped them tightly around him. I clutched him hard, trying to squish free those horrible memories. He returned my gesture and I felt him rest his chin on top of my head. We stayed like that until groans from the alley had me pulling back to see what was going on. The female shifter was starting to pull herself up, her friends still down for the count. They would think twice about taking me on again, and word would spread of this. Somehow, it always happened that way in these communities.

"Let's go back, I need some sleep."

I leaned heavily into Louis, and he took a lot of my weight as we strolled from the alley. It spoke of how absolutely drained I was, both mentally and physically, that I didn't even notice the food piled high on the plates of the supernaturals eating on the street. We also ignored the many eyes which followed as we walked.

"Why didn't the Compasses come after me?" I said, in a sort of slur. I fought for clarity.

Louis quickened our pace and gathered more of my weight into him. "I convinced them to stay behind while I checked on you."

I let loose a few peals of laughter. For some reason the possibilities of how he *convinced* them were endless and amusing.

"I'll just bet they appreciated that."

The sorcerer joined in with my laughter. "Braxton especially was appreciative."

The thought of my dragon shifter sobered any humor. What the hell was I going to do about him and all of these feelings plundering my soul? *And lady parts*.

Seeing Maximus with a mate had opened up something inside of me. I'd been so resolute in trying to keep everything the same, not risking the pack dynamics, but things had changed anyway. Change was going to happen and I didn't want to miss my moment with Braxton because I was afraid. What if I waited too long and never had a chance? He could meet his mate tomorrow. The dragon king could rise and kill us all. The only certainty we had was right now and something told me that five minutes with the dragon was worth any minutes without him.

Louis tipped his eyes down to meet mine. "Just talk to them, Jess. There wasn't a supernatural in Stratford who didn't know how much they loved you. They will never leave you."

I exhaled loudly. "It's not as easy as that, you know how possessive we are. Already vamp chick was giving me the evil eye, and I won't ever ask him to choose between us."

"It will work out, and I'm not opposed to smacking a few of your men into line."

I laughed in a short burst. "Thank you. I might just take you up on that." This sorcerer was actually a pretty badass threat to have in my back pocket. "So quick subject change, but how worried should I be about Mischa?"

His facial expression remained calm. "I'm not sure. The twins are not to be trusted, but something tells me that they are not *evil* in the true sense of the word. We need to take our time, any big reaction will only work to push your sister closer to them."

He made a very good point. We walked in comfortable silence for a few minutes. I decided to ask him something which had been bugging me for a bit. I trusted Louis, but he was filled with secrets.

"You remember when we talked in Stratford, about the dragon marked, and you said you thought they were all killed at birth. If Quale is your brother, shouldn't you have known about this place? About the dragon marked being imprisoned?"

I examined him closely as he answered, scenting his words even though I was pretty sure he was powerful enough to get around my truth and lie hormone detector.

"I never knew what my brother protected here. I just knew that he lived in a sanctuary for supernaturals. It wasn't until I chatted with you about the marked being held in the prison that I started to question further. I contacted Quale and applied a little bit of pressure. He finally admitted that this mountain range had been slowly commandeered over the years by the mystics, and that they housed the marked. Their duty was to protect them until the rise of the king."

Truth. For whatever that was worth with Louis.

"The existence of this place is a heavily guarded secret, Quale shouldn't have told me. But I'm glad he did. I knew this was the perfect exit strategy for you."

My lips quirked into a slight smile. "Thank you. For always staying a step ahead. For helping me."

He kissed the top of my head.

I was quiet for the rest of the walk and Louis let me keep my thoughts. He was strangely relaxing to be around. Despite the immense power vibrating from him, he was still a little less intense than the Compasses. I closed my eyes for the ride up in the box, relieved when I could finally step free from all that metal. The door opened for me, silent, letting me into the cool apartment. Louis peeled off toward the kitchen and I followed my nose and stepped into the living room. Maximus was on the couch, his head buried in his hands. I knew the other quads were in the building, but the vampire was all alone right now.

He shot his face up and I stopped in my tracks. I'd never seen him look so miserable. I wanted to run to his side, throw my arms around him and pull him close. But for the first time I hesitated, he wasn't mine to comfort now, he had someone for that. Someone who would not appreciate my scent all over him.

The vampire stood, filling the space with his giantness. "Don't do that, Jess, don't treat me differently."

I swallowed the lump in my throat, trying my best to calm myself. "Things are different." My scratchy voice irritated me.

Maximus crossed the room, crowding right into me, warming my cold limbs with his heat. "You're my girl, you have been our entire lives." He lifted his head up to stare at the ceiling, as if trying to find the right words to say next. "I love you. I always have." *Truth.* He dropped his face again to meet my gaze. "That love has changed over the years. Sometimes it was platonic, sometimes it was romantic. You have no idea how many times I wished I was Braxton and at least had a shot at being your true mate. But I always knew that you were shifter and I was vampire."

My mouth must have fallen open at some point during his speech. I flicked out my tongue to moisten my lips. I was processing what he was saying, but I don't think the true meaning was actually registering.

"What about Mischa?"

His eyes darkened, and I sensed it was guilt which tugged at his features. "She was you ... but not, if you know what I mean."

Ah crap, no wonder my sister was pissed off.

"Cardia doesn't change anything about us. She knows you are my family, my pack, and that if she makes me choose, I will choose you."

Truth. An absolutely astonishing truth.

"I have no doubt that the shit will hit the ceiling more than once, but eventually our pack will find its dynamics."

I couldn't hold myself back from him any longer, I dived into his arms, and as the strong limbs wrapped around me – lifting me off my feet a few tears finally leaked from my tightly squeezed lids.

"I love you too, Max, I *need* you to know that."

Footsteps sounded behind us. Tyson. "Thank the gods you two finally sorted it out, I've been waiting to get my hands on our disappearing Jessa. I'm going to need one of those hugs too." I pulled back, so happy to see my wizard's smiling brown eyes.

Maximus gave me an extra squeeze, as though he was afraid to let go. "I'm not going anywhere," I whispered against his soft shirt.

He kissed the top of my head before handing me off to Tyson. I sank into the wizard. I was done now. My exhaustion was going to force me to sleep.

Tyson reached down and hauled me into his arms. "I think shower and bed for you, babe. I volunteer to be a shower and bed buddy."

I snorted. "Missed ... you ... Ty." I was all slurring and shit, but he understood.

Braxton and Jacob were waiting in my room. I assumed Louis was still in the kitchen, but he might have taken off, giving me time with my boys. Braxton had the shower already running, steam filling the room. Tyson set me down, steadying my movements so I didn't face-plant. I managed to wave them away, before undressing myself and stepping into the water. I slid closed the glass partition.

"I'm leaving this door open, Jess." Braxton said. "Call out if you need me." His husky tones trailed off as he walked away.

Holy shit, he could have phrased that differently, because I was coming to see with more than a little clarity that I needed him. Goddamn, I needed him.

I forced myself to focus on the simple task of washing away the filth and keeping my legs steady beneath me. My body felt so sensitive as I ran a cloth slowly over my skin. I forced myself to be quick. I needed sleep, but the low ache deep in my stomach was my first warning that I also needed to get laid. I needed sex ... and I had an important decision to make.

I hadn't forgotten what had happened in Faerie. The question of the hour: should I burst the friend-bubble Braxton and I were precariously living in? Dive into all the deliciousness that was my dragon. Or was the risk too great? If I was smart I'd be investigating what sort of nightlife was in this sanctuary and heading out to find myself an available shifter. Play it safe. But that thought just wasn't as appealing as it should have been.

I shut off the water and pushed the door open, letting the cool air wash over my wet skin. I shivered a little; the exhaustion had my metabolism off kilter. Someone had placed some of my clothes on the sink. I pulled on underwear and a mid-drift tank. I liked to sleep naked, but this was probably safer since I knew some of the quads would be with me and we didn't sleep naked together. Most of the time anyway.

I brushed my teeth, and ran a comb through the damp strands of black hair. Hanging up the towel, I padded silently from the bathroom, and almost tripped over my own feet when I saw what was happening in my room. The Compasses had pushed the two big beds together, forming one large sleep surface. All four of them were standing around it, dressed just in shorts, their well-defined chests bare, expanses of tawny skin filling the room. Sometimes they were so alike, it was a little scary.

It had been a very long time since we'd all slept in the same bed. My heart swelled, I had thought that I'd never have this chance again.

I stumbled across and crawled into the middle of the beds. I was always in the center, which meant that I had to sleep on the crack between the two beds, but I didn't care. Jacob slid against the wall, then Braxton, me, Maximus on the other side, and Tyson last. We generally changed around places so everyone had a chance at bonding. The brothers all slept with space between them, but every single one of them crowded into me.

My eyes fluttered shut. I was unable to keep them open any longer. I felt Maximus turn to me, before his fingers linked with my own.

"Your mate is going to kill you," I said.

He chuckled, and his brothers quickly joined in. "She'll be fine, she has no choice but to understand."

"Besides," I heard Tyson quip, "she bagged a Compass, she has nothing to complain about."

"You are ridiculous," I mumbled. "Conceited ass."

The last sensation I had before drifting off was the scent of vampire and dragon wrapping around me as they both turned toward me. I was warm, safe, and I couldn't imagine anything in the world could top this moment.

Chapter 10

I hadn't expected to dream that night. An exhausted brain should be blank, right? Well, apparently that was wrong, very wrong. Apparently an exhausted brain torments you with dreams. Firstly, that ugly one, with Mischa and the other two women. Where the dragons tore into me as I tried to escape across the field. I knew it was a pretty effed up scenario, but I still didn't understand my overwhelming fear.

I was starting to get the feeling that the women were placeholders for the real life twins and that whatever path Mischa was on right now was the one which was going to bring this dream to fruition. I had a semi-conscious thought that I needed to find my sister and soon, she needed to be brought back to the right path.

Warm hands rubbed my back, clearing that dream from my thoughts. I snuggled in closer to that warmth before drifting back into the land of snooze. The next dream hit me hard.

I was in a cave, long and winding, the air so cold I could see puffs of my breath. I marched along at a rapid rate. I knew where I was going, taking turns left and right and left again. Finally I could see an end, a wall, with some circular pattern right in the center of it. As I stepped closer, the image became clearer and I tried to understand what I was seeing. It was like … a compass, or something with four points. But the writing on there was not in English.

Shit, damn. Was this the tomb of the dragon king?

I seemed to know what I was doing, stepping closer until I could reach out a hand and place it against the frigid stone. Each of the four points had a divot at the end, the perfect size for a hand, and then lines ran down from each one. A thumping, dragging noise had me spinning, and now I was facing the way I'd come, my back to the stone. The sound reminded me of the way a dragon's tail dragged when it was bouncing along behind. I braced myself, hands and back flat against the stone as I waited. Shadows entered the curve first, and then a snout followed around. It was definitely a dragon, but in shades of color unlike any I'd seen before. Red and orange, like a sunset.

"Jessa!"

A shriek tore me from my dream world. My eyes flew open as I struggled to free myself from the covers. I was trapped under the heat and weight of Jacob and Tyson. Mischa was standing on the end of the bed. She ignored the Compasses and crawled across the sheets to throw herself onto me.

"You're safe, you're safe." She repeated it over and over.

I managed to wiggle an arm free and loop it around her, hugging her close. I thought moisture hit my cheek, but I couldn't hear any crying, and when she pulled back a few minutes later her face looked dry.

"I was so worried. Where were you?"

The six of us stayed snuggled in the two beds – Tyson shifted to the side so Mischa could sprawl between us – while I quickly detailed our little side adventure to Faerie land. Mischa never interrupted me, her eyes wide, the green very light today. I decided there was no point reiterating the part when I found Maximus in bed with his new mate. Despite the fact we were all together, I could feel the tension between those two. I was pretty sure the vampire was only pretending to be asleep.

"Where have you been?" I asked Mischa when I finished my explanation.

Her eyes darkened to the murky color of moss, her face transforming from light and open into secrets and heaviness.

"I've made some new friends in here, I'd like you to meet them." She crawled backwards off me, the warm sisterly feeling from before evaporating with her vague explanation. "I can see you're busy right now, so later ...okay?"

She spun and started for the door, only turning back at the last minute. "I'm so glad you're okay, Jess, I've missed you a lot. I'm heading over to see Mom and Jonathon. Come find me when you get up."

I gave her a nod and she left the room, closing the door behind her. I was sitting in the bed, my thoughts tumultuous. Something big was going on with Mischa. I'd been worried before, but now ... now I knew it was bad. I needed to know what had happened with her and Maximus, and where exactly she had been spending her time the last three weeks. Maximus would have figured out that Cardia was his mate the day I disappeared, when he fed on her, so Mischa had been pulling away all of that time. She'd lost her sister and her sort-of-boyfriend in an instant.

I pushed down my worry for the moment. It was good for her to be with our parents. Jonathon was usually very switched on when it came to the moods of his pack members. I hoped he was aware and dealing with Mischa. I snuggled myself back down into the warm space between the two males. The

Compasses remained silent, although I could sense some heavy thoughts.

I was still exhausted. I was pretty sure I hadn't slept that long, and the dreams were not allowing me any solid rest. I really just wanted to sleep soundly for a few hours.

I started tossing and turning, trying to get comfortable, when Jacob reached out and captured my hand. He began to sing, a low soothing melody, and just like that I was unable to hold on to my consciousness. I don't care what he said, there's magic in the feys' singing. This time when I drifted off, the dreams stayed far away.

Hours later I awoke naturally, sprawled out on my stomach, both arms under my pillow snuggling it toward me. I felt a thousand times better, refreshed, as I turned myself over, stretching my arms above my head, letting my body elongate right down to pointed toes. Nothing better than a good stretch.

Small particles of light streamed around the room, so when I rolled across to my side I was blindsided by a massive expanse of bare chest.

I froze.

My eyes darted left and right as I tried to figure out what to do. I could see – and scent – that there were no Compasses left in the room except Braxton. We had needed sleep the most; the other boys would have bailed earlier and left us to our rest. My body softened as I studied the face across from me. It was only in sleep that Braxton seemed relaxed, young even. When he was awake it was easy to forget he was only twenty-two, he carried so much strength and domination. The power he wielded was the same as that of the elders.

I scooted a little closer. I couldn't help myself. I was drawn to him and I was starting to see that this was not going away – the need was increasing.

And I didn't want to fight it any longer.

I continued to watch him. There wasn't the slightest sign that he was awake, no change in breathing or even flicker of an eye – when suddenly his lids flew open and piercing blue eyes pinned me to place. I held my breath. No doubt, Braxton and I had reached the point where we had to deal with this thing between us. I felt as if I was going to self-destruct if I didn't touch him. If he didn't touch me. If we didn't ... *damn, I'm in trouble*.

We were silent for many long moments, the flow of energy between us so strong it was almost visible. Braxton reached out a long arm then and cupped his hand around the back of my head. My breath caught in my throat. His other hand scooted behind my ass, and then, with exquisite care – and an anticipation which almost had me moaning – he dragged me closer. So slowly did he close the distance between our bodies.

The few times I allowed myself to dream about being with Braxton, I'd imagined it hard and fast, passions overwhelming us as we lost control. So far it was the opposite: tender and gentle. I wasn't sure if he was savoring our moment or if he was giving me the chance to stop him. But if that's what he was waiting for, he was going to be very disappointed.

At some point I'd made this decision, and now I was following through no matter what the consequences were. The emotions threatening to burst from my chest were so strong, the attraction and years of love I held for him so overwhelming, nothing could tear me from this moment.

My body arched as he continued closing the distance between us, nipples tightening in anticipation of having them pressed against his delicious body. Something he'd surely noticed in my very thin tank. I ran my eyes across him. There was not a flaw on Braxton, he was broad everywhere important, narrow in the hips, with strong muscled legs. I'd seen him naked enough to know he was as endowed as you'd expect any dragon to be. Freaking huge. It kind of scared me a little – well, except that it also had my insides turning into a quivering mess and my panties wet. Besides that part, it was a little daunting.

I parted my lips in anticipation, my breathing heading toward the panting side, but who could blame me.

Braxton's face was calm except for the smallest of smiles which crept up and flashed dimple at me. I was such a freaking sucker for those dimples. I swear the boys only had to dimple up and I turned into a simpering mess. I was pretty good at hiding it from them, but they could have gotten anything from me if they just hit me with enough of their smiles. Braxton especially.

He was still staring, the smile fading out to be replaced by a blazing heat. Exactly like a flame: dangerous and tempting.

"You sure?"

My breath stuttered as he spoke. His huskiness scraped down every nerve ending I possessed.

This was the second time he had asked me to be sure about my choice, and somehow I knew it would be the last time. He was giving me one more out. I was not taking it. That ache which had started low last night was something much bigger today. My lower half was a ball of throbbing need.

Braxton was still slowly inching me toward him; it was torturous, but I was loving every second of it. The anticipation was delicious.

When there was about an inch between us, our bodies humming but not touching yet, he took the hand which had been behind my head and slowly drew it from my back and along my collar bone. He didn't stop there though, his massive hand continued lower, brushing over both of my breasts. My nipples were hard, begging for his attention. He followed the path of my body until his hand rested against my abdomen.

"I can feel your need, your pain…"

I arched up into him again. "Why are you torturing me then?" I was a little pissed that I sounded so breathy, but this was what Braxton did to me and we had barely touched yet. My need was greater than I'd ever felt with any other shifter.

What did this mean? A deep wish I'd held in my heart for a very long time – but had refused to ever seriously consider – flittered through me.

Could Braxton be my mate?

What were the odds that he'd been under my nose the entire time, with me too afraid to risk the friendship.

"I'm not torturing you," he said, leaning in. My eyelids fluttered closed in anticipation of his lips on mine. "I'm prolonging the moment, I'm giving you a chance to run." My eyes opened again. Braxton grinned lazily. "You always run."

He had a point, but that urge was nowhere now. He must have read that in my expression, because his hesitation was replaced with a determination that I was all too familiar with. The moment for doubt was gone and it was time to see what was between us. If we both survived.

His lips hit mine, so full and soft that I sank into him. I'd kissed Braxton a million times before, but nothing like this. This was everything.

The kiss started slow, tantalizingly slow, as his tongue parted my lips and swept inside. He sucked my bottom lip into his mouth and I groaned deep from my throat, almost a purr. As the kiss deepened, so did the wild arc of want between us, and just like that ... it was no longer slow.

I slammed myself into his body and he caught me with both hands beneath my ass, drawing me into his long length. I could feel his desire pressed against my thigh, resulting in harder, frenzied kisses.

I tore my lips free. "Braxton!" It was a growling warning, he'd better stop teasing and start pleasing or I was going to rip his face off.

He grinned right before he lifted me with one hand – how freaking strong was this guy – and suddenly I was back against the headboard. He settled between my legs, both hands sliding up to cup my breasts. I arched again, and in one smooth movement he tore my tank from my body. As the cool air hit my swollen and sensitive skin, I hissed, before moaning as hot hands replaced the material.

"This is the sexiest thing I have ever seen." His voice was vibrating as he traced the dragon mark on my side. I realized he'd never seen the entire image, and right now it was dancing in red and black for him, shifting and moving in the dragon visage.

We clashed eyes. "You are the sexiest thing I have ever seen," he said.

I reached forward and laced both of my hands through the dark hair at the nape of his neck, before tightening my grip and yanking his head to me. I needed more kisses, I had to taste him again.

The gentleness from earlier was lost in the wake of the primal need that had our mouths clashing together and bodies straining for each other. My body knew what it wanted and there was no stopping it now. Thankfully my brain was clouded enough that not a single doubt was present.

Braxton's right hand slid down again, scraping over the front of my panties. I moaned, "Goddamn it, Braxton Compass."

He laughed, he knew exactly what my problem was, but decided to torture me anyway.

"What do you want, Jess? You're going to have to spell it out for me." His low voice was in my ear. I barely even registered what he was saying.

"Touch me," I growled again. "Touch. Me." My sex-deprived-growly voice acted on Braxton the same way as if I'd been on my knees begging for him. Begging wasn't my style, but for Braxton ... nah, not even for him.

My underwear disappeared so fast I wasn't sure if they'd magically vanished or if Braxton was moving with super speed. Long fingers slid along into my wetness. I almost freaking came right then. Why the hell had I waited so long to do this? My body was wound up tighter than hell, and as Braxton continued to stroke, my lower half moved with him. Our mouths found each other again, and I moaned against his lips as he brought me closer and closer to the screaming orgasm that was in my immediate future.

I wrenched my lips free, gasping to fill my lungs. "I need to touch you."

If I was doing this, I was doing it the whole way, and I'd wanted to touch Braxton like this for a long time.

His hooded blue eyes caressed my body. "Your pleasure first."

Damn, this male was going to be testing my alpha all night. I wanted to wrest control from him. I needed to dominate, bite, mark and claim. The only thing saving us was that Braxton and I had established equal dominance a long time ago ... but still.

His hands increased their motion, his thumb stroking the most pleasurable of spots. Pressed firmly against him, I was on fire. He applied the perfect pressure, gliding across every smoldering nerve ending,

In a surge of burning need, the intensity which had been building inside exploded. I tilted my head back, nails biting into Braxton's shoulders as the force of my orgasm ripped through me. It felt as if it started at my toes and built until it ended with my screams of overwhelming pleasure. I forced myself to breathe, more moans emerging as the sensations throbbed. It was the longest, multiple, toe-curling orgasm of my life.

Braxton was growling now, and as I returned to myself and met his gaze, I stilled. The blue of his eyes were threaded with gold, like someone had melted metal through the sky. They were heavy and hypnotic. Braxton's dragon was right there with us, and it seemed as if he was about to lose control. He almost never lost control. And yes, I did totally love that I affected him like that. It was my turn to play now.

I leaned forward as if I was about to kiss him, but right before our lips touched I pounced into the large body and slammed him onto his back. I practically purred as I climbed over and onto him. His fingers still rested against my center, and I was enjoying that sensation.

My black hair fanned out as I leaned down and placed my mouth onto his neck. I bit into him, gentle at first, and then harder as my wolf and dragon rose to the surface. My dragon, especially, had been with me the entire time, so in-tune to Braxton.

My teeth stopped short of breaking his skin, just short. And he let me ... no battle or fighting.

It was his allowance of my control which tamed the tumult of my animals inside. Braxton, the most dominant supernatural I knew, was giving some of that up for me. I'd never seen him give an inch with anyone else, not even his brothers, but he was different with me.

Mate-like.

Once I'd finished my first bite and mark of territory, I couldn't stop myself from leaning in and wrapping my arms around him. His chest was simply the most alluring thing in the world and I just had to touch it. I felt the smooth texture of his mouth as it landed on my shoulder, followed by a tantalizing scrape of stubble as he started kissing along my nape.

I arched back as he moved across my neck, sending the most delicious tingles through to my core. He was kissing everywhere, branding the shit out of me too, so slowly did he claim. God, I wanted him so badly. When his mouth reached my nipples he finally withdrew his fingers from me. I didn't protest, I was wanting those fingers replaced with something else very soon.

Impatient as always, I reached both hands down and managed to tug free his shorts. I slowly lowered them and Braxton shucked them the rest of the way. I eye-screwed the hell out of him, following his long, thick length. I'd seen him naked before, but never aroused to this state. He was … enormous.

I let out a huff of air. "Always were the overachiever, weren't you?"

A bright grin flashed and I found myself caught in the amused gaze of my dragon shifter.

With a growl I dived onto him. My wolf and dragon with me again, I was feeling a little act-on-base-instinct. My hand encircled him and I couldn't close it all the way around. I stroked him once, watching his face, and his lids fluttered, his full lips parting. He hadn't stopped staring at me the last few minutes … we locked gazes.

I really hoped there was no one else in the apartment, because something told me if they were, we weren't keeping these afternoon activities a secret.

I loved running my fingers over the velvet smooth and hardness of him. I loved bringing him pleasure. It had me wetter than I'd ever been before;

we were going to have to move the foreplay along very soon.

As if he'd had the very same thought, Braxton reached down and stilled my hand. In seconds he had flipped us over, reversing positions so I was back on the bottom. He laced our fingers together, and raised both of my hands above my head. Our faces were even with each other. I narrowed my eyes at him.

"I know you don't think you're going to be the dominant one here, Brax." My bared teeth indicated my thoughts on this. I lunged back at him, battling for the top. I might have bitten him a few times, but in the end I was the one on top.

He laughed, flashing all those white teeth and dimples at me. For the first time something calmed the alpha in me. Don't get me wrong, I knew my place in the pack, and Braxton and I would be fighting for control until the day we died. But my wolf and dragon were strangely content. Which gave me a rest in the dominance game. For the moment anyway.

Unable to help myself, I leaned forward and ran my tongue along the indent of his left dimple. His laughter stilled, and I smiled against his face. Men: you just have to know the right buttons. I tilted my head down to see him again, and became ensnared in the blue blaze of his eyes. The gold had faded out, which I wasn't sure if I was happy or sad about.

We stared for endless moments, me sitting on him cowboy style with his arousal pressed intimately against me. Usually I was impatient in sex; I don't waste time, I get in there and go for it. But for some reason I wanted to draw out this first time with Braxton, wanted it to last days and weeks and months. I had this terrible feeling deep down that this might be the only time we had with each other. I didn't need a big revelation to know I loved Braxton, I'd loved him longer than I could remember. But in this emotionally charged moment I was hit hard. I didn't just love Braxton, I *loved* him. I had no idea if we were true mates, but really … fuck true mates and all that fate crap.

I reached forward and pressed my hand to his chest. "I choose you." He knew what I meant. And I had just made myself more vulnerable than I'd ever been. But if there was any supernatural in the world I trusted with my heart, it was Braxton.

He growled from the back of his throat, low and hypnotic, before reaching out a long arm and threading a hand through the hair at the nape of my neck. Damn, even on the bottom, he out-dominated me every day of the week. Luckily I could pretend I was the one in charge.

He pulled my head down to his and kissed me, the gentlest of caresses. "You are mine," he whispered as he pulled away. "Always have been." His eyes darkened; they almost looked black. "We belong together, Jessa Lebron."

He was so right. I leaned down and smashed my lips against his. I couldn't stop myself, my need was taking me over again. He was feeling it too. He met my bruising force, our kisses long, hard. There would be no more pauses this time, nothing short of the end of the world was going to stop us now.

Our kisses continued, and I slid one of my hands down his body to reach between us. I took the length of him into my hand and guided him toward me. There was no need for protection, we didn't carry sexually transmitted diseases and I was still outside my fertile time.

My wetness eased the entrance, but still it was a tight fit. My breath caught as I slid down his massive length. It seemed to go on forever, filling me, touching everything inside. It took my body a few seconds to adjust to the fullness. Braxton growled again, his lashes fluttered closed.

"You are so tight. Feels fucking amazing, Jessa."

I loved that from this position I could see every expression which crossed his face and while it was clear parts of him fought against the lack of control, he allowed it. I rose slowly, before slamming myself down onto his length, pleasure crashing into me, starting low and spreading everywhere. It was like wildfire, burning through me at a rapid rate, as if I could feel every second of pleasure, every receptor inside responding. My pace increased. Braxton had both hands on my hips as he drove up into me. He watched me intently, his focus so strong that nothing would break it.

With a growl, he flipped our positions, his length and heaviness settling deliciously onto me.

His grin was rakish. "Hold tight, Jessa, it's my turn."

I scraped my nails along his shoulders. "You better make it good then, Braxton Compass." There was still some alpha hidden inside of me.

He leaned down to capture my lips. "You have all the control, you know your power."

It was true. I did, and since my animals were content, we didn't have to battle Braxton.

I reached forward and trailed my hands over his broad shoulders, as far as I could reach. He was moving inside of me, fast, hard, and with a skill that was probably going to kill me. I clawed at him again, urging him closer, urging him faster, urging him to go harder with me. I could sense that he was worried about hurting me, but I was a shifter, we were built tough.

I don't really know what changed, but something pushed him over the edge of his control. Braxton placed a hand under my ass and lifted me up off the mattress, which allowed him full access as he slammed into me. I cried out, his strength like nothing I'd ever experienced before. I was in ecstasy.

I wanted to close my eyes, to feel everything that was crashing inside of me without the distraction of Braxton's beautiful face. But I couldn't tear my gaze from him, he had me locked in and there was no escaping. Our pace increased and that low aching buildup was starting from my toes again. My previous orgasm had almost destroyed me with its intensity. I already knew I was not surviving this one.

Braxton lifted me higher, and suddenly we were against the wall. The hard pressure against my back only increased the hard pressure inside of me. He held me without effort, and at this angle opened up an entirely new can of pleasure.

"Brax. Holy fuck!" I was gasping and cursing and trying to sort out what the hell was happening to me. I was unwinding, coming apart, and there was nothing I could do to stop it.

He captured my lips, before pulling back to speak. "I have you, baby, I won't let you fall."

I screamed his name as the world exploded around me. I had no choice but to close my eyes and ride out every second of a pleasure so intense I wasn't sure it was survivable. He continued moving, and the orgasms were unrelenting, ripping through me. I forced my lids up, even though my head was slammed back against the wall. I really wanted to see Braxton's face when he finished.

The eyes I met were melted gold. I could feel stirrings inside of me, the wolf and dragon rising from their cages, their energies intermingling.

I threaded my hands through his hair, moans still falling from my lips. I felt him swell even more inside. He leaned his head forward and our lips met in another scorching kiss. Tasting him was like tasting home. His pace increased and then I watched as he lost all control. When Braxton came, everything stilled, as if time actually halted. We were cocooned in a bubble. I remembered his groaning cry. I remembered him leaning into me, his large frame strong but with the slightest tremble. Then everything went dark.

Chapter 11

The first thing I registered were swirls of light dancing behind my eyelids. I swallowed. My throat felt rough and scratchy, but my insides were warm and content. I rubbed at my face before finally I felt ready to open my eyes. The first few rapid blinks told me that it was much too bright and I went slow, allowing my eyes to adjust. I stared up into a sky of blue, there was not a single cloud marring the perfection.

Questions barraged through my head, and with a gasp I sat up. The last thing I remembered was Braxton, in my bedroom, the best sex of my life. So what the hell happened between then and now? I pulled myself to my feet. I was still naked, as if I'd been transported straight to this place.

I was getting a tad sick of magical assfucks scooting me around the universe like their own personal puppet.

I tried to determine where I was, but I was surrounded by mists or clouds or something. And yet ... there were no clouds in the sky, it was warm and sunny.

"You've arrived at an in-between place, and you have a choice to make."

The orchestra of voices echoed all around me. I didn't bother to turn and look because I could sense that whatever was speaking was everywhere.

"What choice?"

I didn't yell, I didn't think there was a need. I'd be heard even if I whispered.

Swirls of wind preluded speech this time. "You have been chosen, Jessa, to take a burden and to save a race. Chosen often equals sacrifice. What are you willing to sacrifice to save the supernatural people? Would you sacrifice a mate bond with your one true?"

I dropped my gaze to try to gather my thoughts. "Yes, I am pretty sure I would sacrifice my mate bond for the entire supernatural race."

Even I wasn't selfish enough to place myself above hundreds of thousands of lives.

"Would you form a mate bond with someone not of your choosing, if it meant saving the supernatural race?"

I sighed. This was some bullshit magic mumbo jumbo. But just in case I was in the presence of a god or something, I'd try not curse them out. "If you put that kind of magical gun to my head and tell me

I have to get freaky with some stranger for eternity or we all die, then the answer is 'yes, I would.'"

"The choice will be soon."

I growled. "Wait, tell me more of what you speak."

The voice faded out, and the mists swirled around me. The howling winds forced my eyes to shut. I raised both hands and held them over my face to stop my hair from whipping me. Thankfully, the wind finally died out, and I was able to remove my hands to see what was about to ambush me next.

I was standing at the base of two beds. Back in my room. I scented Braxton and I all over the space, not to mention the visible signs – torn covers and askew beds. Had Braxton and I destroyed the room during sex? Seems I might have missed some of our last few moments.

Movement caught my eye and I realized I wasn't alone. Braxton was there. He stood near the door to the bathroom. He had his shorts back on, but was still bare-chested.

"Jess." He took three huge steps across the room and hauled me into his arms.

I wrenched my head back to see his face. "What the hell just happened?" I was clutching at muscles, trying to sort myself out. I didn't know what to think. Had I dreamed the entire misty place?

"You lost consciousness, and then this energy burst from your body. I couldn't get to you." His blue eyes were hard, narrowed, as he ran his gaze across my features. "Do you remember anything?"

He never even flinched as I dug my nails into his arms. I couldn't seem to stop from clinging to him. "I blacked out and then when I came to I was in this weird misty place. There was a presence there…" I tried to catalogue my thoughts. "Almost as if there was a narrator talking to me. It asked if I would sacrifice my mate bond to save all the supernaturals, or if I would mate someone I did not want to."

Braxton dropped his head down, letting it rest against mine, and we stayed like that for a moment. "Shit, that's not good," he eventually said. "A mate bond partially formed between us, Jessa, but … it's not complete."

I startled against him. "What do you mean?"

Low growls were rocking from his chest. It seemed to take him a few moments to be able to speak again. "I don't know, babe. I can only think of one possible explanation." He ran a hand over his face. "Do you remember that story Mom used to tell us, when we'd ask about broken mate bonds?"

No fucking way.

I didn't have to think hard about it. Of the many stories from the Compass parents, that one had stayed with me. Jo had been the supe I'd always gone to for love tales, since I had no mother of my own. Deep down a part of me was always trying to gather facts about mate bonds. I think even back then I'd been trying to figure out how to be with Braxton.

"The one about the lion-shifter?" I asked, barely above a whisper.

We sat on the bed. I was still naked but I knew Braxton didn't mind.

"Yes," he said. "The shifter with the two mates."

I shook my head, there had to be another explanation. That story was an urban legend – the female lion shifter who had two true mates. It was said that when she found the first, a bear shifter, the mate bond didn't properly form, so they didn't realize they were mates. It was only when she found her second mate, a lion shifter, that the bonds kicked in, and it was then she had to choose. Once she made the choice, the bond formed with that supe.

I wrinkled my nose. "We can't seriously be contemplating the thought that I might have two mates?"

Braxton let out a huff of air. "I don't know. What else could it be?" He looked unsure, which was so not my dragon man. Not to mention there was something simmering behind those mesmerizing eyes, something that seemed a lot like pain. Which made me want to punch myself ... in the face.

I tried to think of any other possible scenario. "Maybe it's just about my strange dragon mark, Brax. No reason to jump to the worst conclusions yet. Let's wait and let it play out." I reached up and cupped his cheeks. "Besides, even if it was true, I don't need to find a second *mate*, I choose you."

He quirked an eyebrow. "Unfortunately, my beautiful shifter girl, if this is the same as that female, it's not a decision you can make. Not yet anyway. Remember what Mom said, when the lion found both of her mates, there was some sort of test. In the end the mate best suited to her was the one."

"So this might be what that misty vision was about?" I didn't believe in coincidences, and the weird narrator voices had been talking about mate choices, and now Braxton was saying the same thing.

He touched my face gently. "I guess we'll find out when it happens. For now I'm glad we have the bond even if it is partial. You're right, let's fight one battle at a time."

I could agree to that. No point creating worries, we had enough without searching for more.

Braxton stood and held out a hand to me. "Now we shower, dress, and eat, because I don't know about you, but I've moved to that place past hungry where I'm ready to rip someone's head off."

I took a deep breath. I was hungry too, but that wasn't what filled my mind. "How do you know the mate bond isn't complete?" I took the hand he offered and got to my feet. We strode toward the bathroom, our movements in sync.

A sense of sad unease was heavy in my stomach, threatening to burst up through my body and expel itself from my mouth. I was about two-more-stressful minutes from barfing.

Braxton's hand curved around my neck and began to gently rub. "The same way I know you are really freaked out right now. I can feel you in my heart, but I can't hear you in my head."

It was strange but he was right, I was rocking so many extra emotions in my chest. The tie I had always felt toward Braxton was stronger now. Although, what was he talking about with hearing thoughts?

"Mates can't hear each other's thoughts," I said, as he reached around me and hit the lever on the shower.

Braxton stepped back and gestured for me to enter the stall first. I didn't move straight away, I narrowed my eyes and processed his information. I'd known lots of true mates, even my parents, and not one of them had ever mentioned they could hear the thoughts of the other. It was not written in our history or taught in any of the classes. And we had extensively covered supernatural mates in our kinship and race diversity classes.

Braxton shuffled me back into the stall, and followed. "Dragon shifter mates can. It's a special bond. We don't exactly hear every thought, but we can definitely communicate mentally."

Okay, I did not know that. Why the hell did I not know that?

He read my expression. "No one knows but dragons. We're born instinctively with this knowledge. I figured it wasn't worth sharing."

"Why did you figure that?"

He shrugged, giving me that sexy half-smile. "I chose you a long time ago, Jess. Either you were my true mate and you'd discover the mental speak the fun way, or you weren't and it wasn't worth worrying about what we didn't have."

All I heard from that was: *I chose you.* The extra emotions in my heart swelled.

I was distracted by another one of his devilish grins. "I'll bet you also didn't know that all dragons can communicate with each other while in our beast form."

His shocking revelations continued. Seemed I needed to get some dragon workshops going or something. This information was better hidden than the secrets of the fey.

"Why did I not hear you in Faerie then?"

He lifted me into the water, my question cut off by a cascade of warmth flowing over me. He followed even though he was still wearing a pair of shorts.

"Because you haven't connected intimately to your dragon yet. You're still ... distant. When the true merge happens, you'll understand what I mean."

I melted against him, my hands straining to pull him into me. We'd had sex not that long ago, but it wasn't enough. Something told me it would never be enough. But before I initiated any frisky business, I needed a few answers.

Pressing my breasts against his chest, I glanced up, the slightest of smiles on my lips. "How do I connect to my dragon? And is that the reason I couldn't shift on command when I was falling?" I exhaled, trying to keep my focus despite the distraction in front of me. "We couldn't reach each other. There was this energy wall between us."

Braxton's pupils dilated, his nostrils flaring just slightly as he scented my arousal. His hands started trailing over me, lingering on my mark again. He couldn't seem to help himself, touching it over and over.

"Every dragon shifter is different. Sometimes it's an event, or for others it was simply time. Shift enough and eventually the bond is formed. I expect it will be quick for you. I've never seen a new dragon shifter have such control over their animal."

I definitely had control over her, she was like a big puppy dragon. Most of the time. I was about to let loose with more questions, but suddenly those trailing fingers were right in the sweetest of spots. I threaded my hands behind his head and pretty much climbed his body, giving him better access, but I also now had a direct path to his luscious lips. And I was not wasting one second of this shower.

An hour later we were forced to emerge or we were going to expire from drowning or lack of food. Braxton left me in the room to dress. I wiggled into jeans and pulled on a simple black tank. I found a pair of black Converses in the cupboard. Even though I'd never seen them before they fit perfectly. They were either Mischa's, or a shoe pixie lived in the cupboard. Yep, they were real demi-fey and they loved shoes. Generally, though, they were stealing them, not bringing new ones.

As I stood in front of the mirror to brush out my hair, my eyes were drawn to the shower stall. My thoughts flashed back to the last hour, and I couldn't help the grin which spread across my face. My reflection, I'll admit, looked quite flush and satisfied.

Why the hell had I waited so long to do this with Braxton? I had been so worried that taking this step would destroy the bonds of our friendship, but instead it felt as if we had never been closer. I could feel him in my chest, as if my heart were now twice the size it used to be, more emotions than I'd ever experienced.

No wonder mates got all blissed out and forgot the world for a few years. All I could think about and feel was Braxton, and I seriously hated that we were leaving the bedroom.

Braxton and I were mates ... well, sort of.

Why the frig couldn't anything be simple in my life?

My brush stilled halfway along a stroke. I wondered how Jacob, Tyson, and Maximus would take this. The last thing I wanted was any sort of rift between all of us. I was amazed that things with Maximus and his new mate had been calm so far, but maybe I'd been counting my blessings too soon.

No doubt I'd find out shortly. The Compasses would make their opinions abundantly clear.

"What are you thinking so hard about?"

Braxton's voice did the usual and shot heat right through my body.

"Just wondering how your brothers will take this revelation," I said, before the next random thought burst from my mouth. "Do you want to keep things casual until we figure out what's going on with this mate bond?"

His hooded eyes trailed over me. "No, Jess, there is no casual when it comes to us." He leaned in the doorway, his relaxed pose all sexy. "I have two thoughts about what we do until this mate bond is sorted. The first centers on exclusivity. I want it. I demand it. I will kill any males, besides my brothers, who touch you inappropriately. If your second mates comes along … well, we will deal with it."

There was the dominant dragon shifter that had been missing in the last few hours of gentle play. I had forgotten for a short period that Braxton was a badass – okay, I hadn't forgotten, he wore badassery like a second skin, but he had been tempering it slightly. No more apparently.

"And the second?" There was a hitch in my voice, anticipating what he might say.

He straightened, his presence filling the small bathroom.

"Nothing that happens here will ever change the fact that I love you. I have always loved you. Since we passed puberty, well, it has been as … more than friends. You're my choice, Jessa." There, he'd said it again. Stronger this time with no hesitation. He owned his emotions without missing a beat. Damn, he was perfection.

My heart did something weird, like it stopped beating for about thirty seconds. I was trying to draw in air, but there seemed to be a shortage in this room or something. I shook my head a few times, before stumbling two steps and throwing myself at him. He anticipated the movement and caught me with two hands wrapped around my thighs. Our mouths met in the hardest of kisses.

I wasn't sure when I fell in love with Braxton. Probably it had always been there for me too. I had been particularly harsh and dissatisfied with ninety percent of my past lovers. For a reason I'd never really stopped to identify. But I was well known for never committing; I ran when things were getting serious. The longest relationship I'd ever had was with my Compasses, and that is why I held so strongly to the "friendship only" thing we were rocking.

I had been so afraid that if I started anything with any of them, my commitment-phobia would kick in and ruin everything. Guess I couldn't hold out any longer with Braxton. You could only fight fate for so long, especially with true mates. I was *never* acknowledging a second mate – seriously, that notion could just eff the hell off.

Our kisses tapered off. I squirmed as the need to be naked with him again overwhelmed me. But for now, the growling of my stomach was slightly stronger. I was lowered back to my feet, my Converses sinking into the soft carpet. Wait, how did we get out of the bathroom? This male had my senses all over the place.

We didn't touch again as Braxton led the way from the room, but all this did was increase the tension radiating between us. It was as if we'd broken the seal on the attraction and now there was no tempering it anymore.

The trip out of our silent home and down the elevator was over quickly; we set off for the food street. "So what are we going to tell everyone?" It never crossed my mind for a moment that we would keep it secret. But I also loved my other Compasses and I didn't want to hurt them with this new development.

Braxton actually chuckled. He was in a mighty good mood today. "I don't think any of them are going to be surprised. They've been waiting for this to happen for a long time."

Shit, was I the only one who hadn't been placing bets on the inevitability of me and Braxton hooking up?

"We just tell them the truth?" I wanted to make sure we were on the same page.

He found my gaze. "Yes, we tell them the truth."

Okay, I could do that.

The chattering of hundreds of supes and the distinct smell of the five races hit me hard as we stepped into what seemed to be a central gathering place in the sanctuary. It was around lunchtime, and all of the restaurants were full. I took a moment to enjoy the delicious scents, and my brain starting making a list of what I wanted from each and every place.

What? I was hungry.

Then I heard my name. "Jess! Brax!"

I recognized Jacob's white hair reflecting the artificial sunlight. Still not touching, which seemed to be more obvious than if we'd been holding hands, we crossed the hundred yards to reach our friends. Everyone was there, the Compasses, Mischa, Louis, Quale, even Grace, who I hadn't seen much of. And suddenly I saw him … I took off at a run.

"Dad!" my shriek was loud enough to have heads turning, but I didn't care.

Jonathon Lebron was out of his chair and across the path in seconds, his alpha power surrounding me with the warmth and comfort I'd missed. Strong arms encased me as he pulled me into a firm hug. Just the scent of my father was enough to kick-start countless memories flashing through my mind. Some were shitty, like the years after Lienda had left him, but most were amazing. Besides the Compasses, my dad was the single most important influence in my life. He'd taught me to fight, helped me through my first shift...

I had really missed him

When we finally pulled back I was a little surprised to see moisture ringing his eyes. I'd never seen my dad cry, not even in the dark years after Lienda left – although I think he'd tried to keep that devastated part of himself private. Speaking of, my mother was waiting to the side, and with only a little hesitation I opened my arms and gave her a brief hug. There weren't that many memories associated with her crisp, lemony scent, but I still enjoyed the moment.

"It is so good to see you, Jess, I've missed you," said my father.

I grabbed his hand, pulling him back to the massive table where my family was holed up. "I have missed you so much, but ... food ... I need food."

It was reaching desperate times.

Jonathon threw back his head and laughed, strong white teeth flashing. He had the same blue eyes as me, but his hair was light. Same as Lienda. I had no idea where Mischa and I got our black hair from, but in most other ways I could see a lot of my features in my parents.

Jonathon slid into the chair next to mine. "Nice to know some things haven't changed with you, my little shifter wolf."

Tyson grinned at me from across the table. "So, what you been doing to work up such an appetite, Jessa babe? Thought you were sleeping." Honeysuckle eyes fluttered innocently at me, and as I ran my gaze across the rest of my grinning friends and family I was hit with a realization. They all knew about Braxton and me.

I bared my teeth, no shame forthcoming. I had nothing to hide. I was proud to be with him. Proud to be his mate. I met the wizard's piercing gaze.

"How did you know?"

Tyson lifted his arm and gave a sniff to the top of his forearm, and I realized what had given us away. Sure, we always smelled of each other, but there was a distinct change when anything sexual had occurred. Even though we had showered, we'd fooled around plenty after that.

Jonathon and Lienda were smiling, so I knew they were cool with this new revelation, but I was most worried about the other quads, and my sister. Thankfully Mischa had a broad grin on her face, her eyes twinkling, although I detected a slight shadowing across them. She gave me a thumbs up. That was one pack member accounted for.

"Are you guys okay with this?"

Braxton growled as I directed my question to the other Compasses. He wouldn't care if his brothers were okay with it or not, but I still had to ask. By sleeping together, forming this part mating, we had changed the dynamics of our group. We were supernaturals, so I knew we'd all still share a bed at times – packs liked to stay together – but I wasn't sure what their immediate reactions would be.

There was no hesitation from any of them.

All three reached across to me and placed their hands on top of both of mine.

"As long as you are happy, Jess, we are happy." This was from Tyson, who was uncharacteristically somber, before the smartass returned: "And at least Max is off the hook – you know, since now you're the one messing with the dynamics."

The vampire clipped his brother across the back of the head, although even I could see he wore an expression of relieved happiness. He was okay with me and Braxton. I did briefly wonder if he'd have felt the same way if he hadn't just found his mate. But fate circumvented that little issue for us.

Jacob chuckled. "I think my brothers are turning into whipped bitches, but I'm all good with that. Although I'm instilling a rule right now: no frisky business when we're all in the bed."

I wrinkled my nose in his direction. "In your dreams, Jake."

His chuckles increased. "Hell yeah, only not with my brothers as the other parties."

Okay, overshare much.

Braxton growled again. I pinned him with squinty eyes. "Stop that, Braxton Compass, your growling is giving me a headache." It really wasn't, but I needed to keep on top of his dominance or he'd smother me.

His fierceness faded under his amusement. I tried to ignore the way his smile heated my insides.

Jonathon cleared his throat. "I'm a little surprised you didn't end up being true mates."

Small beads of pain flashed through me as I narrowed my eyes on him. "How do you know we aren't true mates?"

He turned his head as if the fierceness of my reaction surprised him. "Because you would have told us, and I don't sense the sort of energy connection which should be bonding you."

Louis leaned in toward me, his brow wrinkled. "Actually, they are bonded, but it seems to be … there was a problem with the bond."

A variety of expressions shot across the faces around me. There were a lot of furrowed brows.

Braxton and I took turns explaining what had happened, from my journey to the land of the white mists, and Braxton's two mate theory. The

Compasses registered some recognition. They remembered Jo's story too.

I growled. "I'm not exactly happy that fate seems to think I'm going to have to make a choice about my mate." I hadn't even known at the time that this choice bullshit was going to involve Braxton.

Louis tented his hands in front of him, before leaning into them. "That story from Jo is true," he finally said. "The bond between you and Braxton will come to fruition in its own time. But there will be a choice and a challenge. Your young bond will be tested."

"That's some pretty obscure mumbo jumbo bullshit you are muttering there, sorcerer," I snapped.

He was unfazed. "When it's something this rare, and not caused by magic, then obscure is all I got."

Braxton shook his head, his icy eyes taking in everyone at the table. "It doesn't matter, Jess and I will weather any obstacle. We are true mates. I will accept nothing less."

"Yes," I agreed, but the tendrils of fear which were scooting through my veins indicated I was more worried than I was pretending. I couldn't imagine anything in this world, or any other, which could make me doubt Braxton. But I hated overconfidence, it made you stupid, blind to what might be coming right at you. I wanted to be smarter than that. Especially if the choice I'd have to make could save or destroy the entire supernatural race.

We were all distracted as food landed in front of us. I was ecstatic that it seemed to be share platters, a mix of seafood, pasta, and lots of breads. I was too busy for the next little while to talk, but eventually I noticed that Cardia was not here.

"Where's your mate?" I asked Maximus. He slowed his food intake just long enough to answer.

"She's with her nest mates. They're celebrating something."

I stared at him for a few long beats. "You know you don't have to miss out on those moments for us, we understand that you're part of her family now too."

I *sort of* understood that.

His lips narrowed, like he had some heavy thoughts going on. "We decided to take it slowly, this blending of two families. For now, I'm okay with that. I can feel her here." He touched his chest. Lucky bastard didn't have some weird, half-bond thing.

I squinted, trying to see the energy ties that Jonathon had talked of to recognize mates, but I saw nothing.

I caught my sister's eye. She had been quiet for most of the meal, eyes downcast as she finished eating her ridiculously small amount of food. I seriously had to get some cake into her, she was becoming uncomfortably thin – fading away even, which was never a good sign for a shifter.

Melancholy seemed to have settled over her and I wasn't liking it.

She caught my eye. "I'm sorry about your partial bond … maybe you got my share of matehood as well." She attempted a grin, it was a ghost of true happiness.

I realized she must have been pondering my half bond, and behind her pitiful smile I could see the layers of pain radiating from her. Something was wrong with my sister; heartache bled from her. Could this just be about Maximus, or was there more? I needed to take the time and figure out what it was.

"You have a mate out there, Misch, and hopefully it's a little less complicated than my … thing," I said.

Tyson snorted then. "She called you a thing, Brax. God, I love Jess, but she's going to destroy you, man. Run now, run while you can."

I leaned across and punched the wizard on the arm. He ruffled my hair like I hadn't just whacked him. *Ass*.

Pulling back, I met Braxton's blue eyes. The dragon shifter didn't reply to Tyson's assness, but I could see the anticipation of a challenge in his gaze.

I knew he wasn't worried about us. We totally had this.

I was just reaching out to link my hand with his, when a thin, cold voice trailed over us. "Mischa, it's time to introduce us to your sister."

Swiveling around, I focused on the two females about ten feet from us. Judging by the Compass' expressions, they were not friends. Both were blond, a smooth creamy yellow, unnatural, with large eyes that were dark and empty, and stick-thin figures. They looked to be about the same height as me.

Even without the energy of old magic coating them, I knew who they were. The identical expressions, the cold stares. They were the twins who had been breaking out dragon marked from prisons around the world. And corrupting my sister.

Chapter 12

I stood wordlessly, my eyes locked on them. My instincts were screaming that they were the enemy. They looked nothing like the females in my demented little dragon dream, but I knew it was them. I could feel their energy.

Mischa jumped to her feet, and before I could reach out and stop her she had dashed to the females, embracing the closest as if they were the best of friends; then she turned and hugged the other. Neither of them lifted their eyes from me, even over my own sister's shoulder. It was as if they were taunting me, showing me how much they'd infiltrated into Mischa's life, how close they were to her. Something cold was in my hand. I looked down and realized I'd reached out and snatched up one of the knives. It was pretty blunt, but it would work as a weapon.

Mischa had turned now and she waved at me. "Jess, come and meet the girls. They've been waiting for you to return."

I'll bet they had.

When I didn't move, her green eyes darkened, and she did that nibble-on-the-corner-of-her-lip thing. "They've been helping me look for you. I don't know what I would have done without their support."

Both of the twins turned from me then, bestowing my clueless twin with smiles that gave me the creeps, but at least they had lost the dominance contest. They weren't shifters like Mischa and I, though. I couldn't tell which race they were from. I turned to my pack.

"What the hell happened with you all and Mischa while I was gone?" I was mainly directing my soft, but bluntly spoken question at Maximus.

His features hardened, although it looked a little like guilt and a lot like worry flashing across his eyes. "Let's just say she didn't react in a positive manner when I found Cardia."

I had figured that was the issue. But why was she taking it so hard?

Lienda clued me in. "She thinks like a human, not a supernatural. Especially when it comes to love."

On occasion I forgot that Mischa hadn't been raised in the supernatural world, so things like true mates didn't mean anything to her. I had explained to her before that most supernaturals mated within their race, but there was so much more to it.

Supes had three types of relationships: a chosen mateship, which was not a destined match but still committed; a true mateship, which was forever and determined by the fates; and casual relationships.

It wasn't easy to find a true mate, but if you were mated or in a relationship with a supernatural who found their true mate, you had no choice but to accept that it was over. No fighting, arguing, or even thinking twice about it, it was understood and very little drama occurred.

Which is why I never thought for a second that Mischa would take the whole Maximus and his little mate thing so hard. Firstly, I was pretty sure my sister and the vampire had never really been together, they just had this weird flirtation going on. And secondly, she knew they could never be true mates.

But the whole human part of her clearly felt differently. And now to ease her heartache she'd jumped straight into bed with what was quite possibly the enemy.

I catalogued the twin's features. They were like Mischa and I, mostly the same but with a few flairs of difference. One was a little finer boned than her sister, and her hair had orange streaks through the blonde. I was going to call her Orange for the hair, and the other one Lemon.

The fruit twins.

Orange was speaking to me. "We have much to discuss with you, Jessa. You're the fourth of our compass."

I shook my head. "No thanks, Orange. I have my own set of Compasses, I don't need to be the fourth of another."

Jacob cracked up then, he drew the attention of most of the supernaturals in the street.

I snorted. "It wasn't that funny, Jake."

He doubled over as he continued laughing. "Shit, yes, it was funny as hell. You named her Orange. I'll bet the other one is yellow ... no, not yellow." He squinted, his laughter trailing off. "Lemon."

Our pack had clearly spent too much time together over the past twenty years.

Lemon – ignoring the comedian fey – took over the negotiations. "The dragon king rises in a few days, and you're important. Don't you want to fulfill your destiny? You're chosen."

"Chosen for what? To murder everyone?"

She shook her head. "Our destiny isn't to kill anyone–"

"No, but the dragon king will kill the lot of us. I won't be a part of it."

"You have no choice. It's your destiny."

I sighed, shifting my fingers for a better grip on the knife. Jonathon was standing at my side and I could see the tension radiating off him, his hands were clenched. Most of us around the table were standing now. It was like a high-noon showdown. Mischa was looking more and more miserable from where she lingered between the two groups.

I let my wolf and dragon rise to the surface, just enough that my energy was strong. "I'm only going to say this once, so listen up, fruit twins. I am never freeing the dragon king. Never. Ever. Ever. Ever." I drifted my gaze across to Mischa. "You need to step away from them, they are just using you for their own gains. You can't trust them."

Lemon grinned, showing all of her teeth. "Mischa has sworn an oath to help us with this task."

In my head I had already flung the knife into her smug face, somehow I restrained myself. And more than a little of my annoyance was directed toward my twin. Could she really be so stupid as to promise these bitches anything?

Mischa's large eyes widened even further. "No, you never said the task was for the dragon king. You said it was to help proliferate the supernatural race."

Okay, apparently she wasn't stupid, just naïve again … or maybe both. We needed to get her a keeper or something, because she was shithouse at making decisions herself.

"The rise of the dragon king will proliferate the supernatural race. He will bring about a strength and unity which has been sorely missing with all of the divided races." Orange waved her arm in a circle. "Look here at the sanctuary, all different races existing together, all bound because of the mark we wear. That mark is our birthright, our loyalty to the king of all races."

I held up a hand. "I'm going to stop you right there, because the crazy train has already left the station and I think you missed your seat." I sat back down and turned away from them. "I'm done giving you any of my time."

Lemon and Orange took a step toward me, but the growl and wash of power from my father had them pausing. Braxton hadn't said anything, but together with his brothers they were more than intimidating as they stood side by side.

I continued watching the fruit twins, even though I was acting dismissive. They were examining the powerful members of my family. Then they straightened, and dialed back some of the dominance they'd been broadcasting.

"Mischa…" Lienda's voice was soft but to the point. She held out her hand for her daughter to join her.

Thankfully the fruit twins didn't have their slimy grip too tight yet, because there was barely any hesitation before Mischa crossed back to us. I thought for a moment Lemon was going to reach out and grab her, but she didn't.

"We'll see you both soon." I got double grins of malice before the twins faded off.

I turned to Quale. "Tell us everything about those two before I smash you in the face."

I slammed the tip of the knife into the table, lodging its blunt end in about an inch. I was not liking this place, or the freaking dragon mystics.

Louis rubbed a hand over his chin, interrupting before his brother could answer. "Jess, it's not Quale's fault."

I swung my glare around to him. "Like hell it isn't. It's his fault and it's your fault. Why the crap did you send us here? This is like a cult recruiting to raise the freaking evil king. And I'm apparently one of the four females required for the job." Panic and betrayal swelled in my gut, my throat tightened. "Did you know about that? Did you send me here for that reason?"

He reached out to take my hand, but a hard glare from Braxton had him backing off. "No, Jess, I promise it was just about keeping you safe. The sanctuary is the one place the Four will never find you, and it's only for a few more days. Once we pass the thousand year mark, we can make a new plan."

I tried to think. "I have to leave. I can't stay here. I can't be in Romania."

My father took my hand, trying to calm me. "If you're not in the sanctuary or Drago at the time of the rising, you'll die. I can't lose you. If the king rises, we will deal with it." Jonathon's voice had a layer of ice over it. I recognized the tone, he was both worried and pissed.

I rubbed the back of my neck, the tension there becoming painful. "So ... even if I don't help them open the tomb or raise the king or whatever bullshit plan they have, I still have to be here or at Drago? All of the marked do?"

Quale spoke, "That's the rumor, and there is no way to know until the final strike of midnight on the Day."

He said "day" like that was its title.

"Tell me about the twins." I was focused on him again. "How do they break into the prisons?"

Quale looked around, I think to determine if anyone was listening in. I was pretty sure lots of supernaturals were listening in. We were in the middle of a freaking restaurant.

"I'm not totally sure, they keep their secrets very close to their chest. I have guessed at a few skills: they can sense dragon marked supernaturals –

which makes it easy to find them hidden in the prison – and they can also influence the minds of males. Mostly those who are weaker, but still, in every prison they have found someone to help them."

Influencing minds, like controlling other supernaturals? That was both wicked and scary as heck.

"Why don't Mischa and I have cool powers like that?"

Louis answered me. "They're old and have had a long time to develop their abilities. You and Mischa are young, and your powers have been blocked and bound for most of your lives." He turned to my shell-shocked twin. "Mischa's marked powers still are."

I lowered my voice. "Do they have a large dragon mark too?"

There was a few confused looks around the table, but not from Louis. The damn sorcerer always knew everything. Well, clearly not everything, we still had a crap-ton of unanswered questions. But he was on point most of the time.

I explained for the confused. "From what I've seen the supes in here have small dragon marks. Mine is like half my side and back."

Quale shrugged. "I've never seen the twin's marks, and the other mystics haven't either, but I can tell you that there have been none to enter in the last few hundred years which have a large mark."

I was sure that the fruit twins had massive marks too. Why would I be the only one in this compass? Mischa lowered her head but didn't say anything. Her expression troubled me.

Tyson pushed back strands of brown hair. "The spirits – magical essence inside – is urging us to unlock Mischa's mark, let her and Jessa figure out what their twin-abilities are."

"No!" Jonathon's tone was short and hard. "I don't think there could be anything worse right now than releasing more energy for the dragon king to manipulate."

Mischa's chair screeched as she lurched to her feet. "You think I'm weak and stupid. You don't trust me with my powers. Shit, I was raised with humans, I freaking think like one, and you're doing nothing to help me adjust."

She was yelling and waving her hands. Plus she'd just sworn in front of her mother, who had very definite ideas about ladies and bad language.

Mischa turned tail and took off. I could see my parents were about to go after her, but I stopped them. "I'll go. We need to have a bit of a talk, and I think it's better if no one else is there."

I had to get through to her, I couldn't lose my sister, and I sensed a rift between us which hadn't been there before I got lost in Faerie land.

Jonathon gave me another hard hug, a goodbye this time. "We also need to talk, my little wolf. I would like to hear what has been happening since you left us. Including your run-in with the jinn and side-trip to the Faerie dimension."

Nothing slipped past my father, which was why he made such an amazing alpha. Speaking of ... I wondered who was running the shifter pack and council in Stratford. The leaders often left, but only for short periods of time. It would be a little sparse on the American Supernatural Council right now, since Stratford was also missing their magic leader. Kristoff was in Vanguard. Well, I hoped he was, he must have had his trial by now. Another thing I needed to talk with my parents about.

"I'll come and find you after I talk to Misch," I said. With a kiss on my forehead Jonathon let me go.

I caught Braxton's eye as I turned to leave, and the heat in his gaze almost had me abandoning my plans and dragging him back to my room. I forced my hormones down, gave him a wink, and was relieved when he returned the gesture with a simple nod. He was working on his overly possessive temperament. Still, there was a battle going on behind his expressive eyes. For now he was trusting me.

"You call for us if there is any trouble, especially if the twins come back." The low timbre of his voice rocked my girly parts, but I managed to nod without jumping him.

Something light and smooth slipped into my hand. I glanced down to find Louis had given me a small black cell phone. "Untraceable. We all have them. I programmed everyone's numbers in there."

I groaned. "You know I'm going to lose this in like five minutes, right?"

"Five?" Jacob muttered. "She's probably already lost it."

I stuck out my tongue, waving the phone and my middle finger at him. "Not yet, smartass."

With laughter following me I hightailed it out of the food street. I had no idea where my sister was, but instinct was sending me toward our apartment building. I was going to check there first.

Cool and still inside the front hall of our residence, I threw the phone onto the kitchen bench and followed Mischa's scent. She was all wolf and tears right now, a sort of distinct wet dog smell – kidding, wolves' fur didn't smell like dog's.

I tried to figure out what I would say to her, how to offer comfort when I really just wanted to yell at her for being so stupid. I needed to work on the sympathy thing. I was getting worse with old age. I followed the sound of her sniffles into our bedroom.

The door was open so I walked straight in, only to almost bump into Mischa as she stood staring down at the beds which were still all over the place. She lifted her chin and turned to me.

"Looks a little like a battle went on in here," she said, a trace of humor in her voice, which was much better than the tears still sprinkling her lashes.

I snorted, unable to stop chuckles from trickling out. As Mischa's mirth increased she started to laugh with me.

Eventually our amusement faded. I found myself focusing on the bed, flashes of memory shooting through me as I relived the time spent in here with Braxton. I was totally ready for another round, I had not had enough the first time. I'd probably never have enough of him.

Mischa interrupted my adult-rated thoughts.

"I'll admit I'm jealous of you right now."

I forced myself not to snarl. She'd never shown any interest in Braxton, so it must mean something other than what I feared. Of course, my wolf didn't care, she wanted to snarl anyway.

"I might be a virgin, and I'm more than ready to hand that particular card in, but what I want more than anything is someone to call my own."

My wolf calmed, along with my dragoness. They loved my twin too, but possessiveness was part of their animal instinct, and Braxton was ours.

I searched for the right words. Mischa was sensitive, I had no idea how to reassure her. Girls were hard, boys seemed much easier, more straightforward to deal with. I couldn't completely understand her need to belong to someone. It kind of grated on my sense of independence. But what the hell did I know? I'd always had the Compasses and called all of them mine. I had never been alone.

"You will find someone to call yours, Misch. There is no rush, we're young. To be totally honest, I never expected to find my mate anytime soon, but it's Braxton..." Which said it all.

I breathed deeply at the emotions flooding me. There was a new intimacy between Braxton and I now, and it continued to bash against me like a surge of tides. Sure, we'd only been together for half a day, but that full-heart thing was a force living inside my chest. Maybe I had a better idea than I thought of the connection my twin was seeking in her life.

We both dropped onto the edge of the bed. I reached across and grabbed a cushion, pulling it into my lap. "I'm sorry I disappeared on you. I didn't mean to abandon you."

She raised her sad eyes to meet mine. "You didn't do it on purpose, Jess, it just sucked that right when I needed you the most, you were gone. I was so worried about you, trying to deal with Maximus. Trying to hold it together."

"Tell me what happened." I took her hand.

She shrugged. "I cared about him. Like really cared." Her lips twisted into a forced grin. "I hoped we could have something."

I didn't say anything, there wasn't really anything I could say. But as the uncomfortable silence continued, I decided to try to find the right words. "Well, I know Max cares about you a lot, but true mates are forever and complete. There was nothing he could do."

She nodded, "I know, but just because my head knows doesn't mean my heart doesn't hurt." I hugged more tightly around her shoulders. I had never had any unrequited love in my life, but I could imagine the pain.

After a few silent moments I changed the subject to what I really needed to know. "Why are you hanging out with the evil twinly duo?"

She blinked a few times. "You mean Cristy and Shalone?"

I shrugged. "I have zero cares about their real names. They're Orange and Lemon."

She snickered. "Yeah, I get that." There was a pause then, as if she was trying to figure out how to explain her friendship with the twins. She started with a sigh. "When Maximus came back from feeding, we were trying to find you and Braxton. Tyson and Jacob were going crazy, they had Quale up against the tree by his throat, threatening, screaming. It only got worse when Max returned." She twisted her hands in her lap. "He went ballistic. It took us a really long time to calm him down, and the only one who could was … that vampire he'd fed from. Apparently, everyone knew then that they were *true* mates. I, of course, was the clueless outsider as always."

"Damn, I'm sorry, that's tough." I hated being in the dark, feeling stupid. I knew Mischa would be no different. "But you have a mate out there too. Don't forget that happiness is yours to find, so don't give up."

Her eyes were so green; even ringed with red she still looked amazing. I had no doubt there was going to be a supernatural completely captivated by her one day.

"I'm pretty much off men at the moment." Her voice was hard, before breaking right on the end again. "And I have to tell you something…"

I tensed, her breathy whisper was worse than the hard voice. She was not going to be imparting good news.

"Part of the promise I made the twins ... I have to go with them into the Romanian prison, and they said that if you didn't come also, that they couldn't guarantee my safety. That sometimes supes got lost in the prison system and were never seen again."

It was a direct threat, but I could tell that Mischa didn't really see it that way.

"Fuck!" My arm fell off her shoulders as I jumped to my feet. "Why, Mischa? Why the hell would you agree to go into Krakov with them?"

I had a terrible feeling about this as I stood there staring her down. The fruit twins had already freed the marked from that prison, so what did they have to go back in there for?

Mischa rubbed at her face tiredly. "There is a key in there, or a weapon, I'm not totally sure. They promised it was for the benefit of the entire supernatural community. And all four of us would be required to free it."

"You realize that we're the other two points on this compass to free the dragon king, right?"

Mischa rose slowly until we stood face to face. "Yes."

We were mirror images, facing off. "We can't trust them, no matter what bullshit story they feed you about a weapon for the communities. This has something to do with the dragon king."

She dropped her chin. Her submissive pose pissed me off and I fought the urge to capture that chin in my hand and wrench her face upwards.

"They ... they helped me out. I got myself into a little trouble with one of the shifters and they saved my ass."

And in return they assured she was guilted into a suspect scheme to infiltrate the prison. Mischa had given her word, and we tried not to break our word. Words held power, and it wasn't good to tempt the gods with broken promises.

"Can the fruit twins shift into dragons?"

Mischa's full lips parted, my change of subject had surprised her. "No, they're not even shifters. They've never told me which race they're from, but they use magic at times so I think witches. And I know I didn't answer you before when you asked, but their mark is nothing like yours. It's small."

I knew her weird expression at the table had been hiding something. *Damn, damn, damn.* This was horseshit. I had really been hoping that I wasn't the special one within an already chosen bunch. Whatever being north meant, it was not a good thing, I knew that without a doubt. The jinn's words reverberated through my mind.

I was chosen. I was special. I was so freaking screwed.

I expelled the next words through gritted teeth. "When is this brilliant break-and-enter supposed to take place?"

There was no way I'd leave Mischa to do this. I could sense the aura of evil on those bitches, and if I didn't come along I had no doubt they would leave her to the tender care of the prisoners in there. I had no idea how I would convince the Compasses and my father. They would fight us on this.

"Um … uh, it's going to be, uh…" She started stuttering away and I worked very hard not to scream at her. "Tomorrow," she finally finished. "We have to go in tomorrow."

I should have known it would be soon. They were pretty much out of time. The deadline to free the king was upon us, and whatever plans they had to put into play, well, it had to be in the next few days. "I have to tell Dad and the quads."

If something went wrong we would need backup.

Mischa worried at her lips even harder, her teeth leaving marks along the pink softness. "The twins won't like it. Everything is a secret to them, but … I would feel better if Mom and Dad knew."

She was barely even mentioning the Compasses anymore.

"Girl, how long are you going to hold on to this anger toward Maximus? It's not healthy, you have to let it go." I clapped my hands together. "I think what we need right now is a chance to run."

I missed my wolf, and Mischa had definitely not spent enough time learning about her animal. We got a little crazy if we didn't shift reasonably frequently. It was time.

She jumped on the spot, emotions flying across her face so rapidly that I was having trouble cataloguing them all. But she seemed mostly excited.

I was so feeling that. Together we moved from our room. I picked up the cell phone again, and scrolling through found the right numbers. I sent off very brief texts explaining where Mischa and I were heading. Without waiting for replies, I dumped the phone on the bench again and walked with my sister out of the apartment and into the elevator.

Mischa held my hand, both of us hating this shithole-box which was our only means of escaping the building. My twin distracted us both by sharing some of her heartache.

"I'm not mad at the Compasses, Jess, I'm embarrassed that I let myself get so involved in something that wasn't real. It wasn't like Max made me any promises or did anything besides be a good friend. Sure, we flirted, but that seems to be the way with those boys. They flirt as frequently as they breathe. I just wanted it to be real, and trying to deal with my own stupidity–"

"Led you right into another set of stupidity. Aligning yourself with the fruit twins was not your brightest moment."

She sighed. "They were good to me, I won't judge them yet."

"They threatened to leave you in Krakov!"

"They just needed a way to ensure you'd help. It wasn't personal."

Holy shit. Dumbass alert.

Seriously, someone needed to save us from her bleeding heart, they were playing her like a violin. And all of us had to pay now. I was probably going to be caught by the Four and locked under the sea.

It was a relief when the elevator opened again. I pulled my hand free from hers and together we strolled out onto the cobbled path.

"Where do you want to run?" Mischa asked.

"The forest," I said. I was less worried about the jinn now, it felt as if they'd made their point and would wait now to see what eventuated. Besides they could find me anywhere, and the forest was the place our wolves wanted to be. Quale had explained there was a massive expanse of woodlands, and that we were free to use them. There were no pack territories, and with so much space, other shifters rarely ran into each other.

As we stepped into the cool expanse, I felt my body relax. This was home, this was perfect. Mischa startled as footsteps sounded from behind us, but I'd heard them following us for a while. Not to mention there was no denying the power of an alpha.

"Mind if we join you?"

Jonathon and Lienda were already undressing, so it was a rhetorical question at the best.

I turned around and prepared to shed my own clothing. Once I was naked, I called on the energy of my wolf, dropped to all fours and my body flowed and shimmered. I watched ten fingers morph in a single movement into paws. Then I was wolf. No pain, all awesomeness.

Howls rang out around me, and I turned to find my wolf family waiting and ready. Hell yeah, we had never ran together. This was going to be fun.

Chapter 13

"Oh for fuck's sake, you have got to be shitting me?" Maximus had been stomping around cursing like an ogre since Mischa and I had explained about the Romanian prison dilemma. He was only partially vamped, so he hadn't completely lost control. "After Vanguard, I was determined that none of us would be going into any of the prisons again."

Jonathon had his head tented in his hands. "It seems no matter what I do, I can't keep my girls out of danger." He didn't look angry, more pensive, as if calculating odds and formulating a plan.

All of us were spread around the living room of our apartment, the Compasses doing their sexy lean-against-the-wall thing. Though Maximus was currently giving the carpet a workout as he marched and swore.

Mischa dashed across the room and stopped before our father. "I'm so sorry, I didn't realize the trouble I'd be getting into by hanging around with the twins. They seemed so genuine at first and I just needed someone."

After our run, we'd discussed those biatches again, and she was finally starting to see their evilness.

Lienda captured her daughter's hand and pulled her down to sit between her and Dad. "This isn't your fault. They're ancient, wise and manipulative. You could never have comprehended the means they would go to to bring about the prophesy. They're determined to return the king and will stop at nothing."

Jonathon draped his arm over Mischa, pulling her closer. "Your mother is right, so now we just have to figure out how to derail their plans." He directed the rest to all of us. "Mischa must keep her word, and Jessa has no choice here."

Sprawled out on one of the single couches, I clashed eyes with a blue so frosty it pretty much iced all the breath in my lungs. I'd been avoiding Braxton's gaze. I hated when he was upset. Rigid against the wall, he had yet to say anything, which was far scarier than Maximus' blustering, and I was a touch nervous of his next actions.

Unable to stop myself, I rose, needing to cross to him. He straightened and right before I reached him, he opened his arms. I threw myself into his warmth. Both of his hands ended up under my butt as he lifted me into his body. Some of the heaviness in my chest eased.

I heard a growl from Maximus; he was still pissed. Not to mention frustrated – his new vampire mate had been excluded from this little gathering. "Great, Brax is too enamored with our Jess to even voice his protest."

It was better that Cardia wasn't here, she didn't need to jump into our shit-storm of secrets. Though we still had to be careful of our words, Grace was in the room. She still didn't know about my ability to shift into a dragon. I had told my parents after our run through the forest. It was nice to have everything in the open, and even though Jonathon had been a little emotional, he'd handled the news okay.

Braxton didn't lift his eyes from mine, but he did answer his brother. "There is no point arguing, I trust Jess, I trust in her abilities to protect herself and her sister." He held my gaze with a fierceness that had me rendered senseless. "Don't get me wrong, I don't want her to go, but I will not be the male who is always standing in her way."

This was why I loved him, he knew what battles to fight and what ones to walk away from. He was offering me his support, he was supporting Mischa – who already felt like shit – and he was going to help in any way he could.

"Guess it doesn't hurt that I'm pretty unbreakable," I whispered close to his cheek.

His chest rumbled beneath me as he laughed a few times. "Yeah, we would probably be having a different conversation if you weren't."

I let my legs relax from where I'd had them wrapped around Braxton. My body protested, acting all pissed off that I was removing myself. But I was starting to have thoughts which were not appropriate for when my parents were in the room. As if he read that in my suddenly flushed cheeks, Braxton raised his eyebrows at me, a smirk tipping up the corner of his lips and flashing more than a glimpse of dimple.

Friggin' dimples. They were weapons.

When he let me go, I wiggled my way in between him and Jacob, leaning against the wall. Both brothers reached out and draped their huge arms across me. Somehow it worked without completely crushing me under their bulk. I caught the green-eyed wink the fey flashed at me. So far the Braxton-and-me-thing hadn't changed our pack dynamics. Which was a massive freaking relief.

I felt eyes on me and turned to find Louis' keen stare. "What do you think we should do first, Jessa?" he asked.

I leaned forward a little, more than ready to give my thoughts. "If we are going to do this, we have to unlock Mischa's mark. She's vulnerable with only half of herself free, and we need to know if she can shift to dragon." Jonathon wouldn't like it, but it had to be done.

Mischa almost bounced from her place on the couch. "Yes! I'm sick of being the weak one with no knowledge of my abilities. I choose to no longer be the victim."

I flashed her a broad smile. Finally. I was so proud of her for making the choice.

"Will you unlock her powers?" I asked the sorcerer.

He again rested those unusual violet eyes on me. "For you, little sister, I would do anything."

I snorted, and I wasn't the only one. The Compasses turned as one and leveled a single glare in his direction. Of all the things Louis had ever done, his use of the word "sister" seemed to have set them off.

"What did you say?" Tyson was the closest in terms of distance, and as he straightened he blocked my view of Louis. I wasn't tall enough to see over him and he was far too broad to see around. "Jess is not your anything, you need to learn your place."

"Hey!" I muscled my way out of the men. "I think I can speak for myself, Tyson Compass, and I can also kick your ass if you need a reminder."

He arched one of his well-shaped brows at me. "I think I'd enjoy a good ass-kicking, if it was you delivering it." His eyes flicked across to his brothers. Even Maximus had finally stopped pacing and was now standing on the other side of Jacob. "But seriously, Louis needs to take a step back. You're our sister, our pack, and he is not a part of that."

I sighed. "I'm not a possession, I belong to no one."

The clearing of a throat had my lips twitching. I couldn't help but tilt my chin and meet Braxton's stare.

"Okay, I maybe ... sort of ... a very tiny, little, minute amount belong to Braxton Compass." The other quads faces fell. Oh shit balls, they were tugging on my heart.

"Fine, I belong to all of you, as long as you know you belong to me also. And ... Louis is part of that. He is my brother from another mother. We are cool in that way."

Braxton placed his huge, warm hand on the center of my back, his thumb ever so gently rubbing up and down my spine. "I like brother much better than when he was trying to date you, which could only end one way: blood, guts, and magic splattered all over the floor."

I snorted, surprised Louis didn't call Braxton on that statement. The sorcerer must have noticed my expression. He gave a nod, his demeanor content. "I will not argue with his possessiveness. I would not have accepted any less strength from your mate. Braxton is a good fit, he is worthy."

"I concur," said my father, and my heart warmed that Jonathon was happy with my mate.

He wasn't actually that over-protective most of the time. Really, he had spent a lot of my life grieving for Lienda, or absent running his packs and council. But he was a wonderful father, and I would never ask for anything more. And speaking of wolf-mother, in a smooth motion mine stood and walked over to me.

Seeing the look in her eyes, I started to protest, but she swooped in before I could. I was pulled into the warmth of Lienda. And it was kind of nice. I let myself have a real mother-moment for just a few seconds.

I pulled away when I reached the limit of my hug-time; Lienda looked really happy.

Mischa was practically bouncing in her seat now. "Can we unlock the dragon mark? I'm so ready."

I growled as my thoughts were dragged to that moment my mark was released, to that vampire who'd had his hands all over me. The emotions were dulled now. I was mentally healthier, and thought myself lucky I had been saved before anything worse had happened. As a shifter, I was naturally resilient, my wolf stepping in when I needed a break from human emotions.

"You might want to take her outside," Braxton said. He curved an arm around my waist and lifted me back into him, his expression shuttered. "There was a veritable explosion of energy when Jess ... when I found her in that room." That explained the expression, he was having the same dark thoughts as me.

"That is a sound idea," Louis said in his I'm-an-ancient-supe dialect.

My dark thoughts continued further along the path. "Did Kristoff go to prison?" We'd left Stratford before his trial.

Scents of unease trickled through the room. I stepped forward, Braxton's arm sliding off my waist. "What happened?"

Jonathon rose off the couch and met me halfway, face to chest. Even though he wasn't tall for a supernatural, he was still taller than me. "Don't panic, sweet wolf, but there was a bit of a mess-up with the Kristoff trial."

A mess up? What the hell did that even mean?

"The reason it was so easy for Vlad and his cohorts to knock you out and move you around

Vanguard was because they had help … help from Kristo–"

"No shitting way "

"Fuck off."

"What?"

The roars came from the Compasses. I was too pissed to speak. We'd all thought Kristoff's plan to imprison the quads had been a separate incident to the attack-crap which had happened to me inside Vanguard. But now it seemed they had been connected. Jonathon's eye's shifted across the snarling quads and his growl reverberated around the room. He did not like them interrupting, so his wolf popped up to let them know who was boss.

Maximus was clenching and unclenching his fists at his side. "Tell me that you killed that slimy dickbag sorcerer."

Jonathon's words flowed from him in a gale. "We were on our way to do that. Louis, Lienda, and I gained entry to Vanguard, but he wasn't there. No one had noticed yet, but upon investigation he'd been gone for about twelve hours. And … he managed to free Vlad and Scarface."

"I thought they were dead!" I finally found my voice, it was hard enough to shatter glass.

Jonathon's resonance matched mine. "I thought so too, but there is corruption in Vanguard. We need to have a mass turnover of the guards again. It's generally required every few hundred years, and is the most effective way to break the cycle."

I rubbed at my nose. "So you're saying the motherfuckers who tried to rape and torture me, along with the sorcerer who schemed and murdered other supes to frame my boys, are out there running around free. And this is because someone on the inside helped them a second time?" The sort of rage which quite frankly scared the shit out of me rose up through my body. My dragon and wolf were straining with the need to kill, fight, maim.

"They won't be free for long, Jessa babe," Jacob said, the fey's voice less musical than usual. "As soon as we deal with this dragon mark thing and the rise of the king, we will make it our mission to hunt them down."

Some of my red-hot rage subsided, Jacob's words reminding me that I needed to focus on our current problems. Kristoff would just have to take a back seat. But I would not be forgetting. Giselda was going to be minus a father very soon, and if I found out that bitch had anything to do with his scheming, well, she would be in the shallow grave next to him.

Grace rose from where she'd been sitting in the corner of the room. "Why do I get the feeling that I'm the only one here missing a vital piece of evidence?" Clearly she'd had enough of being the quiet mouse in the corner. "Why am I even here, Louis?" She turned her delicate ire toward the sorcerer, who was hovering between the living room and the front door. "You said they would need a healer."

Louis steadied himself. He'd been halfway out of the room, preparing for us to leave and unlock Mischa's dragon mark. His purple eyes focused on her. "They will need a healer. I don't see the future, but I sense paths that should be taken. I have an idea of what is to come." He glided closer to her. "Your destiny is here, Grace, you just need to be patient."

Grace's eyes flicked to Tyson. It was one of the first times I'd seen her even glance in his direction since we'd boarded the plane from Stratford. The wizard lurched forward from his place against the wall. It was like the moment they locked gazes they were connected. He strode the five steps to reach her and she looked helpless, unable to tear herself away.

"What are you talking about, Louis?" asked Maximus.

His question wasn't necessary. All of us could see and scent that something had shifted in the room. Tyson paused, his arm extended as if he was going to pull her toward him.

Grace's face fell, and her eyes crinkled like she was about to cry. "Please don't. I can't take this from you anymore."

She turned away, finally strong enough to tear her eyes from the handsome wizard. The energy between them shattered as she dashed from our apartment, disappearing out of the door. Tyson hesitated for a second, caught by surprise.

"Shit," he finally cursed, before taking off along the same path.

I fought the urge to follow, I hated to see any members of my pack hurting, but I knew this was something they had to work out between themselves. Tyson and Grace's fight had been a long time coming. Plus, we had bigger things to deal with. It was time to unlock Mischa's mark.

I was consumed by many hectic thoughts as we crossed the town center heading toward the forest, so I wasn't the first to notice the large gathering of mystics on the edge of the green tree line. Twelve of them. Which if I remembered correctly, was the entire bunch. They were cloaked, hoods up, and the feeling of something eerie, ominous even, was strong. I recognized Gerard and Quale, plus a few others whose names I didn't know.

Earlier in the day Louis' brother had informed us that he wouldn't be around much. The mystics were balls deep in rituals and cleansings for the rise of the king. Brainless dickbags, couldn't care less about the damage they might be causing.

"What do you want?"

Louis' power laden voice was directed at the line of cloaked ones.

Quale, still near the middle, Gerard to his left. The majority were nameless, faceless members.

One of them spoke: "You need to train with us, the twins must learn of their mark powers." There was the slightest hesitation before he continued. "And we have decided that if the quads want to continue residing in the sanctuary, they must join their powers together. Our people demand to know if they're a threat."

I bared my teeth. "We don't have time for this. Plus, you have no jurisdiction over us."

Quale stepped forward. "If you don't have the basic instruction, the same as all the others who enter the sanctuary, then you will no longer be welcome here."

Okay, great, maybe they did have some authority. We stared them down, but they didn't seem worried.

"In one hour, we'll meet you in the largest of buildings toward the sea side. It is the only one in yellow, you can't miss it." Gerard pointed. All of us could see the building. It towered high and shiny into the air, the color was a pale version of sunflower. "Do not be late. You will still be free to accompany the twins to the prison tomorrow, but today you must train."

As one they turned and marched away. Only Quale looked back with an expression of unease. I could tell that Louis' brother wasn't always cool with what the mystics stood for, but it was his fate to serve the dragon king. It was hard to fight against one's fate.

I pushed back a few strands of free hair, hooking it behind my ears. "So, not to state the obvious, but clearly the twins and the mystics are all in this together."

Louis nodded. "Yes, they all have the same end goal: achieve the prophesy and raise the king. And while they understand that what they're doing could bring about the next world-war of the supernaturals, they don't care. It seems to be programmed into their DNA, as if they're no longer capable of individual thought." His wise eyes rested on Mischa. "Even you have fallen prey to the schematics of this entire endeavor. The only one who doesn't seem affected is … Jessa. I wonder why that is…"

Awesome. Now I was the sole focus of everyone, like a freak-show creature.

"No one controls, Jess," Jacob said, giving me a reprieve from the inspection. The fey was standing off to the side with his hands pressed to the tree, communing with nature. "Except maybe Braxton, but he uses good old fashioned charm and animal magnetism."

I flipped Jacob off, which pretty much said everything I was thinking. Besides, if I denied it, many here would scent the lie. Braxton was close to my back now. I could feel him both there and in my chest, those ghostly ties between us, a sense of connection, more than we'd ever previously shared. And yet still not enough. I wanted the bond complete.

"Stalker much?" I teased in a low voice as his body pressed against the length of mine. I could feel every powerful muscle as they flexed behind me.

His voice was close to my ear. "Until we figure out what is happening to you in regards to the jinn, dragon king, and your mark, well, get used to it. My one and only priority is to keep you safe."

I snaked my hand back and Braxton linked his fingers through mine.

"It has to have something to do with Jessa's mark," said Mischa, interrupting us. "The twins speak as if she's the golden child ... always calling her 'north.' Plus, we all know she's a dual shifter ... one of a kind."

I snorted. "Hey, we don't know that yet. Maybe you're a dual as well."

All I knew was that being unique or different when it came to the dragon king ... well, that was not a good thing. I was starting to get that sick-in-the-gut feeling when I thought about the next few days. So much was going to happen and so much could go wrong. I just wanted to crawl into bed and ignore the next week.

Louis crossed the space to stand before my twin. "Only one way to see if Jessa and Mischa have even more in common than the fact that they are twins. Let's unlock the dragon mark."

Freeing myself from Braxton I crossed the space to stand before Mischa. I took her hands. "Are you sure about this? If you unlock the mark you will be a target for the Four, and they're here in Romania searching for me."

She stared into my eyes, her green tinged with blue today, which she'd definitely inherited from Lienda. Our mother had eyes the color of the ocean, shifting and changing. "I'm not afraid, Jess. I don't want to be half a supernatural anymore, I want to be everything that I was born to be."

I gave her a nod, before stepping back and letting the sorcerer capture her full attention again. I wasn't going to argue. Besides, hopefully in the next few days when the king either rose or didn't, the Four would have no more reason to hunt dragon marked. The whole point was to prevent the rise of the king.

Although ... since the marked were supposed to be his personal army, probably the Four would never stop hunting us. Oh well, we'd just have to kill them. It was on my to-do list anyway.

Louis placed both hands on Mischa's chest, over her heart, the same as he'd done to cloak my energy back in Stratford.

"You're power is still very much locked away," he said as he lifted one hand. He seemed to be pulling something, lowering and raising that free hand, almost like he was unthreading energy which was wrapped around Mischa. "It's different than Jessa's. Even when you were babies I felt the difference, but it's still very strong."

I was worried about Mischa, my insides crawling at the thought of something going wrong for her. To distract myself, while Louis did his sorcerer thing, I dug a little deeper into what he'd just noted.

"Have you ever felt the energy of other marked?" I had been wondering if mine or Mischa's power was like the others.

"Only my brother's, and I think the mystics are different again."

Maximus turned his head as if he scented something. I focused on the direction he was facing and straight away I was hit with vampire. Cardia, his female was moving toward us. Maximus' eyes started to glow, her presence was awakening him.

He paused for a second to wink at me, then he marched away. No male worthy of the title of mate would make his female come all the way to him, he was going to meet her halfway. He disappeared behind a few buildings, but within moments was back, vampiress tucked snugly under his arm. He looked happy, relaxed; his mate had a calming effect on the beast inside.

"Do you look that blissed-out around me?" I said, wiggling my eyebrows at Braxton.

He reached out and traced a single fingertip from the top of my cheekbone all the way down to rest against my bottom lip.

"Blissed out doesn't even begin to describe it." He then replaced that finger with his lips, and I was lost in his kiss for ... who the hell knows how long. Supe males were not afraid to show emotion to their mates, no matter who was around. This sort of love was seen as a strength.

Jacob muttered close by, "Jessa is the Pied Piper of dragons, that's for sure." And I knew he was not just referring to Braxton, but also that strange encounter when we first entered the sanctuary. I'd been steadfast in ignoring the red-dragon incident. I wondered how long I could hide from all the peculiar in my life.

I pulled back from Braxton, although some of my body was reluctant to part ways – wait, how did my leg get around his waist? Shit, I really needed to pay attention. He was dangerous for my concentration and awareness. While untangling myself I noticed Jacob had moved even closer, he was watching me and Braxton. Not in a creepy way, almost wistful.

"You okay with being the last one not in some form of complicated relationship, Jake?" We all knew Tyson and Grace were heading toward … something.

He shook his head, white silky hair stylishly tousled against his forehead. "Yeah, I'm all good with a little less complicated in my life. There are too many females out there for me to want just one. I'll stay unmated for as long as possible, thank you."

Jacob the jackass. It would probably be a sad day when he mated and some of his dick-like behavior disappeared.

I furrowed my brow a little. "Am I the only one who thinks it's odd that two of the Compasses have discovered true mates here in the sanctuary?" I directed my question to the entire group. True matings were rare, so both brothers in such a short period was unusual.

Lienda answered, her expression wistful. "True mated pairs are works of fate. If you need to find them, you will."

Jonathon linked his arm with Lienda. "The energy of the dragon king has started to return. We can feel his cold power leaking into the supernatural world. It has been there for some time now. He is preparing to rise and release his command. This is causing a shift in the great plan, and during moments of war, we always have more supernatural mates."

Well, since fate decided to land me six-and-a-half-feet of beautiful, muscled dragon – it was Braxton Compass for freaks sake – I was not complaining.

Although, I did have a little something to say about this partial bond thing. Not cool, fates. Not freaking cool.

I was determined to eliminate the second mate sooner rather than later. There was no one else for me and I wasn't running anymore, or hiding behind friendship contracts. I would no longer be wasting energy fighting the inevitable. It was now and always Braxton.

Louis brought our attention back to him and Mischa. "Prepare for the final release," he said, his voice just a little strained. The glow from his hands increased as he neared what must be the last key to unlocking her power. All of my nerves rushed back to the forefront.

Then, in the same series of steps I remembered from my dragon bursting free in Vanguard, the light and power ricocheted outwards. I stayed on my feet only because I'd braced myself for it. Mischa dropped to all fours, her screams brutal. I wanted to rush forward and gather her into my arms, but Louis seemed to have thrown up some sort of barrier around them. Jonathon and Lienda were surging forward also.

"If she shifts, she will kill you," Louis warned us.

I banged my hands on the barrier. "She won't kill me, and trust me, the pain is a horrible bitch, so let me get to my sister."

The barrier disappeared. Either I burst through the shield, or Louis allowed me to enter. I was the only one though. I hurled myself down, wrapping my arms around Mischa, whispering nonsense words, rocking her back and forth in the only way I knew how to comfort. She continued to scream. My dragon energy rose up from inside, and for the first time her power responded, as if the two energies had been separated and were now coming together.

With a crack, like lightning striking, our energies collided.

Chapter 14

Ouch. That fuc ... freaking hurt.

The thought was not mine. It took me a few moments longer to realize it was Mischa's. Right, so sure, whatever ... we were just like chilling in each other's heads. Because that is normal. Okay, it kind of was normal for me nowadays.

Surprisingly, I could not only hear her thoughts, but sense her energy connected to mine. It took no effort – almost like instinct – to communicate with her.

So you even censor your curses in your mind.

She froze, as if she was having trouble comprehending what had just happened.

Jess? You're in my head! How the hell are you in my head?

I laughed out loud, which had all the Compasses staring. *I have no idea, our power connected and now we seem to be able to mentally talk.*

She was quiet again, then I sensed a sigh coming from her. *The other twins have a mental connection. It sounds like we're the same.*

I snorted. *We're nothing like them.*

I untangled myself from Mischa, standing and breaking the physical contact. As our hands parted, the mind link disappeared. I could still feel her energy, but in the normal shifter way.

"You can't hear my thoughts, right?" I asked.

She shook her head, standing slowly, as if stretching new muscles. "No, you're gone."

Jonathon's arms wrapped around both of us and pulled us together, and the moment we touched again her energy re-flooded my body.

"You could hear each other's thoughts?" Lienda stood beside her mate, her expression a combination of pleased and pensive.

Mischa stepped out of Jonathon's arms and into her mother's. The connection between us fell again. "Yes, but only when we touch."

Louis' eyes narrowed in interest as he crossed his arms over his broad chest. "The ability will grow as you both become stronger. For now contact is needed, but one day soon you will not have to touch."

Jacob, who had been doing his fey-singing-to-nature thing, trying to calm the energy Mischa had created, suddenly laughed out loud.

He smirked at Braxton. "Better work on Jessa's shielding, Brax, or you might end up banging twins."

Mischa and I lunged at the same time, landing dual punches on his arm. Good to see my sister was turning a little badass in her old age. Jacob rubbed the spot we'd hit, but he should be counting himself lucky. If Braxton had retaliated, the fey would have been walking lame for the rest of his very long life. And he knew it, judging by the way he was edging away. Mischa kicked Jacob again as she walked past him. His dimples flashed, but luckily for him he kept his mouth shut.

"So what are these abilities I should have now?" Mischa asked when she stood center of our group. "I don't have a dragon or demon chilling inside the way Jess described it, but maybe I need to shift first or something. Get a feel for my own fluffy beast."

My fluffy beast elevated her head a little, gave a snort of amusement, then she sank back into her space, so calm, her ancient energy radiating. I almost couldn't believe I used to call her a demon and fear her release. Now she and I had the same bond as me and my wolf. Twin souls.

Mischa was still talking. "There is something inside though, different than my wolf, not like the shifter power."

She closed her eyes and her expression morphed into something serene. Her face suddenly looked like it was carved from stone. I could see civilizations rise and fall in that expression, and I fidgeted waiting for something to happen. My dragon reared up as if she was sensing things I didn't have knowledge of. As Mischa twisted her head to the left, I had my first view of her dragon mark. It was low on her neck, and small. Dammit! There went my hope that I wasn't the only special one with a massive mark. As the others began to notice the red and black marring her skin, more than one set of eyes turned in my direction also. They all knew what this meant, but before anyone could say anything we were distracted by the glow.

A ghostly specter rose from my sister. Like wafts of smoke, it seeped out of her, and then with a sort of pop the image became clear. She was surrounded by a ghost dragon. Braxton moved closer, he was watching Mischa with a laser-like focus. He'd told me that the marked generally gained extra abilities, mimicking dragons but not being able to shift into one. Was this what he referred to?

Jonathon's voice was smooth "Mischa … honey, can you hear me?" I recognized the tone. It was the same he used to talk down a startled shifter, keeping his energy low and calm.

Her eyes flicked open, the green glowing, like twin beams of light, both eerie and beautiful. She seemed to be babbling, even though her tone remained very even. "I'm great. And what the hell is with this eyesight … it's insane. I can see these waves of light. I can scent a million different things on the wind. I feel as if I could fly, but I know I can't."

Braxton strode back to my side, as if he knew I needed to speak with him. He saw the question in my eyes and nodded. "Yes, to my knowledge, this is the usual power of the dragon marked," he said.

I rubbed my temples, attempting to alleviate some of the tension which had decided to settle there. "Why am I the special one?" I lowered my voice to a mutter. "I don't want to be the only dual shifter, I don't want to be north in the freaking compass."

Jacob opened his mouth, but Braxton fixed him with a stare and the fey decided his life was worth more than whatever quip he was about to utter. Maximus stepped into the circle. He'd been standing away with his mate, I think trying not to upset Mischa, especially when she was dealing with her energy being unlocked. Quite considerate for Maximus. I was glad to see my vampire taking control again. It was not natural for him to linger on the outside.

"We should go to the mystics now," he said, his deep tone commanding. "We don't have much time, and the stronger Mischa and Jess are, the better chance we have of thwarting the evil twins and preventing the rise of the king."

Mischa's smile was genuine. "Max is right, I feel so much going on inside right now, but there is so much more. I want more."

Maximus' smile was light. He seemed happy that some of the tension between Mischa and him had eased, which of course only pissed off his newly minted mate. Cardia didn't say anything, but I was reading her narrowed eyes and furrowed brows.

Mischa's ghostly dragon and shining eyes started to fade away; she'd either learned how to pull it back or had lost control of the marked power. Either way, Maximus was right, we needed to learn about our power. What being a marked meant exactly.

It was time to find the mystics, get this training shit out of the way.

It was mutually decided that Jacob, Maximus and Cardia would grab us some food for the road. Who knew how long we would be training with the mystics. And I was quite worried about my recent weight loss. I needed cake. Lots of freaking cake. Cardia paused beside me, just before everyone dispersed. I could tell it was a deliberate pause.

She didn't vamp out on me, and wasn't even close to powerful enough to roll me, so I could stare her straight in the eyes. "I hope we can be friends," she said, her voice smooth and sweet. I had the strangest feeling that she was speaking the words but wasn't feeling them. I hated fake. I really hoped it was just that she was trying to get a sense of our pack before jumping right in.

I ran my eyes over her. Damn, she was so freaking cute, all petite and pretty, not the type I thought Maximus would end up with. I'd expected tall and strong. But I wouldn't underestimate Cardia. She'd been chosen for him and that had to mean something.

I threw her a bone. Sort of: "The Compasses are my pack, my family. You're now family. But it's going to take time, there are dynamics which will need to slowly adjust." I got to my main point. "The reality is: don't fuck with my boys and I'm sure we'll be friends."

I'd never had much use for chick friends, so competitive and annoying, but having Mischa around had demonstrated that there were benefits. I needed to give Cardia a chance – for Maximus.

She gave me a measured stare before smiling, seemingly satisfied with our conversation, and crossing back to her mate. They three of them –

Jacob included – wandered off toward the food street.

Lienda and Jonathon had already left with Mischa between them. My twin had been chatting away. I hadn't seen her this animated before. She was positively glowing. The dragon marked energy flowed through her body and she was flying high on the power. I strode across to join Braxton and Louis, who had been waiting for me. We were quiet as we crossed the town toward the mystics building. I walked between them, and while there was no immediate tension, it didn't exactly feel friendly either.

Braxton was the first to speak. "Explain to me this whole brother-sister thing you two have going on?"

Louis grinned, and I couldn't help returning it. I let the sorcerer explain, it was his story, and I didn't know how much of it he wanted other supernaturals to know. He told Braxton pretty much everything – about his lost love, his isolation, the connection he felt when he touched me as a baby. Braxton didn't interrupt, letting the sorcerer talk as much as he wanted. As I stared between the two of them, it became startlingly clear how similar they were – both commanding, powerful, and unafraid of anything. Louis actually fit in really well with the Compass quads.

We crossed the last of the pebbled path, reaching the building we'd been directed to. A few lower level witches scurried out of our way, leaving the doorway free – yeah, we were badasses.

Just before we entered Braxton faced the sorcerer, his expression neutral. "It's no secret that males don't like other males around their mates, and I'm no exception with Jessa. Reality is, dragons are usually the worst of all supernaturals. We guard what is ours with a ferocity that would scare almost everyone ... except you – nothing scares you." I sensed the slightest tone of grudging admiration from Braxton. "I accept what you say is the truth. I will allow this friendship."

Woah! He did not just say that. "Hang on just one freaking second! Allow ... allow the friendship?" I poked my finger directly into Braxton's chest. "I'll choose my own friends and no bossy ass dragon is going to change that. You have a problem with any of my friends, you come and talk to me."

His blue eyes darkened and as usual he enjoyed watching me lose my shit, although he didn't back down. The next eight hundred years or so were going to be volatile to say the very least. Males were so annoying with their posturing, possessive bullshit.

Louis laughed, distracting us. We didn't break the stare-off, but some of the tension eased. The slightest of smiles crossed Braxton's full lips and I got a flash of dimple. I was staying strong though, I would not let his sexiness break me. If he dominated me in decisions like this, he always would. It was in his nature.

"Let's call it a tie?" he said, mimicking back what I'd said a hundred times to him over the years. My heart swelled at the love that laced his words.

"I promise I won't threaten your friends without running it by your first. But if I think they don't have pure and honorable intentions, I will destroy them. Do you understand me? There is only so much I can tolerate, Jess, and you have to understand that you are it for me. You are it." He was fierce. "There is no other, and there will be no other. So I will fight to the death and beyond to keep you."

My legs trembled, just the slightest motion, but he saw. His words were like lava, flowing through my body and into my soul. The jump from friends to lovers had been a quick progression, but in reality, we'd been moving this way for a long time. I'd just been too pigheaded to see it. Braxton had been patiently waiting for me. I knew I never saw him with other women because he'd never wanted me to.

"How long have you loved me for?" I couldn't hide my honest curiosity.

Louis laughed again. "You're cute. Obtuse, but cute."

I flipped him off. "Shut it, sorcerer, you don't get to butt in here."

Braxton reached out and captured my hand, his thumb rubbing over the soft, fleshy part of my palm. "I've loved you since we were children, but as a mate since we were about sixteen." His eyes held me captive. "Do you remember that season we both came into our powers? We'd just learned to shift and the emotions were so overwhelming. Dealing with new energies, our animals, it was a crazy time."

I nodded, that was not an experience I imagined I'd ever forget.

"We'd just come back from running in the forest, all of us and you. You shifted to human and were standing in the vines, naked, dirt all over you. You threw back your head and laughed at whatever moronic thing Jake had said." Braxton's voice was huskier now. "Seeing you there hit me like never before. I couldn't move, I couldn't breathe, I couldn't take my eyes from you. Fuck... I was slammed by my feelings. I don't know why it was that moment, I'd seen you that way a million times, but I knew then that you were mine."

I stepped closer, my right hand rising to rest over his heart. "I'm sorry it took me so long to catch up."

Every part of me was filled with emotion. I remembered what Louis had told me long ago, that without the lows you couldn't really feel the highs. I couldn't imagine anything higher.

Braxton shook his head, stepping even closer to me, my hand squashed between us. "It wasn't that you had to catch up, you had to let go of your fears. And since you're one hell of a brave supernatural, I knew it couldn't take you long."

It had been fear holding me back, and I was still afraid. I whispered the terror I held deep in my soul. "What if we lose this? Why the hell do I have a second mate?"

He cupped my chin, gently dragging my gaze back up to meet his. "Never going to happen. This is just another trial for us, but we will slay it as we always do."

Our cliché romance book moment was ended by the appearance of a bunch of gray haired cloaked fey dudes. Obviously women's liberation never reached the dragon mystics. They were a penis-heavy bunch.

"Are you ready?" asked Quale, stepping forward, no qualms about interrupting my moment.

From what I could see, below the cowl of his cloak, his expression was serious. "We do not share the secrets of the dragon lightly. Many argued against allowing any who are closely associated with the quads into the inner circle. But I will not permit us to take sides in this war. We are the council to the king, yes, but we are also part of the supernatural community."

Most of the mystics looked unhappy by his words. But they didn't voice any objections today. For some reason they seemed to both admire and fear Quale.

He turned to Braxton. "Where are your brothers? We need you to join together so we know what we are dealing with."

"They're on their way," Braxton said.

I was guessing the mystics wanted to determine if they had to eliminate their enemies today, which is why we had the full showing of cloaked grays. I was sure this "forced joining" would have been demanded a lot earlier if not for all the disappearing into Faerie and such. Seems they had decided now was the time.

This thought had my insides turning. I didn't like that the mystics were so unknown. Quale spoke as if they were just fey who acted as council to the king. But what if the hidden powers they supposedly possessed were enough to take out my boys? I seriously doubted it, but that didn't completely alleviate my concerns.

Not to mention I could sense other supernaturals inside the building. Quite a few actually. The mystic's plan wasn't completely terrible. They knew it was better to try and take the Compasses out before they got too strong. They did not want another set of Four to contend with. My boys were still young in the supernatural world, and had never joined powers before.

What the mystics failed to understand was that even without their powers joined, the Compasses were beyond anything they'd dealt with before. I never knew the Four when they were young of course, but in my head, they hadn't been on the level of my quads. Sure, I was biased – probably the most biased supernatural you'd ever meet. Maybe their parents, Jo and Jack were as bad, but us three definitely formed the basis for the quads' fan club. The other members consisted of the simpering fools in Stratford, females who thought they could tame a Compass.

Oh shit, I was one of them now, one of those females I'd always pitied. Gone all soft for a male. Love did a real number on you. I barely recognized the hardass I used to be. I was all soft and fluffy … my wolf was like a goddamn kitty cat.

Quale waved us forward. "Since our time is limited we'll start with the twins, the quads will be last."

We joined my parents and Mischa. All of us followed the grays through the double glass doors. The sanctuary was so weird. On one hand it was all natural, with its forest and ice-land and desert and ocean, and on the other they had all of this advanced tech stuff everywhere. Such a mix of old and new, natural and manufactured. Magic laced through all of it, though. Ancient power had created this place and something told me it would stand through any war.

Once inside the pale yellow, shiny, glassed building, we moved through what looked like a foyer of sorts and then ... of course ... into an elevator. I closed my eyes, though I felt I was dealing a little better with the caging. Thankfully, it was a short trip, and with a ding the metal doors slid across and I opened my eyes in time to exit with everyone.

The room was massive, a single expanse without any pillars to break the space. The black rubber floors had a spongy feel, and I envisaged that this was a training ground of sorts, perfect for fighting. Standing along the far wall, which was about a hundred yards across, were two dozen supernaturals. As we closed the gap between them and us, I could sense there was a mix of the five races. A few vampires, three shifters – no wolves –

wizards, fey, and two demi-fey: a centaur and a pixie.

"Do you think the reason we never knew if demi-fey were marked was because they were either in prison or in the sanctuary?" I murmured to Braxton, thinking back to our conversation in Vanguard.

"Yes," Quale, the eavesdropper, said, "their elders almost never hide them, they are handed over straight away. They also have the least amount of marked representatives. But they *are* represented across the full range of demi-fey."

I couldn't pull my eyes from the group against the wall. Thrills of excitement started to build like small sparks in my stomach. I wanted to see these powers, I wanted to know what the mark was capable of, I wanted to know if I was the only one who could shift to dragon. Surely, if there were any others the mystics would know. They clearly trained all new arrivals.

The mystics formed a line, their hoods dropped back to reveal their strange silver-gray hair, and for once all of their faces were clear to be seen. I liked that, so much was revealed in facial expressions. Gerard and Quale were center again.

One of the grays on the end waved us forward toward the supernaturals lined up against the wall. "Jessa and Mischa, join the group. Observe at first, then you should attempt to access the natural power of the mark."

I might have rolled my eyes at Braxton and Louis, my exasperation rising to the surface. I hated school, and immediately this reminded me of class. *Boring*.

Mischa and I fell into the right side of the group, she next to a vampire and I on the end.

The rest of our pack and family moved across to wait off to the side, close enough to see but not get in the way. The mystics lined up in front of us, poised and very still. The hybrid feyness of their energy was still strange. I wasn't a fan of their weirdness, but I'd put up with it for now. I didn't anticipate that we'd be stuck in the sanctuary for much longer.

A mystic I wasn't familiar with started to talk. He had expressive, very dark brown eyes and the most perfect skin I had ever seen. Rich and dark, like freshly ground Arabica beans. The contrast to his hair was pronounced, and yet, it also wasn't. He pulled it off no problem.

The beautiful male moved along the line of the marked. "It's important that all of you know we have been observing the dragon marked for a thousand years, and so far there are three traits that each possesses. Number one, longevity of life. You will age until maturity and then no more. We have marked here, some of the first ever born, who look no older than early twenties. You might know that the marked are almost impervious to death. There are some weapons in Faerie which can inflict enough injury to kill, but on Earth you need to fear very little."

Interesting, so the jinn knew what it was doing by sending me to Faerie.

"The second skill the marked possess is the ability to sense other marked. Your energy calls to each other, and in some ways it is as if you are one big collective. You can tap into each other and form a single unit of power."

Great! Just fucking awesome. The dragon king could not have designed his army any better, a big bunch of pack-like, immortal drones. He probably had mind control over us too. Although ... it would explain why I'd been so drawn to the Vanguard prison, desperate to go back there to try to free those prisoners.

"We believe the king, when he rises, will be able to communicate with all of you at one time. Collectively."

Braxton was grim faced, legs slightly apart and arms crossed over his chest. Listening and not happy. He wasn't the only one. I was also feeling "not happy" right now with this entire bullshit endeavor.

"Lastly, you all possess the ability to call on the spirit of the dragon. Touch the power inside and a small facet of the king's power will become yours. Senses heightened, strength heightened, speed heightened. Basically, you will mimic much of the ability a dragon possesses."

I raised my hand but didn't wait to be called on. "Have any marked ever like ... shifted into a dragon?" It had to be asked, even though I was almost certain I was the special cupcake of the year.

The mystics observed me for a moment, almost as if they couldn't believe anyone was questioning them during their "talking moment." *Get used to it.*

Quale answered: "No, to our knowledge there have never been any to actually take the form of a dragon. As you probably know, there are no dragon shifters who are marked. They don't need to be, they are already called to the king's cause, and they have far greater skills and strength than the marked."

I nodded a few times as if that was an awesome and legitimate answer. Meanwhile, on the inside I was having a mini freak-out. Definitely a special cupcake. *Fuck a duck.*

The mystic from before started talking again, shooting me a dirty glare. "As I was saying, these are the three traits present in all marked, no matter which of the races you fall under. We are here to cultivate these qualities so that when the king rises, you will not be taken by surprise."

I raised my hand again, and with a sigh he quirked a single eyebrow at me. Which was quite a skill. "Why the hell are you helping the king? He's evil and an asshole. One supernatural should not rule everything."

I heard laughter, and a quick glance told me that I was amusing my parents, Louis, and Braxton.

The mystic walked toward me. So far he was the only one of them to break the line and move around. "What makes you think everything is so black and white? Good, evil, they are two sides of the same coin. How do you know the king was not trying to usurp a corrupt supernatural world? How do you know his intentions were not virtuous and honorable?"

Truth. He spoke in the certainty he believed, so it rang distinctly of truth.

He was about two feet from me, so I stalked myself closer, stopping when we were face to face. "It might be true that I don't know the king's intentions, but then neither do you. How do you know that by allowing the king to rise again, you're not bringing about the destruction of the supernatural world?" I could feel the eyes of the other marked on me; they were listening closely. "We all know in the last thousand years nothing really terrible has happened within our prison communities. Sure, there were a few wars and battles, but mostly it has been peaceful. That is what we know. You, on the other hand, are simply guessing because you have never even met the king. All you have are your inherited memories and abilities as his council. You know nothing."

Clapping broke the tension and drew all of our attentions. Louis was grinning lazily, applauding in slow motion. "You should listen to her, she speaks truth and reason. Something I think the mystics sorely lack."

His laughing eyes flicked across to Quale, and I was pleased to see his brother simply flip him off. Uncharacteristic behavior for a member of this somber group, but it was a nice little insight into Quale's developing relationship with the powerful sorcerer.

The mystic in front of me turned his back, dismissing my words in the only way he could, and moved back to join his lineup of grays.

He didn't miss another beat, picking up the speech from where he'd been interrupted before. "We are here to strengthen your bond with each other and to learn how to call on the spirit of the dragon. Reach inside to the place of the mark. It should be easy to find, it is foreign to your other race energy. If you're a vampire, it will exist near the home of your beast, but you will know it's different. For the fey, your elemental powers are clear; you will find the marked energy nearby."

It definitely did not feel that way for me. I had a wolf and a dragon chilling inside, creatures I could pretty much see with my mind's eye. I could call on either of them if I wanted to – hopefully without the issues I had the last time I tried to connect to my fluffy beast – but there was no way I would shift into my dragon here. The mystics were already suspicious of me, I didn't need any more supes to know about my unusual mark and abilities.

The reasonably well lit room started to sparkle, and I realized the supernaturals around me had called on their energy and were now surrounded by the same sort of ghost dragon I'd seen on Mischa. I wasn't sure what to do. I searched around inside. My dragon flicked her tail at me; I could tell she wanted to know if I needed her. I gave her a mental pat with some of my energy and she was content to lie down again. But nope, there was no ghostly specter energy there for me to touch.

The delusional mystic who was doing all the talking was also apparently a smartass. "Having a problem?" His tone was all smug and mocking.

I shrugged. "Nope, maybe I'm not the same as the other marked. There doesn't seem to be any spirit energy inside."

My words all rang of truth, not that I knew if the mystics could sense that or not.

His pupils darted left and right, as if trying to ferret out my secrets.

"We were told that your mark was far larger than any other here. Surely, you must have a greater connection to spirit?"

I shrugged again. "Don't know what to tell you."

He met the eye of another mystic. Gerard, I realized. He would have been the one to tell him of the mark.

Ignoring everything else for a moment, I turned to Mischa. "So are you, like, connected to all of these supes?"

I wanted to understand what was happening between the marked. I could actually see the dragon specters intermingling. They did seem to be forming bonds in the smoky stuff.

Mischa nodded. "Yes, it's as if I can feel their life force, or their energy. I know exactly where each one is. I could find them with my eyes closed."

She was interrupted by Quale. "Now it is time to really tap into the powers. I want you all to tell us what is on the back wall."

All heads lifted to stare out across the massive space. I had noticed when we walked in, that there had been words painted on the far wall, but I hadn't paid attention to what it said. Now, even with my wolf eyes, I couldn't see the image clear enough, it was too far away. I had a suspicion that in dragon form I'd have seen to that wall and beyond, but I wasn't connected enough to my dragon to partially shift, so I wouldn't even try.

It seemed the marked had no eyesight problems. Even Mischa was muttering away next to me before shrieking in joy as she finally managed to zoom her eyesight out far enough.

"This is incredible. I can't even imagine what it feels like for you to be an actual—"

I cut her off with a loud cough. Even though she had been whispering, there were too many ears in this place.

"Still nothing, Jessa?" Quale was watching us, his eyes flicking between Mischa and me.

I shook my head. "No, I can't seem to find the dragon marked energy. But I'll keep trying."

The rest of the afternoon was filled with the mystics teaching the marked how to tap into their dragon abilities. I'd never seen supernaturals jump higher, run faster, or react quicker. They were enhanced, and that worked for fighting also. Lucky for Mischa, this wasn't a fight class. Judging on the demonstration between a vampire and a wizard – she would have gotten her ass handed to her. I'd been impressed, especially as the vampire gained the upper hand and threw the wizard about fifty yards across the room and into a wall. The wizard recovered quickly enough. It seemed their bodies were like super soldiers when they were calling on the dragon spirit.

This was the only part of the training I wanted to join in on, I was pretty sure I could tap into my wolf and have a shot at fighting. I wasn't skilled or connected enough to use my dragon yet, but something told me once I had better control over my shift, I'd be able to use her extra senses in a similar way to the dragon spirit.

All of the Compasses were in the room now, having trickled in slowly over the last hour, bringing food and goodness. Since I had no dragon spirit, I was able to sit out of most activities, hanging with my boys enjoying all the scrumptiousness of my first love – food. Grace and Tyson were back to ignoring each other, peeling off to opposite sides of the group. I was going to guess that the pair definitely did not do enough arguing. Their shit still wasn't resolved.

"What's with you and Grace?" I asked the wizard during a quiet moment.

He growled, running a hand through his hair. "Frigged if I know, I can't understand that woman to save my life."

I snorted. "Keep calling her 'woman' and you probably won't have a life."

He shook his head. I could see the tension was wearing him down. "I most probably deserve the silent treatment, but I never thought I'd want to hear someone's thoughts so much. Shit, even yelling would be better."

I reached out and took his hand. He needed the comfort.

I remembered what that had been like, the uncertainty, fear, longing. Seemed he was the one now who wanted something more, and Grace was the one not ready.

Many boring hours later, the marked training was done and it was time for the mystics to focus on my quads. I was leaning against the wall, Braxton on one side with his arm wrapped tightly around me, and Jacob on the other. Just as the dragon marked supes started to exit the room, one of the mystics slithered past. He paused near my group. "Any luck finding your spirit?"

They were such asshats. I bared my teeth slightly, my eyes flat as they locked on him. "If I find it, you'll be the first to know."

He blinked at me once or twice before backing away slowly. It would be nice to think he was scared of me, but most probably the quads had been doing something off to the side. They were kings of the scary face.

"They think you're deliberately not following their instructions," Braxton said, his voice close to my ear.

I nodded. "I know, but that's better than them knowing the truth. They're on the king's team, and unless the stories about him were very exaggerated, I will never stand with the king. I don't want him to ever know I'm a dual shifter. He will use me, and I will not be used."

Braxton leaned in and nuzzled me, partly comforting and partly pantie-drenching. He was sporting the slightest stubble today, and as he rubbed against my cheek the sensation was deliciously hot.

Louis appeared at our side. Braxton's dimples disappeared as he leveled a stare at the sorcerer. "You better have a really good reason to be interrupting us, magic man, or Jessa is going to be sticking you back together with tape."

Truth.

Louis let out a huff of air. "No need to start breaking things you can't afford, the mystics need you." Braxton and I had been too distracted to notice that the room was now empty of the other marked.

The dragon shifter released me, muttering something under his breath. I could tell he was a little pissed, but I actually didn't mind the interruption. I loved the delicious buildup, the teasing. As long as it didn't go on for too long, then I'd be cranky ... to put it mildly.

Braxton pressed a lingering kiss to my lips. "Don't go anywhere," he said, "I'll be right back."

He strode across the room to join his brothers, and I forced myself to see through the haze of sexual need, and focus. This was the joining of my boys' powers. Nervous tension flooded me, washing away the fire which had been blazing through my veins. What was going to happen? Would their joining give them the same urges as the Four, the urge to hunt and imprison dragon marked?

Chapter 15

"What have you done to our famous dragon shifter?"

Louis' question distracted me for a moment. "What do you mean?" I wrinkled my nose at the sorcerer before turning back to the quads.

Braxton looked slightly bored, as if he had not a single care about what was going to happen next. But I could tell by the rigidness in his jaw and semi-hooded state of his eyes that he wasn't as calm as he portrayed. None of us knew what was going to transpire after the joining of their power.

"You're wearing quite an interesting look right now, Jess." Louis' grin was as wide as his damn, arrogant face. "That dragon has you all wrapped up in emotions."

I snorted. "You've been mated, you know how it is."

Louis' face fell, the amusement disappearing, and I wanted to smack myself. Damn, why did I bring that up?

He finally answered, his voice more brittle than usual. "She wasn't ... we weren't true mates. But it didn't matter. The fates made a mistake, she was my chosen one."

I tried to school my expression. I had assumed from the way he'd spoken, the depth of his anguish, that she'd been his true mate, but apparently not. I reached out and rested my hand against his shoulder. We didn't speak again, but I wanted him to know I was here for him. He wasn't alone anymore. Louis felt things so deeply, hiding it behind power and his jovial attitude, but he loved with all of his heart. Braxton was the same. This was what made them so dynamic ... so amazing.

Now that I knew what it was like to be *truly* loved by Braxton, well, Louis was right ... I was different. I had officially lost all chill. I didn't even care who knew it. If supes didn't like me all loved-up, well, they could suck it. I was happy. I'd always been happy, but this was like an entirely new level.

I was granted a reprieve from my thoughts when the quads' training started.

Quale was the one in charge now. He looked a little hesitant as he addressed the four Compasses. Might have been the way they were standing with their "get fucked" expressions in full force.

"There is only one way to know if you four are going to pose a threat to us or the king. We have sworn an oath to ... remain loyal to the command of our leader. Many of the mystics did not agree with Gerard's decision to allow you entry to the sanctuary, though we understood that the circumstances were a little unusual with Jessa's odd mark. We voted, and the only way you will continue to be welcome here is if you join your powers together and don't pose a threat to us in the sanctuary. The compulsion to hunt marked will be strong, you won't be able to fight it."

Jacob pulled a face in my direction, clearly loving the heck out of this lecture. I forced myself not to laugh at him. Sensing that this was going to take a long time, I slid myself against the wall. Grace – who looked pretty miserable – dropped next to me, and Cardia hesitantly sat on the other side of us, keeping a reasonable space between me and her. I was glad to see she was taking the no-rush thing seriously. I slid my hand across and grasped Grace's hand.

"You okay?" I asked, without looking in her direction. I really didn't want her to cry or anything.

She kind of snorted before returning my hand squeeze. "Tyson and I have been playing this game for a long time now, even though he was slow to figure it out." She paused, before sighing, her voice barely a whisper. "I'm just not sure I want to play anymore."

Oh, I got that. I totally got it. There was only so much a heart could take, but I had to give it a shot. For Tyson.

"Don't give up on him, Grace, Ty has a good heart, and I think you two could be happy. True mates or not."

That was the bottom line, they didn't know if there was more between them than just anger and raging attraction. And right now, I could see that Grace wasn't ready to find out.

I noticed then that the quads had stopped pretending to listen to Quale. All of them were staring in our direction, like a force-of-nature smacking us in the face, strong, swift, and breathtaking. Grace and my conversation died off as we became caught in the Compass magnetism. Assholes. They sucked you in and never let go. I shook my head before flipping them off. They needed to focus on the mystics right now. With shakes of their heads, and small grins, they finally turned back to the cloaks. Tyson lingered the longest, his expression unreadable.

"I don't know if I can walk away," Grace said, her voice almost inaudible. "Damn, every female in Stratford would give their right arm to have a Compass."

Despite her anger, there were still tendrils of awe from her. It wasn't exactly the same for me, I'd always had the Compasses. I'd never had to fight for their love or attention. I was very lucky in that regard. But Grace was extra right, I was even more blessed now. True mates was a really strange and beautiful concept.

Generally when a supe stumbled across their true mate they had never met that supernatural before. So while there was an instant connection, there were also many unknowns. For me it was different. I'd known and loved Braxton for a really long time. The history and memories were already there, the bonds strong. Which meant I was feeling a tad overwhelmed by the sheer intensity of our new mateship.

Out of nowhere, an ache started low and dull in my chest, odd and out of place. My head jerked up and there was Mischa, her eyes locked on the three of us. She had been near the back of the room with our parents, but my newly formed twin bond was telling me that something in the way us females were grouped against the wall had upset her. Made her feel on the outside again. Mischa's face showcased about a zillion facets of anguish. With a stifled cry, she stumbled away and left the room. I lurched to my feet to stop her, but she took off like a shot.

Shit!

I really wanted to stay here with the Compasses, I needed to know what was going to happen. I was afraid that if they decided to go all crazy-marked-hunters, there weren't many supernaturals here who could stand against them. Only Louis and my father had a possible shot. But I also knew deep in my soul that this thing with Mischa was important too. I started to follow her path, it was time to deal with my twin's drama. I was just about at the elevators when Lienda halted me with a hand on my arm. "I'll go, Jess, you have other responsibilities."

I blinked a few times at my mother. "Are you sure? I don't mind."

I sort of did, but I was giving this "nice supe" thing a try. Must be all the love pheromones confusing me.

Lienda kissed my cheek and I barely even flinched. See, emotional growth was my bitch. "I'm happy to go," she said. "I haven't seen my daughter much lately. It seems we might need a mother daughter chat. I'm worried about her."

She wasn't the only one.

I tried not to let it upset me that she'd said "my daughter." I was her daughter too. But I knew that with so many years between us, it was going to be difficult bridging that gap. For reals ... I could have used mother-daughter chats myself over the years. But there was no point dwelling on the past. Had to move forward. Like I told Mischa, there was no other direction to go in.

"You're my daughter too," Lienda rushed to add. Either everyone was a mind reader, or I wore my emotions on my face. She wrapped an arm around me. "I love you, but Mischa is just a little more alone than you are, a little less independent. Children need different things from their parents, it doesn't mean I love you less. You just need me less."

It was true, I didn't really need Lienda anymore. I'd learned not to need her.

Lienda gave me a lopsided grin before leaning in and kissing me on the cheek again. I rubbed my face, stepping back. I was at my kiss limit now. With one last shake of her blond hair, she laughed as she turned and hurried out the door.

I strolled back. Nothing in the room had changed: four bored Compasses surrounded by a group of mystics. No one looked to be connected yet. I was wondering what the holdup was when I noticed that a circle of white stones had been placed on the floor surrounding the quads, crystals like those we occasionally used in magic class, primarily for protection spells. The mystics were creating a protective zone just in case the boys lost their shit. Probably a good idea.

One of the mystics was activating the stones, spelling them one by one with magic of the fey. As he moved to the next, fizzling energy followed his path.

I settled in beside Jonathon, next to his warmth and power. It reminded me of home and pack and alpha comforts. I needed the comfort, something to ease my nerves. My eyes briefly alighted on Cardia and Grace still against the wall, both staring at the quads. Grace looked sort of mesmerized and Cardia, even more so, as she locked in on Maximus. That was the face of an obsessed, loved up, supe.

Screw that, I might be riding this mate-ship thing too, but I was not following Braxton around like a lost puppy. I forced myself not to stare at my dragon, and focused on this weird spot on the floor instead. It was white, like a fleck of paint or something.

After about eight seconds of this, I sighed.

"They're starting," said Jonathon, and joy crackled through me. I now had a legitimate reason to be staring.

I lifted my head only to realize that all four Compasses were watching me, wearing the widest of grins. Double dimples and all. I sucked in rapidly. Being the sole focus of their attention was like being zapped by electricity, no matter how many times it had happened over the years. I flipped up my middle finger, because even though I had no idea what they were thinking, I knew it was going to be something asshole-worthy. With the Compasses, that was a given.

The mystic had just finished up on the final white rock – eight in total. The moment he stood, energy beamed out, crisscrossing the room and surrounding my boys, thankfully distracting them from whatever nefarious thoughts had brought out those four, identical, shit-eating grins that had been facing me.

I met my father's gaze. "Do you think the protection dome is necessary? Is there really a possibility that by joining, they are just going to completely lose their shit and start trying to kill marked?"

He was focused on the center of the room. "Sometimes control takes a while," he said. "After a few times joining, they should have the same mental-control of the Four, but the first times can be a little dicey."

Control of the Four. That was exactly what we wanted … said no one ever. I wanted the Four to cease to exist, and I wanted to be the one to wipe them off the face of the Earth. But … when everything was all said and done, I had to keep reminding myself that if the dragon king rose, the supernatural community would need them for the fight. I wondered what role my quads would hold if the king rose?

Everyone fell silent as Quale addressed the Compasses. "You are free now to join your power. I believe you have been instructed on the manner in which to do this?"

Four heads, just one single nod. I was surprised. After twenty years of friendship there weren't many secrets left in our pack, but I had no idea when they'd been instructed on joining their power. They had had a few private classes in the history of supernaturals, and in Family Ties class … it had to have been during these lessons.

They'd told me at the time those classes had been about the unique abilities of multiples – a class I probably should have attended also, but back then my twin status had been a hugely guarded secret.

Wanting to see everything that was about to happen I shuffled forward, Jonathon stayed by my side. If I didn't know any better, I'd say he was acting all bodyguard-like, which meant he didn't have that much faith in the protective ring surrounding the boys. I couldn't really blame him. It was always better to be safe than sorry with the Compasses. They often did … the unexpected.

For the first time, since entering the dome, unease flittered across the quad's faces. But they also looked intrigued. I could tell they wanted to know what their calling was, but were concerned about the damage they might wrought. A concern we all wore.

I felt the surge of power then, even through the shielded cage. The boys were starting their joining.

Maximus vamped out first, energy drifting over his hair and down his body. Suddenly everything about him was changed, and yet he was also the same. It was hard to describe. His hair grew richer in color, his eyes black as a night sky, his skin glowing a tawny color. His fangs elongated and his body increased to even more massive proportions. He was spectacular. I could see Cardia licking her lips as she dragged lustful eyes over him, but along with her clear attraction, there was also dilation of pupils, paling of her skin, accelerated heartbeat. She was like the rest of us, fearing what this change might bring to her very recently discovered mate. I had the same fears churning inside of me, only times four, as I loved all of the Compasses.

Jacob was next. He called on the elements, and even here, inside a glass and metal building, they came to him. The most prominent was fire, definitely his specialty, whipping in burning arcs around his head and down his left arm. His right hand held a single ball of water, like a large dewdrop. Wind thrashed around his blond hair, and the scent of fresh dirt filled the room as earth responded beneath his feet. Green eyes burned as energy surrounded him and joy split across his face. The elements made him feel alive.

Tyson stepped up. He would be the least showy. Much of his power relied on spells and nature. Yet, as he spoke rhythmically, spell casting, chanting too low for me to hear, energy cascaded over him, a subtle glow, which like Maximus enhanced his already dangerously beautiful features. Grace drew forward now. I'd been mostly focused on my boys, so I hadn't realized that the healer witch and vampiress had left the wall and were now just on the outside of the barrier, as if they had to move closer to the Compasses – the quads' overabundance of life force drawing all of us like magnets.

Tyson and Maximus had predator eyes locked on their girls. Their energies filled the huge space, and I was starting to understand what everyone was worried about. Individually, the quads were so powerful. What the hell was going to happen when they fully joined with each other?

All coherent thought fled when it was Braxton's turn. He would finish the quartet of energy. I knew he couldn't shift into dragon, there wasn't enough room in the dome. He dropped his head, light reflecting off his black hair, and then it hit me what he was going to do. I scooted further forward, not wanting to miss a single thing. This was something very few shifters had ever achieved.

A fusion shift.

I'd seen Braxton succeed at this once, in shifting class. He had been the youngest to ever achieve this feat. This wouldn't be like the dragon spirit Mischa had called, this was attaining a form somewhere between man and beast. Almost like the *loup-garou* myth, which humans both feared and worshipped. That Braxton could fusion shift so young was one of the reasons he was considered to be so very powerful.

Lines of scales formed on his cheeks, before spreading down his neck and across his arms. There weren't enough blue and black scales to be creepy, but enough to look scary and dominating. His eyes glowed the yellow of the dragon, and his body became much bigger, his clothing tore as it stretched to accommodate his new form. Which was almost double his regular size. Suddenly I was just like the other girls, my dragon straining inside to get to her mate, my feet pushing me forward, fear of the unknown flooding me. As I moved Jonathon stuck to me in the same way bitch stuck to Giselda. Permanently.

The four Compasses, their powers surrounding them, was a true sight to behold.

One of the mystics moved closer. "Now you will join."

Shit. He probably should have stated that as less of an order. Sure enough, all four Compasses turned blazing eyes on him, their stares hard ... scary as all hell. Especially with so much power riding them.

"Apologies." Quale, always the diplomat, stepped forward. He'd been standing off to the side with Louis. "We'd really appreciate it if you'd attempt to merge as one now."

I swear everyone in the room rolled their eyes right then. Seriously, what a condescending dick. But I was coming to expect that from these fey hybrid tools. The Compasses fell into a circle of sorts, their backs to us in the room. I saw them lock eyes, and I knew they were communicating.

Mirroring expressions rippled across their features. After a few moments they started to chant, and I was close enough now to hear the words. My dragon had won in her quest to move toward Braxton.

"How will they join?" I whispered to Jonathon. I'd always been under the impression that these sort of callings came to the supe, not the other way around.

His reply was almost inaudible. "Their joining should have been allowed to arrive naturally." He confirmed my thoughts. "Time and growth of powers would have taken care of the timing. Now they will have to use a spell to push forward the process."

"How do you know this?" I *needed* to understand what was happening to the boys.

"All multiples can join, the quads are just on another level, and involves a calling," he said.

The quads started to chant.

Brother as one, we will be, brothers as one. Power of four, join as one, power of four will never be undone. United!

They chanted the first part, before shouting "united" to finish. Three times they repeated the phrase and each time the energy coating them rose, moving above their heads, swirling, and then as the four of them bled their individual power, it formed a peak above them. Energy flashed outward, filling the room with a single wave of light. I tensed as it shot through me, but there was no kickback at all. It just flowed through our bodies and off into the universe.

I looked up after the wave had passed me and froze.

Grace's voice was barely a whisper. "Holy fuck me."

Cardia and the witch healer were slowly moving closer to us, and I couldn't blame them. The boys were even scaring me, and I had never been scared of them in my life.

The quads were not like the Four – they didn't look identical or anything – but they were the most alike I'd ever seen them, as if facets of each of them had blended into the others. Braxton's hair was a little lighter, Jacob's a little darker, all of them with a highlighted golden brown sheen. All of their eyes were black, their skin the same shade of tawny brown – at least their faces remained true to them. Braxton's scales were gone, as were the four elemental powers which had surrounded Jacob. They were awash in a glowing energy, power thrumming in the room. Four sets of black eyes leveled on me.

"Why are they staring me down?" I was proud that my voice didn't tremor. They wore the look of a predator – well, four predators to be exact – who all seemed to have found what they were hunting.

Footsteps echoed from the back of the room, near the elevators. I wanted to spin around, hating anyone unknown coming at my back, but the far greater danger was in front of me. I didn't turn from the dome.

A high, familiar voice sounded across the space. "They are the same as the others, they are not natural. They need to be eliminated."

Okay, now I was turning around. No one talked about eliminating my boys without getting their ass kicked. Louis and Jonathon fell in beside me as we faced off with the fruit twins. And Mischa. My sister had clearly run straight back into the arms of those crazy ass bitches. I glared at Mischa, who remained quiet but didn't back down from her place in the terrible trio.

"They are unnatural," Orange said again.

Her words triggered a memory. This moment screamed of the dragon dream – where I'd stood on the opposite sides to Mischa in a war I knew nothing of. Those obscure references which had scared me, made sense now. They'd been talking about the Compasses. Didn't these bitches know I would never turn on the quads? Not in this life, the next or the one after that.

"There are only two unnatural *things* in this room," I said, "and neither of them are inside that dome." I was determined not to reveal an ounce of my worry or fear but the reality was, the fruit twins were complete and total unknown elements and they did actually scare me a little. Loose cannons are always tough to judge, and I already knew they were slimy and scheming. I preferred foes who came straight at me, I wasn't great with underhanded. I wished we could have just killed them, but since murder was frowned upon in the supernatural world and I still had a trial pending in Stratford, I probably should find a more diplomatic solution.

Lemon took over the bullshit advice. "You will see tomorrow, there are greater things awaiting you than being mated to a dragon shifter. After we retrieve the weapon from Krakov, you will have little loyalty to those abominations."

Louis and Jonathon both reached out at the same time and captured my arms. I looked down to find my hands partially shifted into claws and my knees bent.

"Let me go!" I snarled, my voice deeper as my anger took control. "Let. Me. Go!"

My voice was suddenly overpowered by another, a roar much louder, darker, and spine chillingly scary. Braxton had moved forward in the protective dome, standing as close as he could to the edge without touching the white beams of energy – both hands clenched at his side, eyes locked on me like a heat-seeking-missile.

Air whooshed around me as Louis and Jonathon stepped away, both of them holding their arms aloft.

"No one is touching her, Braxton." Jonathon was using his calm-down-crazy-shifter voice.

The moment I realized that Braxton's reaction was about me, slivers of cool started to thread through my previous rage. Now, I couldn't focus on anything but my mate; his expression was terrifying me to my very core. And apparently I wasn't the only one. Hearing a scuffle, I whipped back around and all I saw of the terrible trio was the ass ends of them as they scurried into the elevator.

Weak. I'd scented weakness on them from the start, and this fatal flaw was why they actually worried me. They would not come at me with honor, they would lie, cheat, and manipulate to get what they wanted. My biggest disappointment was Mischa.

She was a Lebron. Wolves do not cower in the shadow of others. We're a pack, we stick together, we don't lie with snakes. You lie with snakes, you either become a snake, or you get bitten and die.

I was guessing that Lienda either hadn't found her or Mischa had ignored our mother. It was time for someone to have a slightly stronger chat with her. Judging by the expression on Jonathon's face, and the low rumbles that spurted from his throat every so often, he was going to be the one. She would learn the power of an alpha wolf, that was for sure. The leniency she'd been receiving was about to come to a swift end.

I hadn't forgotten about Braxton. I was giving him a few moments to calm down. But when I couldn't keep my eyes from him for any longer … holy crap on crackers – okay, there'd been no calming. He'd separated himself from his brothers, blue flames licking across his tawny skin. Still right on the edge of the barrier.

As soon as we locked eyes, I couldn't stop myself from stepping toward him. The scent of fear was filling the room. Everyone was afraid. Even Jacob, Tyson and Maximus were keeping a decent distance between them and their brother.

It was a struggle to pull my eyes from the semi-shifted dragon-fire-ball in front of me but I did look away long enough to see that the other Compasses were back to their own hair colors. Why was Braxton still twice his regular size? He remained in a semi state of fusion, minus the scales.

Was he still my Braxton?

I wasn't even sure he recognized me, and if his calling was to hunt marked … were they right? Would he actually hurt me once freed from this cage? I had to physically stop myself from crying out, the slices of fear and hurt ricocheting through me were enough to double me over. I drew on the strength of my dragon and wolf, I needed them to keep me semi-calm.

Braxton's attention never wavered from me, locked in with an animalistic intensity. The mystics were in a sort of semi-circle, no doubt trying to conjure some sort of protective magics to use against the quads. I couldn't stop myself from taking another step toward the dragon shifter, pausing at the edge of the cage. He was like a statue carved from the smoothest of stone. I barely recognized my best friend. Gone was that twinkle in his eye, that mirth which always curved one side of his full lips.

"W-what...?" I stuttered, not even sure what to say. "What the hell is up with Braxton?"

I could sense no one was standing close to me. Even my father held himself back.

Louis answered me from about ten feet away. "Braxton's not quite himself right now. He has merged fully with the dragon, so he is very much a fusion of man and beast. Which in some ways is worse than being full dragon."

"What do you mean worse?" I asked, without removing my eyes from Braxton. The dragon shifter's flames increased every time I looked away.

"He has the strength and instincts of an animal, but with the human emotions attached. Human emotions which are increased a hundred fold. Fear, love, jealousy, anger and ... pain."

My heart lurched.

Pain. Oh hells no! I could live with a lot of things, but not Braxton's pain.

My fear disappeared, I rocked forward and slammed my hands against the barrier. Energy blasted me back, not enough to hurt or knock me off my feet, but I still ended up away from the cage.

"Disable the magic," I was shouting without even realizing it. Deep down I knew I was acting irrationally. Braxton could kill everyone in this room and I wanted to just free him.

I didn't throw myself at the barrier again, and no one approached me. Probably because they didn't want to touch me and rile the dragon shifter even more.

It was then he must have decided that he'd had enough. He moved swiftly, his arm almost a blur as he reached forward for the barrier, and all it took was a blast of his energy. A partial shift of hand to talon, and the cage simply fell away.

Note to self, dragons are badass.

Braxton did not pause, flowing smooth as honey, the blue fires flickering as he strode to me.

Second note to self, dragons are scary.

"Jessa, do not run from him."

The unnecessary warning came from my father, who had moved himself a little closer. I could scent him at my back. Probably five feet away. Jonathon definitely loved me. Nothing else would have a supe braving a dragon's wrath.

Louis was close too. "I'm almost a hundred percent certain that he won't hurt you, Jessa, but you are the only one safe right now."

Almost a hundred percent ... I liked those odds.

Braxton paused right in front of me, and the heat he was radiating called to me. My dragon unfurled herself from where she was caged, opened her mouth, and bellowed as the flames filled her with energy. It was like a shot of adrenalin and I knew I couldn't stay out of Braxton's arms any longer. I threw myself at him, not caring if I was burnt alive. All I cared about was getting to my dragon.

A split second of shock softened the formidable planes of his face. He dropped the flames a moment before my body hit his. I felt the graze of burning heat but then it was gone. The flash of disappointment which flickered through me was madness. No one wanted to be burnt alive, right? That would just be weird.

I wrapped my arms around Braxton's shoulders, he was far too gigantic for me to reach any further. He was still in his extra hulked out form, so I was like ten feet off the ground, twin bands of steel holding me with a sort of desperate need.

Something shifted between us. Bonds grew deeper, the semi-frazzled mate link intensified – but still would not completely merge. This partial bond was messing with my head, I just wanted to know how to fix it. At this point Braxton must have started to shrink back to his normal size; my arms were able to close a little further around him.

Before I could speak he was moving, striding from the room. I lifted my face from where it was pressed to his chest.

"Put me down."

My command received a single raised eyebrow as he stared down at me, but he didn't drop me and he didn't stop moving.

I growled, narrowing my eyes. "Put me down now, Braxton, or so help me I'm going to remove your testicles from their comfortable resting place."

Some of the tension from his face eased, and my reward was a flash of dimple as his eyes ran across my face. I tried again: "Listen, dude, we're establishing our roles now, and I play submissive to no one."

Okay, *yes,* I had been a little more submissive than normal in the bedroom, but I think I was just overwhelmed because it was Braxton. It sort of knocked me for six. In fact our entire coming together had thrown me off my game. But I had to step up at some point or he would be dominating me forever. Which would lead to bloodshed in the end.

At the elevators, before he stepped into the metal cage, he lowered me slowly and suddenly I had a use for my legs again – you know, since the Compasses seemed to think they were just for show.

To give myself a breather from his intensity, I threw a quick glance over my shoulder. The room was still recovering from the quads' joining – and Braxton's ... whatever that was. My other boys looked to be doing okay. Tyson was standing close to Grace, but the witch was doing her best to ignore him. I wondered how long she was going to be able to hold out. Tyson was relentless when he set his mind to something. Maximus and Cardia looked to be two minutes from banging right against the wall. Seriously, get a freaking room.

Jacob noticed my appraisal, raising one eyebrow at me. He was asking if I was okay. I gave him a single nod. I could handle Braxton. I was clearly born to handle him since we were true mates. Besides, either their calling hadn't been to hunt marked, or they were strong enough to fight it, since no one had been attacked yet.

Jacob blew me a kiss. His gentle smile faded away as he turned to speak with Louis. Everyone in the room seemed okay. I knew eventually the mystics would start grilling the shit out of the quads, trying to find out what had happened when they joined. What their calling was.

Braxton drew my attention again by stepping into the elevator. He stood there, waiting for me to make the decision. It wasn't a real choice though. I belonged with Braxton. I would follow him anywhere.

I walked inside. The doors slid closed, and for the first time I felt nervous around my shifter-mate. It was as if a sliver of "stranger" had bled into the relationship. Time to bring some normalcy back.

"So what happened in that cage? Do you have a calling?"

Braxton hadn't said one word since turning into fire-dragon-man, so when he finally answered, the low huskiness of his voice had my blood boiling.

"We received a calling. We're the weapon to fight the dragon king. We do not care for the marked, only the king. He will be destroyed."

There was a slightly robotic, hypnotic trill to his tone. Which was as freaky as fuck, and I hoped it was just an aftereffect of the joining energy. I also wished he wouldn't be so creepy with all the "we" stuff. I did not want them to ever be like the Four. They were evil assholes.

I settled myself back against his side. "So you and the Four are a perfect team. One to destroy or capture the marked and the other to destroy or capture the king."

Braxton's warm gaze rested on me. "We will protect you, Jessa, and we will destroy the king."

I tried to contain my feelings of dread. I could feel in my soul that the next few days would be a turning point in this whole dragon king saga. The supernatural world would never be the same. Would the Compasses and I come out with our pack still intact?

Chapter 16

It was early the next morning, the day of the Krakov break and enter, and all of us were gathered around the living area. Mischa had just popped in to tell us she was bringing the twins across, and then we had to go. Jonathon and Lienda hadn't been able to find her yesterday afternoon, and so far no one had had the chance to throttle the shit out of her, which is what she needed.

I was squeezed into a couch, Maximus on one side and Jacob on the other. They were doing the whole invade my space thing again. Jacob was singing, very low, keeping my nerves at bay. His beautiful fey songs were the ultimate comfort.

My eyes drifted across to where Braxton was against the wall, Tyson slouched next to him. Blood rushed to my face as mental images of yesterday afternoon flashed across my mind.

After leaving the training building, Braxton and I had decided to take a run through the forest. He had a lot of energy to work off. We'd stayed in human form, holding hands, enjoying the closeness. In the center of the forest area we'd run across a massive waterfall which descended down to a lake. It was the most beautiful thing I'd ever seen. Right up until Braxton stripped off his clothes and dived into the water.

After many moments of staring and drooling, I'd eventually gotten naked and joined him. Which of course, quickly turned to touching, heating the lake to hot tub temperatures. Two hours later I'd been satisfied, and wrinkly. Braxton was skilled in many ways. I wanted to ask him where he learned his art, but I was afraid I'd hunt the bitch down and kill her. I'd thank her first of course, and then I'd have to rip her face off. It was just one of those things.

Especially if she taught him that thing he did with his tongue.

I had to squeeze my legs together even thinking back to the image of his dark hair parked firmly between my thighs and the way he–

"Are you blushing, Jessa babe?" asked Jacob. My thoughts came to a screeching halt. The fey had a knowing look on his face. He went back to humming under his breath. Smug bastard.

I punched him. "I'm not blushing, just suffocating. You're all oversized."

I was grateful when Louis's voice filled the room. "Did you know Mischa's new best friends, the twins, were born the same year at the Four?" He directed his words toward Jonathon.

My father's expression was serious as he leaned forward in his chair. "So, if that set of quads and twins were born on the same year, and my twins and the Compasses were born the same year – there has to be a connection."

Yep, all twelve of us were connected to the dragon king – on opposite sides of course, but connected nonetheless. It was too big a coincidence to ignore.

"Jess, we need you to try and keep things under control in Krakov," Jonathon said. "Clearly the twins have some sort of special means of infiltrating the prisons. For all of the breakouts, there was not a single trace they were ever there."

It was really annoying that we might be giving the fruit twins any advantage this close to the "rise of the king." It worried me what this weapon was.

"What do you want me to do about Mischa? If things go to shit in there, I need a way to get both of us out."

I was locked into this friggin' scheme because of Mischa, but I wouldn't leave her to the mercy of those bitches.

Jonathon sat up straighter, even though he was already as rigid as an army sergeant. "Braxton, Louis, and I will be there, inside the walls. I've set us up through the legitimate channels, arranging an official tour with the lead guard. This is common when a council leader arrives in another prison territory. We will get to you if you need us. The other Compasses will stay here in the sanctuary, to make sure everybody is safe should anything go wrong."

Jacob's voice was as hard as diamond. "We should be there. Jessa is our responsibility to keep safe." Tyson joined him in protest.

Maximus nodded, a little less vocal. He had a mate to guard now, so I couldn't be the vampire's only priority.

"I'll protect her," Braxton said. "If too many of us show up, it will create suspicion."

Maximus finally said: "If things go to shit – if Jessa is in trouble – do not hesitate to get us. I expect to be informed immediately."

Louis and Braxton both nodded, and an exchange of hard glares seemed to seal this male bonding moment. I sat a little straighter ... so we had a cover story, but how was I going to be able to SOS them if things went asshole up?

Which they were sure to.

Louis was standing in the doorway like the purple-eyed magic man he was. Somehow I just knew he was going to be the key to this being a success.

Sure enough, the grin which spread across his face was my first indication that he was about to reveal the brilliant plan. "I will place a spell on you, somewhere concealed. Touch it and speak the activation words, and we will come for you."

Sometimes it was obvious how very lucky we were to have Louis on our side. For more than one reason it was a fortunate day when he decided that instead of killing me as a baby, he would big brother me.

"Is it a tracker?" I wanted to know the exact specifications of the spell he would place on me.

Louis nodded. "Yes, I'll be able to track you, and once you activate the spell I can hear what is going on also. So try not to scream too loudly, I'm already going a little deaf in my old age."

I had no idea how old Louis actually was. He looked late twenties, so a few hundred years at least. I wiggled my way out of the depths of the couch, past the long limbs pinning me down. Maximus reached out and cupped one of his hands under my butt and basically threw me across the room. I stumbled only once before regaining my footing. Lucky I had supernatural reflexes, or I'd probably be facedown with my teeth through my lip.

I arched my eyebrows at him. "Thank you for that, asshulk. Maybe next time a little less oomph."

Laughter rang out from various places around the room.

Jacob was the loudest. "Asshulk…" He snorted. "She totally nailed you."

Maximus' long arm swung around and clipped the fey right up the side of the head, knocking him completely out of his chair. Which did nothing to halt his snorting chuckles – though they were a little quieter to avoid a second smack from the muscled vampire.

Ignoring the quads, I strode over to Louis. I was wearing jeans, shit-kicker army style boots, and a black tank. When we were ready to leave, I'd throw a jacket over the whole thing. Enough protection from whatever was coming at me. Although, I didn't have many easily accessible spots for Louis to place this "help button" on me.

I stopped right in front of him and he assessed me lazily, starting at my feet and working up to the top of my head. He was about halfway through when heat caressed my back and I knew we had a third in our little group – Braxton behind me, not touching, but staking his claim all the same.

"You better think long and hard about where you decided to touch her, mage." The tone was casual, but even a deaf idiot could hear the warning in his words.

Louis' grin got even broader. I really wished he didn't find such joy in tormenting the quads. "Oh don't you worry, lizard, I am thinking very long and *hard* about where to put my hands on Jessa."

I kicked Louis.

He had been expecting the attack to come from Braxton, so my boot landed cleanly in his gut and knocked him five feet across the room. Loud clunks followed my footsteps as I stomped after him.

The grin was still in place, although there was a little more feral in the eyes as he stared up at me. "Don't, Louis." Wisps of growl laced my words. "Just put the effing tracker on me."

He was on his feet like a bullet. I never even saw him use his hands or legs. "Apologies, I merely like to rile up the reptile. He is a little touchy where you are concerned."

Braxton placed both of his hands on my shoulders. "Touchy doesn't even begin to cover my emotional stability when it comes to Jessa."

"I respect that." Louis was suddenly somber, something I rarely saw, because he was always projecting an aura of jovialness. But I suspected we saw more of the real Louis in the brief moments he was serious than in all the other times put together. "I would not have approved of a mate for Jessa who showed anything less than the true devotion I see in your eyes. You are a worthy mate for her."

Jonathon laughed. "Why do I feel as if my father role has been usurped right out from under me?"

I squeezed Braxton's hands before turning and crossing the room to my parents. I hugged my dad, throwing my arms tightly around him. "Thanks for being so awesome. I take it for granted, but I appreciate you."

He hugged me back, and his strength made me feel safe. My dad had always been a hero to me, as if he could fix anything that broke. No matter what. Even when he was mourning for Lienda, he'd always been my dad.

I smiled as we pulled back, my voice huskier than usual. "Thanks for not being a hardass. For respecting my ability to make my own choices."

His eyes flicked up over my head and he scanned the room, before coming back to me. "You already had four males following you around and keeping you out of trouble. I never worried, especially after my little chat with the Compasses around puberty. Once I explained how easy it was for a body to disappear, the dynamics worked perfectly."

A snort of laughter left me. I could just imagine my father lecturing the quads, all of them towering over him in height, but easily smacked down by his power. "Well, you all did good," I said. "Really good."

Our family moment was interrupted by the sound of the front door opening and boots clicking across the entrance. Three sets, and the scents were quite citrusy. Okay, they didn't really smell like lemon and orange, but I knew it was them anyway. And Mischa.

I closed my eyes for a brief second, before taking a deep breath and turning around to stand next to Jonathon.

"Looks like it's game on. Distract them for me so I can get the spell put on by Louis," I murmured to my father.

"You got it."

Jonathon intercepted the trio at the edge of the kitchen. Louis and Braxton strode across to me, using their bulk to help block us from the room.

Louis peered down. "You ready?" I nodded once and lifted up the hem of my shirt. I had made the decision to have the mark on my stomach, it would be hidden but still easy for me to reach if needed.

A warm hand landed on my abdomen, just above the line of my jeans. I flinched as the heat turned to burning and then a sharp jab followed. Louis removed his hand and set my shirt in place again.

"All done." His voice was low. "To activate, place your palm on the same spot and speak your mate's name."

I smiled. Louis had picked the one person I'd be calling for if I ended up in trouble, no matter if it activated a tracker or not.

As Louis and Braxton stepped clear, the twins nailed me with identical glares.

"We have lingered for too long," Orange said, standing arms akimbo, hands on hips.

Both twins were dressed in black leather, right down to what looked like whips curled up on the side of their legs. I had a few daggers and knives scattered around my person, but I was guessing they had even more stashed on themselves. My sister was in jeans and a long-sleeved shirt, all black, but thankfully she wasn't part of the leather gang yet.

The twins turned and made their way out of the room. Mischa followed, without even a glance for Lienda, who had been hovering close to her. The wolf-mama looked pissed, but there was also fear in those blue-green eyes.

We all held the same worries, Mischa was distancing herself from us and that was bad for a pack animal. Rogue wolves were dangerous, humanity bleeding from them until they became more animalistic. She had the fruit twins, but when they abandoned her, and no doubt they would, the devastation to her animal soul would be monumental.

I grabbed the trench style jacket that I'd left over the end of the couch, the lining thick enough to keep me warm in the snowy outer of the sanctuary. I found myself moving to hug Lienda before we left. When the hell had I became the hugger of the family?

Her voice was low in my ear. "Be safe, and look after Mischa. But I want you to promise that you won't save her over your own safety. Mischa is old enough to make her own decisions. I won't lose both daughters."

I didn't say anything, I just tightened my arms a little more. It was nice that Lienda made it very clear that she had no favorites between us.

Next to jump on the Jessa hug train was Jacob, his earthy scent familiar as he wrapped me in his arms. "I love you, Jessa babe," he said, "you got this. Don't turn your back on those evil bitches, and suspect everyone." He sang me a few lines of my favorite song, and I was thankful for the moments of calm.

I pulled away, leaving him with a kiss on the cheek. Maximus almost squeezed the life from me, and Tyson's eyes flashed gold as he kissed the top of my head. I got a little emotional at that point and marched myself out of the room. I wasn't pessimistic enough to think this was the last time I'd see them, but I didn't have the best feeling about the entire thing. I didn't trust the twins at all, and I knew anything could happen.

Jonathon, Louis and Braxton were a few steps behind me; I fought to focus my emotions. Now was not the time to dwell on what might happen in the next hours

I barely noticed the ride down in the elevator. All four of us were quiet, caught up in our own thoughts. Braxton's warmth pressed along my side as we leaned back together against the wall. His presence worked better than anything at keeping fear at bay.

Mischa and the twins waited for us in front of our building. Standing with them was Quale.

"What are you doing here?" I asked the mystic. Yeah, it was blunt, but we had no time for niceties.

He didn't pretend to be a moron, answering me succinctly. "You need me to drop the magical barriers."

Right. I'd forgotten about that. Louis was going to create a step-though for us, but it wouldn't work from within the sanctuary – the ancient magics which protected this place were too strong.

"How come you could step-through to Faerie then?" I asked Louis.

He shrugged. "It's much more difficult from inside the barriers, I'd rather not expend that sort of energy right now. It's easy enough to exit the sanctuary first."

Fair enough.

We started to walk, following the gray-haired fey. I oriented myself to keep the fruit twins in sight. I knew they had something planned, I wasn't letting them get the drop on me. I wanted a shot at preempting their next move.

Mischa strode into view, and all of my worries returned. Just seeing her drawn features, the way she trailed those two bitches. This shit had to end.

I caught up to her, reaching out to link my arm through hers. I spoke before she could.

"Look, I don't get what is going on with you, I have no idea what they offered you, but I need you to remember … you're my sister. My twin. No matter what, you belong in our pack."

Mischa blinked rapidly before opening her mouth. I cut her off.

"No, there is nothing to say now. You clearly have an alliance with them and we have no choice but to follow through on this promise. But you and I both know that once the dragon king is dead, they're going to run their asses underground and hide for eternity." *If I haven't already killed them by that point.* "And then, Misch, I will be right here for you." My twin was fighting an internal battle, now was not the time for me to turn my back on her.

She bit her lip, suppressing whatever emotions wanted to emerge. We both knew it wasn't the place to show our weaknesses, but I had to try. I had to extend a hand because I was pretty sure that should I lose my twin, the devastation would be all encompassing.

With a last nod, I let go of her arm and fell back to Braxton. He ran a hand over my hair and I knew he was proud of my moment of maturity. As long as he didn't expect them too often.

We strode without pause through the center part of the sanctuary, weaving our way around buildings. Our group was quiet, watchful, each of us making sure the other didn't screw with us behind our backs. I was thankful there were more people in this group I trusted than I didn't.

It took us longer than usual to reach the desert area. There were lots of supernaturals milling around in various activities, getting in our way. It seemed we were going to cross out of this place by the same route which brought us in from the mountain. I hesitated, just barely, before stepping onto the red sand. The temperature immediately changed, heat flooding through all of us. We were reasonably rugged-up to prepare for the chill of outside, so sweaty butt crack was now in all of our immediate futures.

Awesome.

Braxton moved to my side, and Louis on the other. I didn't question their actions. They were on the same wavelength as me. This was where the dragons and jinn liked to play ball, and both of them had already proven that they had some sort of *interest* in me, and now was not the time to battle with either.

We made it halfway through without incident. Braxton was the first to notice something amiss. I followed his line of sight and ground to a halt.

"What the actual hell is going on here?" I said, breathless as I tried to wrap my head around the sheer amazement of what I was seeing.

Orange actually gave me an answer of sorts. "They know we're leaving the sanctuary, they're acting as a guard. They are called to the four of the compass."

A line of dragons, I shit you not, at least twenty, and not all of them from the desert zone. I could see the wash of blue and greens on some who bore a distinct resemblance to ocean serpents, and the smaller dragons of dark greens and earthy browns who I recognized as forest dwellers, and lastly, the most magnificent were the icy blue of the winter beasts.

Braxton seemed both awed and fierce as he tucked me in closer to his side. I could see a part of him wanted to run to the dragons, be with the wild brothers from which his animal descended, but the fear was real also. He was afraid to lose me, and I didn't have the words to reassure him. I had no idea what the next few days were going to bring, and I especially didn't want to be the north in the dragon king compass. Whatever the hell that meant. All I did know was that it looked as if it didn't much matter what either Braxton or I wanted.

Louis was blunt. "Let's keep moving. They are merely curious for now, but we don't have time if that curiosity turns into something more."

He ushered us along, silent Quale leading us through the rocky terrain. The tension radiating from Braxton was palpable, his energy actually tingling along my body everywhere we were touching. My eyes flicked back to the line of dragons, following, but never closing the distance between us. It did seem that they were protecting our backs, making sure we made it out safely.

"I never wanted this for you, Jess."

I spun my head to find Jonathon close. His eyes were flashing with so many emotions. I had never seen the strong alpha so shaken. "This mark has taken so much from our lives, ripped our family apart, and now it's as if we are all strangers."

I looked to Mischa. My twin was watching us closely, her eyes a little shimmery.

"We should have fought harder to stay together. You and I should have run with Lienda and Mischa. I'm so sorry, I put my pack and council responsibilities before my family and I have never regretted anything more than that."

Louis moved aside so I could fall in next to my father. We hadn't stopped moving, we were almost out of the desert now and approaching the stone spiraling path out of this sanctuary.

I took Jonathon's hand. "You did the best you could, Dad. I have no doubts, it's easy to look back in hindsight, but you sacrificed a lot so that we might live and have a chance to rebuild our family. We have hundreds of years ahead of us, we just need to get past this tiny snafu in our path. I don't blame you at all, and I love you as much as I always have."

I was speaking for Mischa as well, hoping she was holding on to the bonds of family, especially when it came to trusting her new buddies. Jonathon squeezed my hand, a smile blooming across his face as he released me. He had scented truth in my words, and it calmed his wolf.

As we started along the rock, I glanced back over my shoulder to find the line of dragons had disappeared. I faltered minutely. What the … how could twenty or more massive lizards just fade out?

With that level of mad skills, dragons could literally take over the world if they had the numbers.

Which is exactly what the king knew when he created the marked.

My hand was in Braxton's now, his thumb rubbing up and down the pad, the motion soothing. It reminded me of the millions of times he had calmed away my worries and hurts. I tilted my head up to him and he knew without any words what I wanted. He dropped the briefest of kisses onto my lips. Soft, with just the flick of tongue, it had me groaning very low under my breath. He would be the death of me, but shit, what a way to go.

His grin was perfect as he pulled away, all dimples and flashing white teeth. He looked happy, which I was coming to realize made me pretty happy too. Yeah, I was a sap.

In no time we reached the end of the path, the yellow barrier sparkling in the dimness. It felt like a thousand years ago that I ran out of the car and threw myself into this mountain. So much had happened, and yet it was really no time at all.

Quale stepped closer to the exit. "Are you all ready? You must move through quickly so I can return the protections. The Four are out there, and should they make it inside, they'll be too strong for us to battle."

The fruit twins scowled simultaneously at the mention of the hunter quads. If they'd all been born the same year, then no doubt they'd crossed paths with them many times, especially since they were marked, and those damn hunters were good at their jobs. I wondered who had hunted the marked before they were born, and how the twins had remained free, unlike so many other marked.

Questions for another day.

Quale muttered a few words and the barrier dropped. Wind howled. The real world appeared to be having a snowstorm of the ass-kicking variety. Awesome. The sanctuary was like being in another realm, one completely controlled by magic, right down to the weather. The seven of us stepped free, leaving the mystic behind. I noticed the brothers exchange a glance before the yellow shield was back up, blocking Quale from view.

I hugged my arms to my body, and shimmied closer to Braxton. The warmth of his body was like stepping into a hot bath. Without saying anything he wrapped his arms around me.

"Come on." Louis had to shout to be heard over the temperamental weather, even with supernatural senses. Peering around Braxton's bulk – although not removing myself from his arms because I wasn't an idiot – I could see that Louis had the step-through already open.

I took an extra second to hug myself very tightly to Braxton. This might be the last moment of happiness I had for a while and I was going to milk the hell out of it.

He lifted me closer to his face and said, "It will be okay, I will keep you safe."

Snow coated our faces and I raised mine to meet him in another kiss. Now might not be the best time for a make out session, but really ... who gives a shit.

Eventually, though, we had no choice but to rejoin reality. I was back on my feet, and with our hands tightly linked Braxton and I made our way to the rest of the group, standing in front of Louis' doorway. I met the sorcerer's purple eyes and knowledge of what the next few hours was all about flooded back in. It was time. We were going to Krakov.

Chapter 17

The step-through took us from a snowstormed mountain range down into a valley of sorts. Concealed within this valley was a medium sized town. I was going to guess this was the gateway community which protected Krakov. Which thankfully meant that there'd only be supernaturals here. We wouldn't have to hide our *otherness*.

It appeared to be laid out similarly to Stratford, but with the more snow friendly style of chalet dwellings. These homes surrounded a few large square "meeting hall" structures.

It was still freezing, but the area was protected from the worst of the storm. The scenery looked familiar, so I assumed we were still in the same region of Romania – in the Carpathian Mountains. From what I could see from our higher vantage point, the area was probably around ten miles in diameter, nestled down in what looked like the crater of a volcano. Mountain ranges encased the quaint little town.

"This is Bruvnest," said Louis. "Their securities are breachable because I've been here before, but there is no easy way into Krakov." His regal features shifted to the bitch twins … yeah, I'd upgraded them from fruit. "It's your party now, *ladies*. Whatever plan you have set in motion, you'd better move your asses. The townsfolk are starting to catch on that we are here."

He wasn't even kidding. Members of the community were emerging from wherever they had been. Rugged, they had the distinct size and appearance of our familiar supernatural races. I wasn't surprised to see they had a lot of trolls here. They were always around mountains and rocky areas.

I heard the townsfolk murmuring amongst themselves. No one spoke English. It sounded Eastern European … Romanian. Which would make sense, you know, since that's where we were. As they closed in, I could hear them more clearly.

"*Ce naiba?*" was a popular phrase.

Louis was keeping an eye on them, his gaze unwavering, streams of power emanating from him.

"Do you know what they are saying?" I asked him, since he looked to be following their conversations.

He chuckled. "Something along the lines of 'what the hell?' I don't think they're impressed to see us appear inside their securities."

Couldn't blame them for that. Their one job was to protect the barriers and the prison, and we'd just strolled right in. The twins were acting pretty indifferent toward the townsfolk drawing closer to us. They joined hands, and while there was nothing obvious about what they were doing, I could see the energy bleeding off them. Then they started to sing. It was a low, haunting melody, which seeped through my skin and settled into my blood. I could feel the notes wanting to twirl their way into my mind, but I was strong enough to hold them at bay.

The conversations from the townsfolk trickled off and silence descended over the snowcapped community. Then they started to retreat back into their hut-style homes and other buildings – seemingly without thought – away from where they had clearly been coming to confront the intruders.

As their song died off I narrowed my eyes on the twins. "What did you do to them? What the hell are your powers?"

Louis was the one to answer. "I'm surprised you've managed to keep this little secret to yourselves," he said. "I recognize that song. You're sirens, and you also have persuasion."

Finally we knew the race of the twins. *Sirens.* The elusive female fey. Generally they only had power over males, but I didn't have any idea what "persuasion" was. Obviously something which could influence an entire town.

Louis must have noticed my confused expression. "The twins are very old, and the older fey can sometimes harness a type of influencing energy. We call it persuasion. Sirens are already blessed with persuasive power. Seems these two have tapped into it further."

I leaned forward, hands on my hips. "Are you saying you can control people? Make them bend to your will?"

Orange laughed in a derisive manner. "If that was the case, we wouldn't have needed to use Mischa to force your hand. We can send *suggestions*, but there is no force. Most supernaturals simply do not have the strength of will to even realize their thoughts are not their own. With suspicious supes, such as prison community members, we don't hide our presence, we influence them to believe we are one of them, not a threat. They ignore us after that."

Lemon piped up. "It is especially strong with males."

Braxton crossed his arms over his chest. "Only some males."

They both nodded, and I realized they must have at some point tried to control my dragon shifter. *Stupid bitches*.

At least much of the mystery around the fruit twins made sense now. "Since you're sirens, and the prisons are filled with an overabundance of males in charge … they pretty much escort you right in, don't they?"

Supernaturals were not generally sexist – aside from the male-oriented mystics – females were equal in all manner, and in many instances superior. But for some reason males were more interested in working in the prison system. The councils were always trying to tempt females into prison jobs, but we seemed to favor the running of the gateway communities.

Orange's face was hard, her dark eyes flashing at me. "It is not common knowledge that we're fey, we work very hard to conceal it. We would appreciate it if you didn't spread this information around."

I flipped them off. "Appreciate this, bitch. I owe you nothing. Let's get this freaking show on the road. I have no interest in any sort of girl bonding."

Yeah, I was pissed. But they had pushed some sensitive nerves, threatening Mischa. I was not playing nice.

Orange hissed, lurching forward as if to attack. Her sister halted her with a little shake of her yellow hair and the fight died out of Orange's eyes. They seemed to be communicating silently again. I knew they could do that mind speak like Mischa and I, and since they were old and powerful, probably didn't even have to touch.

Speaking of, my zombie-like sister continued to just stand there observing and not reacting to anything. Despite my worry, there was also a portion of my anger reserved for her. Dad seemed to have the same thoughts, his icy eyes locked on her as well.

I knew one thing from growing up with him – he was pretty lenient in lots of ways, but the few rules he had, he expected them to be carried out without question. And one of them was to have your pack members' back, no matter what. Mischa was majorly failing at that one today. There was no time to deal with her right now, we just had to hope we lasted long enough to have the family fight I was seeing in our future.

The twins led us along the edge of town. A couple of faces turned in our direction, but no one approached us. We ended up at the base of a massive cliff face. There were a few craggy overhanging crevices scattered over the surface, but mostly it looked like a single sheet of bumpy rock.

Orange turned just enough for me to see her beaky nose and squinty eyes. "Follow our footsteps exactly,"

Ominous words. No doubt there would be plenty of security measures we had to circumvent to make it into Krakov. Prison securities were not to be taken lightly.

The twins approached the wall and I sighed as they placed their hands onto the rock. *Fan-freaking-tastic*. We were climbing. I was a wolf, we didn't climb. Mischa moved in right behind them and I watched as she positioned her hands exactly where Lemon's feet had just been. The divots they were using to climb seemed to be invisible, so unless you knew where they were, you were not getting up the rock. Jonathon pushed me forward, nodding to indicate I should follow them.

"Are you not coming up this way?" I blinked stiffly, the icy air freezing my eyelashes.

He shook his head. "Sorry, Jessa, this is not the main entrance."

Louis tilted his head to capture my gaze. "Don't forget about…" He trailed off, pointing toward my stomach. He lowered his voice further. "We can be there within minutes, but for our plan to work we must check in to our official appointment."

Jonathon brushed a hand over my cheek. "The twins explained earlier that if we all followed, there was more chance of us getting caught. Their powers only extend so far." His blue eyes softened. "We will be close by though, so call if you need us."

He stepped aside and let Braxton crowd into me. The dragon didn't look happy. "This goes against my better judgment, Jess, but promise me that you will not let your guard down for a second. Not even with Mischa."

I bobbed my head a few times. He didn't have to worry about that. A part of my sister had gone to the dark side and she wasn't to be trusted.

"I choose you." I leaned in closer. "I love you." I'd said it a million times before, but now it meant something more. And I was running out of chances to tell him.

He growled. "Don't do that. I will see you again very soon."

"Just in case," I murmured.

His lips hit mine then, and the kiss held a taste of fear, before it softened up and I could feel his true emotions. That kiss told me he loved me. Desperately. Passionately. Forever.

Somehow I pulled myself from him, turning to face the cliff. *Shit,* the girls were already halfway up. So much for me following their exact path.

"I can help with that," Louis said.

My feet were suddenly off the ground. Looked like this wolf was both climbing and flying today. Lucky I was part dragon too.

Despite the strange sensation of floating into the sky, I didn't flinch. I was hardening myself, to prepare for what was coming. The bad feeling I'd had for days was increasing, my instincts were screaming at me to bail, but unlike my sister I was loyal and wouldn't throw her off the cliff. Not yet anyway. But she'd better start proving she was worthy of all of us.

My eyes stayed locked on the three men for as long as possible, especially Braxton, who had both hands pressed into the rock as if he was a heartbeat from following me. I had to look away when I reached Mischa; Louis deposited me against the cliff. The magic held long enough for me to find the divots. My gloved fingers slotted into the deep spots, and it was actually pretty easy to scale up. I glanced back down again, but there was no one at the bottom anymore. The ache in my heart deepened.

I again pushed down my sorrow, focusing my thoughts on what the hell the weapon might be; if the twins wanted it, it had to be important.

About halfway up the massive cliff Orange disappeared. Hanging out as far as I could, I tried to see what was happening above, but she had definitely vanished. Then, as soon as the next twin poofed into nothingness, I knew we had reached Krakov's entry point. I hurried up after Mischa, making sure to stay in her foot grooves.

Five more feet and Mischa was gone, her boots almost kicking me in the head as she shimmied her way into the secret doorway. As I reached for the next handhold, I had to scramble higher to find the opening. I knew it was stupid, but I closed my eyes for the split second it took me to pass through the fake rock wall. I opened them to find my head and upper body in a small cave alcove. I pulled the rest of myself over the edge and stood. The other three waited briefly before they started to move again.

Orange said: "We just came through the back entrance to Krakov. Stay close."

I didn't reply, my dirty looks were speaking volumes. Mischa was a little slower to follow. She blinked a few times at me. Either her eyeballs were freezing from the icy cold or she was trying not to cry. I held her gaze until she shook off the emotions and turned away again.

The cave started to narrow into a tunnel of sorts, growing darker the further we got from the secret cliff doorway. Enough light for my wolf eyes, but I think a human would have struggled. This area seemed like every other cave I'd ever been in, but if that was really the case, why was every single hair on my body standing on end? Why were my wolf senses on high alert? – not to mention my dragon, prowling the walls of her cage, almost as if she was on patrol.

I had a sudden thought. And with a burst of speed I grabbed my sister's hand. The connection between us flared to life, but with no visible energy for the other twins to pick up on.

Did you tell them about my ability to shift to dragon?

I needed to know. I was most probably walking right into a trap, and my dragon felt like a secret weapon of sorts, which it wouldn't be if they already knew about her.

Mischa's wide green eyes met mine, she withdrew her hand, and for a moment I thought she was going to ignore my question. Thankfully, before I had to beat it out of her, she gave her head a shake. She followed that up with a sad little smile, and I knew that for now my secret was safe with her. There was some loyalty there deep down.

I wish I knew the real reason she continued to run back to these manipulators. Their siren persuasion was only supposed to work on males and those unaware or easily susceptible. Had Mischa's heartache and misplaced trust weakened her mind that much? It felt like there was something else. In order to save Mischa, I had to know what continued to pull her back. I would bide my time. One of them would slip up sooner or later.

The tunnel was long, winding, and freezing, but I left my arms loose at my sides. I didn't want to waste a second if I needed to fight.

"Where did this entrance come from?" I found myself asking.

Neither of the twins turned back, but one of them still answered. "This was where they took the prisoners to dispose of them. They would be magically bound and tossed off the cliff. Falling to their death." There was a brief pause. "It was easy enough for the townspeople to accept that they'd died trying to escape."

Especially since their magical binds would have disappeared upon their demise. Very harsh. We didn't have the death penalty in the prison system, so I assumed it was for those who they wanted to *secretly* dispose of. Corruption was rife in all organizations, and ours was no different. Cover stories were easy. It was simple work to spin a story when you had all the power and the other was dead.

We continued in silence, the path unchanging. I was about to ask how much further when unnatural illumination started to filter along the corridor and I knew we were closing in on something. Rounding a corner, I saw the bars first, threading across the path, blocking us from moving forward. No worries though, for Siren One and Siren Two. The twins approached the male guard and he didn't even hesitate to hit a button. The bars slid across, and as I passed through I noticed how vapid his expression was, pupils fully dilated. His loss of control was obvious.

Yeah, it was a wicked power. Shame it had to be in the hands of these fucktards. A clank signaled that the door had closed behind us, and just like that I found myself in a row of cells.

We were in Krakov.

The cells ran along our left side – the right was the roughened stone – extending as far as I could see. The atmosphere was tense, this place had a very bad vibe to it. The cells I could see were occupied by a variety of supernaturals, from all of the races. A lot were demi-fey. These inmates seemed *harder* than the criminals in Vanguard, eyes dead, brows furrowed, lines of stress across their features. They looked old, and supes didn't look old until the last few years of their lives.

I found it strange that none of them glanced up as we moved past. We weren't quiet. Our footsteps scraped the stone and our scents should have tipped them off to our presence.

Orange must have noticed my confusion. "This prison is harsher than Vanguard. The worst of the worst are sent here. There are spells on their cells, like a one way glass. We can see in but they can't see or hear out."

Well, that would explain it. And harsh was an understatement. These prisoners were basically in solitary confinement, cut off from all contact with others. For shifters, and many of the other races, it was a torture worse than death.

Lemon picked up the conversation. "They don't separate the races in here. These cells simply wind their way through and around this mountain."

"So basically this entire mountain is Krakov?" I tried to wrap my head around the logistics of this. Cells just winding themselves deeper and deeper into the rock.

The twins nodded. "Yes, they allow them out of their cells for a few hours a week, but nothing like the free mingling time you have at Vanguard. It's not in your best interest to find yourself jailed in here."

No wonder the faces in the cells were so desperate and desolate, crushed down to shells of supernaturals. I hoped every single one of them deserved to be in this sort of situation, because otherwise ... I couldn't even think about it.

"The dragon marked that were in here ... was it this bad for them?" Mischa asked. For the first time in ages, real emotion creased her face.

A dark fury swooped across the twin's features, an identically swift and brutal expression. "Yes," was all Lemon said, but the tone of the word said so much more than that.

My own anger was ignited – babies and children in this environment. The Four and any other members of the supernatural community who took part in this needed to spend a few years in a prison. Or dead. Yeah, they needed to spend a few years dead, because there was no redemption for what they had done to hundreds of innocents.

This knowledge might have slanted the actions of the fruit twins in a new light, breaking in to save all the marked – except I knew they hadn't just done it to save them. They'd also been looking for Mischa and me. Selfish actions to free a megalomaniac king.

I remained on high alert as we wound along the corridor of prisoners, forcing myself not to watch the bleak faces behind the magic glass. I closed my ears to the rambling mutterings, the screams, the animal-like noises. Nothing I could do to help them. I wondered if Jonathon knew how harsh this prison was. Surely there had to be some sort of regulations on treatment of prisoners. It would be better to kill them than continue a lifetime of torture. Supernaturals lived for a very long time.

We encountered three more barred gates, but each time there was at least one male on guard, and they were more than helpful to the twins. I'd thought they were so badass when I'd first heard that two females were breaking out the dragon marked, but they were pretty much escorted right in and out. No risk. No badassery required. *Posers*.

The worst of all was the fact that so many supes had a weak enough mind that they could be influenced, although I knew it was harder to fight when taken unawares. And the twins were old and powerful. But still.

The cold was increasing as we traversed further into the mountain, and the path seemed to be tilted downwards, heading straight into the basement of this damned place, which gave me a very uneasy feeling. So much stone surrounded us now.

My wolf and dragon both started to growl and I had to cut off that line of thought to calm them down. And myself. Mostly myself, because I was starting to get a claustrophobic freak-out feeling.

"How much further?" I finally snarled, unable to stand the silent walking any longer.

Lemon graced me with a smirk. "Almost there, wolf. The weapon is in the very lowest dungeon of this prison. Where the oldest, most powerful and most evil prisoners rest."

Awesome. And if we were truly lucky, these prisoners would all escape just before we got down there. You know, just for kicks.

With a sigh I settled in for the rest of the long walk. Eventually, we reached a sort of t-section and the twins chose to go left, the path started descending quite steeply. I was still trying to build an image of Krakov in my head. This place reminded me of underground images of ant hills, or the chambers below the pyramids in Egypt. The only light in this section was from small crystals embedded high in the stone walls.

"What was down the other path?" I asked, finding the t-section odd.

I couldn't see which twin, but I thought it was Orange who answered. "That's the mingling area. They take fifty prisoners at a time – any more and they don't have enough guards to control them. This happens twice a week, for a few hours per group."

Only twice a week. These prisoners must be literally insane.

"How is it that you know so much about the inner workings of the prisons?" These bitches were so suspect. I wished Dad or the quads were here. I was going to need someone in my corner. I was outnumbered and lacking vital information.

"We're old, we have been moving through the supernatural world for a long time. And Krakov is a prison which is important to us." Orange again, and surprisingly forthcoming with information. Usually when the crazy ones are loose lipped it's because they are about to kill you. But surely the twins knew they couldn't kill me. They were marked also, and had the same lack of vulnerabilities.

But maybe they knew what our weaknesses were. I wasn't surprised that the Four didn't know, no one was going to broadcast it to them, but I sort of thought the twins might have the knowledge.

The cold was starting to bother me. It was icy enough to take my breath away and freeze my eyeballs. Moisture gathered on my lashes, and my lips felt dry and chapped. I was dreaming of food, a warm bed, and a naked Braxton. Maybe I could eat my food off a naked Braxton while in bed. Yes ... yes, that was a great plan.

I knew when we neared the lower levels of the prison. The energy grew strong, the securities pressing. The elements woven into the bars of the prisoner's cells were visible, and on instinct I shied closer to the stone side. For the first time in ages my eyes alighted on the prisoners. I blinked a few times. Unlike the sad souls up higher, all of the ones down here were sitting perfectly still, making no noise, and all staring straight at their bars as if they could see through the magic one-way-glass. The only reassurance was that their eyes didn't follow me, but still it felt eerily like they could see what was happening.

In this row I recognized a few famous supernatural criminals. From what I could remember of history class, this appeared to be the section for crims who had created massive publicity in the human world. I growled as a familiar face came into view – a sorcerer, his white eyes identifying him immediately. I wasn't sure of his real name, the text referred to him as *The Rostov Ripper*. He was a serial killer of the worst kind. He loved young girls, luring them in, raping and torturing them. A pity that his incarceration didn't include daily disembowelment. I was actually a little surprised he was still alive. The high security and separation in this prison had allowed him to keep his head. Which was a fucking shame.

There were three gates in this small section alone, eight guards, and the only one to even look twice at us was a female shifter, and she was immediately silenced by her partner with a right hook to the jaw. This was how all the female guards we'd seen had been subdued, which pissed me off so bad. The twins were manipulative assholes; they cared for no one but themselves. Typical sirens, so used to controlling males that they thought they could control everything.

When we reached the end of the path, there were no more bars, and no deviation off the path. It was a stone wall, dead end.

"So what's the plan now?" I was quite proud by the level of sarcasm present in my words.

They turned and their twin grins were freaking unnerving. I wanted to punch both of them in the nose.

They spoke together. "Now, we open the wall."

Sure, of course. Open the wall.

"How are you going to do that?" I asked. My hackles raised as the two of them closed in on either side of me. I backed up a little, both hands held slightly aloft so I could fight them if needed.

Orange flashed her dark eyes in my direction, followed by white teeth. "Easy, just a little blood offering."

A little what the what? *Not on my watch, sister, I bleed for no one.* I never even donated blood to Maximus, and I loved him more than life. I started to back up faster, keeping a certain amount of distance between me and them. They stopped pursuing me about halfway along this small section, and I was just wondering what the hell they were doing when they both spun and pounced on my moronic sister.

371

I didn't hesitate to change directions, but I knew I was too far away to get there in time. All I could do was watch in horror.

They were far more skilled than she was. It took no time for Orange to produce a knife, and with a move any expert would be proud of, she plunged it into Mischa's side, sliding it between her ribs. A gasping yelp escaped from my twin's mouth, and she collapsed immediately. I could hear her ragged breathing and knew they'd punctured her lung.

My initial fly kick smashed Lemon in the back of the head, slamming her face first into the stone. She bounced back up without pause and spun to engage me. A trickle of blood ran down her cheek, scraped from where she'd hit the wall. I growled, my hands shifting into claws as I gouged at her. I had to get to Mischa and Lemon was in my way.

Over her shoulder I noticed Orange reaching down to hoist my twin into her arms. Furious, I clocked Lemon, my elbow smashing her jaw. But again I couldn't reach Mischa in time. Orange sent her flying toward the wall blocking the path.

Blood splattered as she hit the rock, and then I sensed the magic. A burst of power shot out through us, ancient, strong – like Louis' magic always felt.

Lemon tried to duck by me. I swung around and punched her. I got a good hit in because she was distracted – trying to reach her sister. Perfect opportunity. I punched her again, dodging her feeble attempts to defend herself, and finally my elbow put her down. This time she stayed there. Kicking her once in the gut, I leapt across her body and moved to help Mischa.

The ground rumbled and I skidded over the rocks to reach my twin, yanking her into my arms, pulling her away from the falling debris. Whatever the bitch twins had done was bringing down the wall. With a bang it disintegrated, rocks rolling out across the floor, leaving behind an entrance into what looked like another small stone area.

The twins both stood above where I was cradling Mischa and stared down at me.

"Follow or your sister will die." Orange looked excited, and that scared me more than her anger.

I could hear Mischa's wheezing, her small whimpers sending panicky trills down my spine. I forced my panic into anger, sneering as growls fell from my mouth. "Marked can't die."

The twins glanced at each other before turning back to me and, synchronized, both laughed, the dead, empty laughter of crazy people. "Of course the marked can die, and the countdown is on for Mischa. You don't want to delay."

Truth. I knew those bitches held the key to our mortality.

Without removing my eyes from them, I slowly stood, my sister's slender form cradled in my arms. "Hurry the fuck up, and you better hope and pray that Mischa is okay."

I shut down my emotions, schooling my features, before following them through that entrance – I had to shift Mischa around so she would fit – and into the next tunnel. The moment I got a free hand I was going to activate my tracker. Mischa was fading, and something told me I was going to need help myself in the next few minutes.

Chapter 18

Mischa stared up at me, her wide green eyes glassy. Shock and pain had set in.

She blinked a few times, bubbles of watery blood forming at the corner of her mouth, and it took her more than one attempt to make a noise. I had to move very close to hear what she was saying.

"I'm ... I ... I'm sor ... sorry, Jess. Said would ... get ... Max..." She trailed off, her head falling back against me as she ran out of steam.

I could feel the warmth of her blood still seeping out of her side. Her shifter healing should be slowing that flow. Why the heck was it taking so long? My eyes darted toward the twins. Was that knife infused with silver? I tilted my head over and sniffed at her wound. The burning tingle indicated there was definitely silver involved.

"Enough screwing around." The command came from one of the fruity bitch twins. "Move your ass, Jessa."

My head flew up, and for the first time I noticed the new area we'd stepped into.

"Oh screw me sideways," I groaned, frantically looking left and right. I knew this place, I'd seen it before ... in a dream.

It was a stone tunnel, about five feet wide and twenty long, ending with a massive symbol against a rocky wall. A compass symbol, the four points perfectly clear in the dim light.

"What the hell is this weapon?" I snarled, moving closer, almost as if I couldn't help myself. The symbol was calling to me. I had a burning need to see it more clearly.

Orange and Lemon were already standing before the image, one on either side, facing me. "The dragon king had a scepter that he used to rule the races. It is needed to free him."

I shook my head. "I won't help you. I don't care what you want from me, I'm taking my sister and getting out of here." I spun on my heel, forcing myself to leave. It was tough, like dragging myself through sticky taffy. The compass pulled me back to it. I had to focus all of my energy just to take a step.

Laughter rang out, washing down the corridor, but I didn't stop. I made it to the doorway in the stone, turning sidelong so I could fit back through again. Truth was, I preferred the hall with all the serial killer sociopaths over the twins.

Orange's voice followed me along passageway. "Two things are going to happen, Jessa. Firstly, Mischa will never stop bleeding without us. The knife was coated in silver, and a spell which cannot be reversed by any but us." No matter how far I walked, her voice continued to follow. "Second ... every guard you have to go through to escape from Krakov is going to bring you back to us. We control the male mind, you have no chance."

Shit. She was right. I could not get out of this place on my own. It was too narrow for my dragon, and in animal form I couldn't carry Mischa. My sister was now slipping in and out of consciousness, and considering her blood was starting to soak the floor beneath us, I knew they were right about the wound healing.

I growled as Orange spoke again. "Help us and we will make sure your sister is healed, and we'll give you the weapon. You can have it. The dragon king will not rise for two more days, so you will have time to try and hide it from us."

It wasn't as if I had much of a choice.

I exhaled deeply before turning back to the direction I'd just come from. The twins were a long way from me now, still standing on either side of the compass mark. Knowing I couldn't run from this, I stomped along, my arms barely registering the strain of holding Mischa. It took me no time to reach them.

"What do I have to do?"

I spoke each word slowly, trying to figure out how to kill them with jagged words and angry looks.

"Blood," Lemon said, "we just need a little of your blood."

I took a step back, before gently lowering my sister to the floor. Straightening again I made my way across to the twins. They must have sensed my compliance, because they turned their backs on me and faced the compass. Knowing this could be my best chance, I slipped my hand beneath my shirt, my hand slick with Mischa's blood. I could feel the spell on my skin. Laying my palm across it, I called for Braxton. Out loud and mentally. Just in case it required one or the other. Orange flipped her head around, looking first at me and then down the hall.

"Your friends can't save you. Just give us what we want and no one else needs to get hurt."

I trusted them about zero out of a million, so it was easy to ignore every word they shot at me. *Braxton.* I tried again, but … shit, something was wrong. The spell was still cold against my skin, and I knew if it had been activated I'd have felt heat. What the eff was going on? Louis would not have made a mistake. He said I needed to say the name of my mate, which was Braxton. So what was wrong?

"Blood!" Lemon was more demanding than her sister.

I flipped her off, and with a pounce quicker than a shifter cat, she had Mischa in her arms. "You want to see your sister suffer more? She still has one lung functioning, but maybe if she was drowning in her own blood, it would hurry you along."

Shit. Fuck. Ass. Balls. Why had I put her on the ground? I needed free hands to fight, but I'd also let them have their only leverage back. I must have hit my head on the way in here or something. This time it was Lemon who had the knife in her hand, and as she lifted her arm to plunge it into the other side of Mischa's body, I lurched forward.

"Stop!" I screamed. "Take my friggin' blood, but you better hope that Mischa and I die after this, because I am making it my life mission to kill you both."

I leveled a hard gaze on each of them so they knew how serious I was.

Orange snatched my right hand. I almost wrenched my arm back. Touching her was like touching poison ivy. My skin immediately itched. My palm burned as she slashed across the fleshy pad. Silver would keep this wound open for a lot longer. Blood immediately eased to the surface before spilling free.

Orange dragged me two steps to the wall and slammed that palm down onto the north groove in the compass. So this was what they meant by me being north. Damn jinn, and damn everyone else for not giving me more information.

Lemon took my sister's hand and placed it on the south point. No need for a cut, Mischa was already bleeding everywhere. Then the twins sliced their own hands, the final blood for east and west. As the four of our palms sat in the divots on our compass, an unnatural wind flooded along the corridor. I shivered as the first icy strands touched me, and then gasped as it turned to a burning heat. It was as if two seasons had simultaneously flooded across the prison.

The twins started to chant, their words melodic, almost song-like: *"Summon, arise, you are called. Be one, fulfill the curse, right the wrong. Bring back which was lost so long ago. Open the door to the inbetween."*

I did not like the sound of that one bit. I tried to yank my hand back, but it was as if my blood was the strongest glue in existence. The wind picked up, howling as it shifted between the iciest cold I'd ever felt to the heat of a hundred suns.

"Summon, arise, you are called. Larkspur!"

They finished on a shout and suddenly my palm was burning and I still couldn't pull it away. I slipped my free hand onto my stomach again. I had to try the spell, I needed help.

This was about more than a freaking scepter, the power here was off the charts.

"Who are you calling?" I shouted. "Who is Larkspur?"

My hand was on Louis' spell again, and as I asked my question I mentally screamed for Braxton. I needed him, I needed my mate. The spot on my stomach flared to life.

The compass image started to shake, the entire wall trembling. Just when I thought my arm was going to vibrate right off, I managed to wrench my hand free, cradling my burning palm. After a few moments, when the pain didn't subside, I unclenched my hand and examined it.

What the shit?

Imprinted on my palm was the symbol that had been etched above the north divot, burned into my skin. Orange shoved me backwards. I hadn't been expecting it and hit the deck hard. Mischa followed, tossed at me by Lemon.

I caught my sister, before locking in on the bitches again. I gasped. One of the twins held a weapon. Did that just appear from the compass? *Was this the weapon?* The scepter was aptly named, looking exactly like the ones held by ancient rulers. Gold, with a giant stone on top, sort of like an opal, shot through with many different colors, the other end tapered down to a point. While I was examining it, Lemon leaned herself back and slammed the opal right into the center of the vibrating compass symbol.

A blast of energy shot us all back; it took all of my strength to keep hold of Mischa. My entire body was aching as I reached up to push my hair from my face. The rod remained lodged in the center of the compass symbol, the vibration increasing, the walls around us shaking. Lemon had fallen next to me.

"What have you done?" I screamed over the noise.

She smiled, her teeth a little bloodstained, but her joy apparent. "We freed the king."

"What?" My whisper was lost in the noise. "But we still have a few days."

She heard the last part, flashing those bloody teeth at me again. "That thousand years had nothing to do with Larkspur, and everything to do with you."

I know I was straining to hear her over the noise, but did she just say it was to do with me?

"Just before he was captured he sent out his energy to touch one shifter. To be his mate. Your blood was the key to him rising." She dropped her head back with a clunk. "We fulfilled our calling. Larkspur will rule again."

Larkspur? Why had no one ever told me that was the king's name? I thought for sure his first name was "dragon" and his last "king," since that was the only way he was ever referred to. And seriously, was I really supposed to believe that the thousand year thing was about me?

I coughed as the burning on my stomach continued to thrum. It was painful, but I also knew it meant my family was on their way. I just had to hold out long enough until help arrived.

The grinding rumble grew louder, and my odds of holding out had just dropped dramatically. The compass emblem was spinning, in a blur of speed too fast for me to track. Within seconds the mark was unrecognizable. It didn't take a genius to figure out that this compass was a doorway to somewhere else. I was just praying the damn king didn't step through. I'd hold on to the faint hope the bitch twins had made a mistake.

The portal opened and natural light flooded over the dirty stone floors. I was transfixed, staring into the land which lay on the other side. It reminded me of the *otherness* of Faerie, but not the Faerie land I had been to. This one was desolate, barren, dead. The heat which had been alternating with the cold winds was now more pronounced than ever. The small section I could see … flashes of black glinted off the red planes, and then … roars exploded across the hall. Oh God, it was so loud, my eardrums felt as if they were about to explode.

The hole in the wall was widening, the landscape beyond becoming clear. I could see out into the fiery world of red rock and lava falls.

"Where the hell is that?" I bit out, not really asking anyone in particular.

Lemon answered. "That's the land between, the dead zone. It is the place of banishment for those too evil for the prisons."

What the actual freak? I swallowed loudly. "You'd better shift your ugly old ass up and get that shit closed. What sort of creatures will you be letting in?"

"We only allow the king. He was called."

Our conversation was cut off when Orange dragged herself across the floor, halting beside Mischa. She reached out a hand and touched my sister's ribs. In a rapid movement I shot out my free hand and gripped her around the throat.

"What, the eff, are you doing?" My voice was low, soft. I was already planning her murder in my head.

"Sealing the wound," she choked out around my hold. "I'm tired of slipping in her blood."

I tightened my grip enough to leave a decent bruise. Orange said nothing. Eventually I had to let her go; I wanted Mischa repaired. I kept a close eye, making sure she did nothing but close the wound.

She was fast, her power leaving tingles on my tongue as it coated the room. But she did as she said, the wound was sealed. My sister was deathly white as I reached out and felt for her pulse. It was weak, erratic. I hoped she would be okay now that her blood was staying on the inside. Plus she was marked, she couldn't die from blood loss, could she?

I must have murmured something about that out loud, because Lemon snorted. "The king is free, all marked can now die." She took great delight in telling me this.

Say what? What happened to our immortality? And more importantly, if the marked could die...

"I guess that means you both can die now too." I gently set my sister aside, standing in a smooth motion. Shit was about to get real.

I was preparing to launch in their direction when a deep voice shattered the room. "You might be my beloved, but I cannot have you hurt my daughters." The powerful timbre echoed off the rock and froze my feet to the spot.

Dread settling heavily in my gut, I turned, hoping like heck I was wrong, but somehow I knew who would be stepping through that portal. Sure enough, as I faced my fear, a massive male filled the gateway, blocking the burning world behind him.

He was tall, bigger than any of the Compasses, with dark honey-blond hair and piercing eyes of undetermined color ... maybe gray. Dressed all in black, like a weird armor made from ... fuck, it looked like scales, which shimmered as he moved. He stepped into the room and I fell to my knees. His power was strong and it was sweet, like a river of honey washing over me. I knew I would drown if this continued, but it was so sweet and tantalizing, I didn't even care.

Something tapped at a corner of my mind. It took me a few heartbeats to realize it was my dragon. She'd crawled out of her space in my center, her energy now prowling around my head. I didn't hesitate, reaching for her, knowing she might be my one chance to fight the king. With a flash of ancient energy – power which felt methodically cold, but with a touch of dragon heat – clarity returned to me, clearing the vestiges of the spell I was under. I regained thought, and remembered who I was.

Jessa Lebron, daughter of Jonathon, mate of Braxton, and nothing to do with this imposter.

I rose, my movements calculated. That bastard had rolled me good, but he wouldn't catch me off guard again. First thing first ... had he said Lemon and Orange were his...

"Daughters?" The bitch twins were next to me, one on either side like they were ready to capture me should I run. "You're the daughters of the dragon king? How is that even possible?"

They had been born years after he had been decapitated. Speaking of, how the heck was his head back on his body? Someone needed to check their sword, because head and neck looked to be firmly attached.

Larkspur decided to answer me. "When I went into battle, I had their mother hidden away and put into a sleep stasis to hide her energy. I did not want her used against me. I planned on releasing her from the spell when I returned." A cold anger washed over him, freezing the brutal planes of his face. "I never returned, so the spell lasted a very long time. Eventually it wore off. She was pregnant at the time."

I curled my lips at the pair. These lying hags had been doing their father's duties for too many years now. "You also called me 'beloved.' You had a mate ... and I already have a mate. I am not your anything."

I spat the last lot of words at him. My dragon roared at the same time; she did not like the dragon king. I wasn't sure when it had happened, probably a long time ago, but she was attached to Braxton. She had chosen him and so had I. And as if I had summoned him, there was a shout from behind me. The spot on my stomach pulsed and I knew help had arrived.

But I was afraid now. I couldn't let him hurt my family.

When the king's gaze finally lifted from me, his cold eyes trailing across the powerful group which were moving along the tunnel toward us, I took the opportunity and lunged for him, pulling a blade from my boot. The king's gray eyes flicked back just in time. He rolled backwards, catching me in his arms, my knife buried to the hilt in his chest.

"I knew you couldn't resist me." His tone and smile was all charm, but it didn't reach his eyes, and I found the lack of dimples disconcerting.

"Jessa!" Braxton's roar shook the foundation of the stone around us. "Get away from him!"

Easier said than done, Larkspur had me firmly locked in his muscular arms and he was making no move to release me. I kicked out, aiming for his balls, because that might be my one chance to cause him pain. Judging by the lack of reaction to the dagger, he was immune to most hurts. But testicles were sensitive for even the toughest of males.

He laughed as I struggled, his hold tightening until I couldn't breathe.

"Let her go, Larkspur," said Louis, energy gathered in his hands. I noticed that my dad had shifted into a wolf.

Maximus stepped forward. He was all vamped out – wait, what were the other Compasses and Grace doing here? My eyes flicked down to Mischa ... Grace was here and she could save her.

Jonathon must have had the same idea. He sprinted forward, his four legs faster than any of us on two, bit down on Mischa's jacket, dragging his daughter back to safety. No one stopped him. The bad guys did not care for that particular twin anymore, she had no further use. Me, on the other hand, well, I was the king's freaking mate or something.

Not in this fucking lifetime

The king loosened his hold again. "I am not your mate, I already have a mate," I repeated as soon as I had enough breath. I couldn't take my eyes off Braxton. He looked like he was about to tear apart the entire place. He was ten feet from us, I think afraid the king would hurt me if he moved closer.

"You mean the shifter?" Larkspur eyes turned the color of a stormy night sky, dark with flickers of starlight dotted around. "If you forsake that mateship and stay with me, I will spare their lives. As the only dual shifter in existence, you have to make a choice. You have two mates, but there can only be one."

How did he know I was a dual shifter? Was my ability something to do with the king?

"I choose Braxton," I spat at him. "Always and forever."

I locked in on my Compass, his blue eyes were hard and so bright I almost couldn't look at them.

The dragon king laughed. "It's not as simple as that. The fates expect you to give us equal time to determine true mates. You have had twenty-two years with Braxton, so I deserve the same chance."

Lie. He was lying about that, and I was astonished he didn't have the power to mask the fluctuation of hormones.

Louis strode forward, spells gathered in his hands. Tyson was right by his side and I knew they were combining their power to create a bigger spell. I didn't even care if they killed me to get to the king, the supernatural community needed to be protected.

I locked eyes with my best friends – I included Louis in that group now. "Do it. Take him out."

Larkspur chortled again. The sound was going to feature heavily in my nightmares from now on. "Not today, my fellow magic users. I'm going to take my mate and leave. Play nice with my daughters."

"Father!" Orange screamed. "They will kill us."

He threw them both a hard look. "If you're weak enough to be killed at the hand of these pathetic youngsters, then I have no need for you."

Despite his earlier entreaty not to kill his daughters, he truly didn't give a shit about them. He dismissed them with a coldness that told everyone present how dead he was inside. He had no emotion, no caring. He would destroy the world to gain what he wanted.

I screamed then as power descended over the room, and if I thought he'd rolled me before, that was nothing on now. The tantalizing sweetness of the honey flowed again, filling me, drowning my senses. Locked in the arms of a psychotic dragon-shifter-sorcerer, I knew he was about to take me off to worlds unknown. The last thing I saw was Braxton's face, lines of fury on his ancient features. I would have given anything to be in his arms instead of this asshole's. But I knew he would come for me. The Compasses, Louis, my dad, would never stop, I just had to hold out long enough for them to find me.

Chapter 19
Braxton

Jessa! Mine!

The stone wall magicked itself back to being solid and darkness snapped the world into a fucking hellhole. Need had me throwing my body against the stone. Again. Again.

It crumbled but didn't give.

I felt the head of the twin closest to me in my hand. She blasted out at me with power, but the dragon was immune. I snapped her neck. A twist, no thought, just action. Her lifeless body fell away.

Yes, they can fucking die!

Everyone needed to die.

Turning, smelling pulsing hearts that my fists wanted to crush the life out of, three bodies threw themselves at me. They were me. I could feel their kinship, their sameness, but they were not Jessa. I pushed them aside, threw them like leaves, and the cave rumbled as they hit the walls.

"Brax," one of them tried again. I looked harder. "Brax," Maximus said. "Focus, we have to think. Thinking will find Jessa, not killing."

I stumbled, letting go of my brother, and my legs collapsed out from under me.

"Jessa."

The anger inside was like a rushing flood of lava, burning, reshaping, reforming as it moved. Jessa had been gone for no more than five seconds and already I was different, death housed in the body of a supernatural. I wanted blood ... I needed blood.

I stood. The blue flames were back, their light flickering off the underground tunnels, off the stunned and furious faces around me. Maximus stepped to my side, Jacob and Tyson on the other, although they kept some distance. I had thrown them away in my initial rage, and my control was not much better now.

My body vibrated, like it did when my dragon was fighting me for control, which he was right now. Thoughts were like blades slicing through my mind ... memories ... images. The male had her, had laid his hands on her, had touched the one that was mine to protect, mine to cherish. Mine forever.

No one touched my mate.

"What do we do?" Maximus' voice was shot to shit, graveled as he fought his vampire beast inside. "How the fuck do we get her back?"

My ability to form a coherent sentence was gone. All I wanted to do was fight, and kill. I wanted to rip this world to pieces and continue destroying until someone returned my mate to me.

I roared, lunged again, reaching for anything to smash. But I couldn't move. Waves of magic surrounded me ... enough to slow my movements. It wouldn't hold me for long.

I locked a male in my gaze. Fucking sorcerer. This had something to do with him, he always knew too much, was always everywhere.

"Where did he take her?" My voice did not sound normal. It was thrumming with energy from my dragon.

To his credit, Louis was the only one who didn't take a step back, although the strain of holding me showed. Grace was still crouched over Mischa doing whatever she was doing to save her. I didn't care. She was another person whose weakness had cost Jessa.

Then I saw the flash of yellow on the floor. Expelling an extra blast of energy, I broke through Louis' containment spell and strode across to the other twin. I doused the flames before reaching out and slamming my hand around her throat.

"You will take us to the lair of the dragon king."

Her face was red, bulging as she tried to fight me. But there was no chance. "You. Killed. My. Sister," she choked out, her eyes filled with pain.

"Yes."

Her eyes rolled back in her head a little. With reluctance I loosened my grip.

"I will never tell you," she gasped and wheezed.

I felt Maximus at my back. "Oh, you will, you will be begging to tell us this information." Vampire was riding my brother. "I'm laying down the odds now. Ten hours."

Jacob snorted. "If Braxton remains like this, I'm going with two hours."

I lifted my lips. The grin released some of the insanity I was holding inside. For the first time the twin seemed to fear me. She knew now. I was going to take her apart, piece by piece.

"Eight minutes," I said, and she looked blank. "That's how long it will take to have you begging for death. You are going to die, that's a given, but the amount of pain you experience before leaving this earth, that is completely up to you."

My brothers fell in beside me, the four of us linking again. Our calling thrummed through us, the impulse to fight the king. He had our Jessa, and blood would rain across the world until we got her back.

Please, if you loved this book, could you do me a huge favor and post a review on your favourite retailer and/or Goodreads. Reviews are so valuable to independent authors and I'd appreciate your feedback. Thank you for all the love and support, I have been totally blown away by the total love-fest toward Jessa and the Compasses. I heart you all a lot! – Jaymin ☺

About the Author

Jaymin Eve loves surrounding herself with the best things in life: a good book, chocolate and her two little girls. She's been writing for about ten years and now it's settled into her blood and she can't get it out. Not that she wants to.

She'd love to hear from you, so find her at Facebook:
https://www.facebook.com/JayminEve.Author
Mailing list: www.jaymineve.com
Email: jaymineve@gmail.com

Printed in Great Britain
by Amazon